Believe

the first book in the series 'Believe'

Believe

Published by The Conrad Press in the United Kingdom 2021

Tel: +44(0)1227 472 874
www.theconradpress.com
info@theconradpress.com

ISBN 978-1-914913-38-9

Copyright ©Angie Bailey, 2021

Typesetting and Cover Design by: Charlotte Mouncey, www.bookstyle.co.uk
The Conrad Press logo was designed by Maria Priestley.

Printed and bound in Great Britain by Clays Ltd, Elcograf S.p.A.

Believe

Angie Bailey

For Charley, Dexter and Jackson,
You are my heart,
You are my soul,
You are my magic.

Chapter 1

Abigale Johnson was born into a family of Never-Believers. She had two brothers, an older, Peter, and a younger, George. Both boys were tinged with grey, their skin had a greyish stony tone, that made their blue-grey eyes appear dull and sad.

Even though Peter was fifteen and George was ten, the roots of their mousy-brown hair were already grey. Typical of Never-Believer children. The life of no Christmases, no birthdays, no smiling, and the complete lack of magic, wonder and celebration, turns them prematurely grey and typically mean.

These boys, however, were meaner than the average Never-Believer brothers. They fought constantly and viciously. Pulling Abigale's hair at every opportunity. Pushing and shoving her, teasing her to the brink of tears. More so on the days they got tired of fighting with each other, joining forces to terrorise Abigale. They were either the worst of enemies or the best of friends, in both instances, Abigale was more often than not the target of their hate.

Peter thought himself way above his station, with barely emerging muscles he spent hours in front of the mirror.

Everything about Peter was spiky. His features were pointy and sharp, and just as cutting as his contemptible attitude. Which was always hurtful and mean. He was forever moulding the spikiness of his grey-rooted hair, in a bid to somehow make him more appealing to Never-Believer girls.

Abigale hesitated a second too long at Peter's bedroom door, making eye contact with his reflection which she instantly regretted.

'What? Guttergale!' Peter shouted, 'What you looking at?' he paused admiring himself, 'Perfection?' Peter flexed his nothingness then whispered menacingly to Abigale, 'Don't look in my mirror, *you'll* crack it, Guttergale.'

George emerged from his room, his plumpness nearly filling his doorway. He had bulging grey-blue eyes framed by thick-rimmed, black glasses that hung on the end of his rounded nose.

He always seemed to have a piece of bread in his hand and crumbs around his absurdly, small mouth. So small in fact, that Abigale was always surprised by how much food fitted inside it. His cheeks were always bursting full of food, like an overgrown mousy-brown, grey-rooted hamster.

He waddled around, huge for his age, unaware of his size or other people's personal space.

George began to charge, he was surprisingly swift for his size, catching Abigale off guard. He outstretched his chubby hand to give her an extra shove into Peter's wooden door frame, making sure he heard a thud.

'Owwwww!' cried Abigale, George's bulbous frame holding her there, the door frame wedged between her shoulder blades, trapped.

'Get out of that, Guttergale! Good one, George,' Peter gave George a high-five, smirking as they tag-teamed her.

George pushed Abigale harder against the door fame, Abigale pleaded to him, 'Please George, you're crushing me.'

Shoving another slice of bread into his mouth the crumbs

tumbling everywhere he mocked, 'Did you hear that, Peter? I thought I heard something?'

'Nope, I can't hear a thing,' Peter's face was full of fake astonishment, looking quickly from side to side one hand cupping his ear, giving George the cue to push harder.

A voice of authority then broke the boys' wicked shenanigans, calling Peter and George to immediate attention, 'What's going on here?' Mrs Johnson clipped, appearing suddenly at the top of the stairs.

'Nothing Mumsie,' oozed George with smarm, just like he always did. His voice so sickly sweet it made Abigale's teeth hurt. Mrs Johnson gave the boys the once-over. Patting George on the head she turned on her heels and headed back down the stairs, giving absolutely no recognition to Abigale.

Abigale lowered her head, she knew her mother never cared for her. A point that George and Peter exploited at every opportunity.

'She doesn't even know you exist,' George spat, his voice just low enough to be out of Mrs Johnson's ear shot.

'It's worse than that, George,' Peter scoffed, 'Mum hates her, everything about her is wrong,' Peter looked Abigale up and down as she froze against the door. 'Your hair is wrong,' he pulled one of her plaits jolting her head down, causing a burning sensation in Abigale's neck.

George planted his hand hard in Abigale's face, 'Your face is wrong,' he joined in smiling as a piece of bread covered in his spittle stuck to Abigale's cheek.

'Mum even spelt your name wrong you're that much of a wrongen,' Peter cackled at his own wit. He returned to his mirror flicking his head from side to side as if the movement would increase the spike in his hair, tiny droplets of gel splattered the room.

Mr Johnson was waiting for Mrs Johnson at the bottom of the stairs. Oblivious to his surroundings and consumed with his own important thoughts. He too ignored this obvious display of bullying as he kept his head firmly engrossed in the newspaper.

Mr and Mrs Johnson were the worst Never-Believer parents ever, at barely forty, their hair had already turned completely grey.

Mr Johnson had been entirely grey by the time he reached twenty, after having his spirit broken time after time, disappointment after disappointment, he was bitter through and through.

Mr Johnson was rounded, like George. He had the same thick, black-rimmed glasses that sat at the edge of his rounded nose. Cold, grey-blue eyes that made you shiver when he ran them over your skin, like ice being thrown all over your body. Eyes of pure and utter emptiness.

Mr Johnson liked nothing more than to ridicule everything about Believers. He would find holes in their principles and celebrations and siphon every ounce of happiness out of their customs.

This act only saddened his own spirit, scaring his soul more by the day. Meanness ran through his veins.

'Have you heard this?' Mr Johnson called to Mrs Johnson as she descended the stairs. 'Singing at strangers' doors in the snow!' he scoffed reading the *Never Gazette*. 'Utter ridiculousness, pointless venture, singing to strangers indeed,' he pushed his glasses up his nose with indignation, 'Carolling they called it, ridiculous name, carolling!' he sniggered, shaking his head in disbelief.

'Pitiful people,' Mrs Johnson joined in, sucking in her lips filling her voice with contempt.

Mrs Johnson makes my heart ache and my throat tighten. Believers are taught that mothers are the heart of their belief system. They are the people that teach you love, kindness and most importantly, make you believe in magic.

Mrs Johnson was not this kind of mother. Mrs Johnson barely even cared her children existed, barely touched them, barely loved them. Actually, she didn't love them, she loved herself.

Mrs Johnson was twice as conceited as Peter, spending hours in front of the mirror, priming and primping her grey nothingness. She shared Peter's sharpness in features, other than she too had a rounded nose that looked rather odd against her sharpness. It looked virtually cut out and planted in the centre of her face, like it didn't quite belong. But it somehow added to her severe look.

Mrs Johnson's hair was a dark, murky grey, cut into a sharp pointy bob that followed the angle of her jawline. Her eyes were grey with a purple hue. She held an expression of deep coldness, giving the impression that the meeting of her gaze could turn you to stone.

The only thing Mrs Johnson believed in was her own superiority and righteousness. Abigale was pleased she didn't engage with her, she could hear her mother now, it would have been all her fault.

Stand up straight, you lazy girl, Mrs Johnson would correct. *You should be neither seen nor heard, insolent girl,* she would scorn, *where is it?* she would ask, *it,* meaning Abigale. *Where is she?*

Abigale's mind raced with all the mean things her mother would say. Sometimes she thought Mrs Johnson was unable to even say her name. The sheer mention of it appeared to leave a horrible taste in her mouth.

Maybe the boys were right, thought Abigale. Maybe she was all wrong just like her name.

Mrs Johnson appeared to take pleasure in picking holes in everything about Abigale. She wanted to be the belle of her grey family ball. Abigale hindered that. Mrs Johnson shopped, moaned, and encouraged meanness in her boys. That was all she did. And all she was really good at.

The thing that filled Mrs Johnson with pride the most was the greyness that consumed their rather modest semi-detected, four-bedroom house.

The outside was covered in a wash of polished pebble-grey, which gave a medium-grey, shiny element to the walls. The rims around the windows and doors in a darker charcoal-grey, with the front door being as black as a witch's blackest cat.

The greyness set off the rows of alternating black and white roses that straddled the concrete grey path which wound up towards the front door.

The front door had the strangest knocker, an odd silvery-grey. The colour was called Never-Grey. It was the symbol of the Never-Believers. Five circles, two at the top and three at the bottom, inside each circle, was a tiny, black-onyx stone and each circle stood for the Believer's celebrations, hope and dreams. A stone cross laid on top covering the circles. Symbolising that they are forbidden for Never-Believers.

The knocker would have been considered Art Nouveau, chic in fact, if what it stood for wasn't so sad. The inside was much the same, each room in a different shade of grey, black, or off-white.

Hallways in Goose Down grey with a Smokey Ash wooden floor throughout the downstairs. While upstairs was covered in a dark, vintage-grey carpet, or at least that's what Mrs Johnson called it. To everyone else, it was just grey and cold.

Abigale was surrounded by these horrid, mean, and spiteful Never-Believers.

Abigale, however, was different. She spent most of her hours avoiding her family, locked in the greyness of her room. Staring at her Misty Mountain grey curtains, grey bedding, grey dressing table, grey, grey, grey, grey, grey.

Abigale had just turned thirteen, not that you would know, as there was no party, no cards, not even a recognition of what day it was from her family. She only knew it was her birthday because of the yearly birth chart.

The Yearly Academia Birth Chart hung on the kitchen wall, which marked the years from birth until you reached eighteen where you were then expected to leave home for The Pearl Grey Never-Believer University. The chart had big grey letters penning the names Peter, Abigale, and George.

Underneath each name a tally of lines for each year that passed since their birth. Four horizontal lines and then a fifth line that strikes through the middle to create bundles of five years. So, Peter had three lots of five, George had two lots, and Abigale's was two lots of five, with three extra lines.

That's how she knew she was thirteen, she saw Mrs Johnson add that third line. Once they reached eighteen marks it was time for them to leave and Mr and Mrs Johnson could not wait.

Abigale, however, did not feel thirteen, although she did not know what thirteen should feel like. With no recognition of birthdays, other than the marking of a line. It was like most of her life had been insignificant, it never actually started.

Abigale was somehow different from her Never-Believer family. Her hair didn't have any grey roots, it was a shiny, caramel colour from root to tip. Parted down the middle into two plaits that hung down past her shoulders. Her skin although pale, was not grey, much to Mrs Johnson's annoyance. Her features were a complete mixture of Mr and Mrs Johnson, not sharp nor rounded. Her eyes were a warm hazel with flecks of emerald-green. Neither cold, nor icy, but somehow mesmerizing.

Sometimes when alone in her room she would think of what it might be like to be a Believer. How did they live? How did they celebrate? What were these things called parties?

Abigale would sit in front of her mirror, not for vanity but to practice, or rather try, her best to smile. Even though it hurt sometimes, she liked to try.

Smiling however, is banned for Never-Believers. She would try desperately to make the corners of her smile reach the top of her cheeks. But she could not do it for long, as it would make her cheeks rosy and pink, then Mrs Johnson would know what she had been up to. Which meant Abigale would be punished and have to stand in front of the family and recite the Never-Believers vow:

'We don't believe in celebration or rejoicing in fables,
There should be no special dinners upon our family tables,

To believe in the fabricated is to be consumed with stupidity,
The life we are meant to lead is straight,
uniformed, full of utmost rigidity,
I believe in things that are real, the air, the plants,
and the large oak trees,
There's no such thing as birthdays, Christmas,
or fictitious fairies,
I do not smile, I do not play,
I do not dream the day away,
Never-Believers are the truth, the nothing and the now,
Grey is the foreverness and not to believe is my vow.'

After saying the Never-Believer's vow, Abigale's glow got a little dimmer, her spirit a little darker. Sometimes she would even find a tiny grey hair amongst her caramel-brown plaits.

It was another time marked that she shouldn't practice that smile that made her cheeks rosy. Her eyes would glisten, but not with hope and not with dreams, but with the salty tears she desperately tried to not let roll down her pale faded cheeks. This was what the Never-Believers' vow was made for. To sadden you into the greyness, wherein the Never-Believers thrive.

In comparison to the rest of the Johnson's, although sharing the same air of sadness that engulfs Never-Believers, Abigale stood out as the outcast of the family. Being the outcast though, did have its benefits, as she was practically left alone by every-one, other than when her brothers wanted to make her life a misery. Unfortunately, today, was one of those days for Abigale. She was desperately trying not to let her brothers see they were getting to her.

Peter was now pulling at her plaits again shouting, 'Ugly, plain and pitiful, is what you are Guttergale,' Abigale eyes welled trying to hide the pain of the tugging, 'Guttergale belongs in the gutter, stinky, smelly, Guttergale!' Peter continued in a sing-song spiteful voice. George was completely blocking any kind of escape she might make.

George joined the cruel chant with crumbs from his latest slice of bread, spitting and tumbling from his overfull, tiny mouth, 'Guttergale, Guttergale!' he taunted from the charcoal-grey painted doorway, in a half laugh, half pig snarl.

'I think Mum and Dad should leave Guttergale here and not take her to Auntie Violet's with the rest of us, she only makes everyone miserable,' jeered Peter.

Abigale only wished she could be left at home and not go to horrid Aunt Violet's. How someone so dull, bleak, and mean could have such a lovely, colourful name such as Violet, Abigale could never fathom.

Abigale's usual plan when Peter and George were like this, was to stay as still and as silent as possible. In the hope they would get bored soon enough and leave to go and annoy each other.

Today seemed a particularly long time she was having to stand infinitely still. She even tried holding her breath to make the stillness stiller. Eventfully, thanks to the shrill of Mrs Johnson coming back up the stairs, 'We are leaving in one hour! You three better be packed and ready to go, or else!'

Finally, Abigale was relinquished from Peter's torturous words and the sputtering of half-eaten breadcrumbs bouncing off George's face. They all darted to their rooms to finish packing, panic-stricken by Mrs Johnson's threat of 'or else!'

Chapter 2

Abigale stood at the open, black-painted front door dissecting the Never-Believer embellished knocker with her eyes. The circles covered over with the bulky, stone-silver cross gave the cold banishing to anything fun, light-hearted, or magical.

Hugging herself she felt a shiver run down her back. Abigale noticed dew drops on the tips of the black and white roses that led up to the house, making the roses seem like they were shivering too. The wind caught the petals and speckles of dew fell to the ground, the drops splashing timelessly on the winding grey concrete path.

Abigale didn't want to go on the family trip to Aunt Violet's, she could think of nothing worse than being stuck on a train for three hours with her family. Sat in between Peter and George, with Peter flicking hair gel over her as he meticulously spiked his hair in different directions. Relentlessly posing and sending pictures of himself to his legion of followers on ShatterNatter.

Then, George sitting the other side of her, holding his grey lunch box stuffed with a whole loaf of bread. This would keep George munching for the whole three hours. Crumbs full of saliva, tumbled down his chin and onto Abigale's pleated charcoal-grey dress. Abigale would be almost wet with George's spit by the time they reached Greystone Station, where cold, heartless Aunt Violet would be waiting. She would be with Mitsey, her vicious grey spotted Jack Russell. Standing there, all pointy and stern, pale and straight faced. Even Mitsey the dog, looked sullen.

Abigale would sit as still as she possibly could, not to be noticed and not to be picked on.

Abigale had never actually seen a Believer in real life. There was meant to be towns full of Believers, but Abigale didn't know where these could possibly be. She always heard Mr Johnson protesting to Mrs Johnson, 'We must keep those despicable, deluded Believers far from children,' he would dictate, 'The like of Enchanters and Utopians must never reach our towns, with their stories of Fairy Godmothers and Tooth Fairies,' which was always followed by a scoff of utter disbelief.

'Utter Nonsense, Fairy Godmothers and Tooth Fairies, disgusting! Pretending the existence of magic,' Mrs Johnson would repeat in a splutter of revulsion, agreeing with everything Mr Johnson said.

Fairy Godmothers and Tooth fairies, what are such things? Abigale thought they sounded wonderful. But she knew better than to let these thoughts cross her mind, especially as she was now being watched. Mrs Johnson's sixth sense seemed to heighten and home in on Abigale every time she thought of something non-grey.

'Guttergale doesn't even look alive!' Peter said standing on the steely-grey carpet, one hand on the black banister in the middle of the stairway, the other pointing sharply at Abigale. 'Look at her standing so still… Oi, Guttergale!' Peter shouted.

Mrs Johnson emerged from the kitchen wearing a grey-mink fur coat, with matching hat, and scarf. Looking like she was ready to meet a Scandinavian prince, totally overdressed for a train journey.

As usual Mrs Johnson didn't even bother to correct or scold Peter for how he spoke to Abigale. In fact, it looked like she almost enjoyed it.

'Peter, can you not linger on the stairway, we will be late,' clipped Mrs Johnson.

Peter ran down the stairs with the swiftness of a pouncing Cheetah, putting on his grey-tweed coat, black gloves, and black-leather boots with elegant ease. George was wearing the same outfit but didn't quite carry it off with the style and grace that Peter did.

George's coat was snug around the middle. The buttons bulging, the coat gaping, exposing the brilliant white shirt underneath. The black leather boots gathered at the bottom of George's calf, unable to glide smoothly up his rounded legs. George's gloves however, fit perfectly.

Mrs Johnson picked up her grey, leather snakeskin bag and stood by Abigale, looming over her intimidatingly. Mrs Johnson called in a high pitch shrill, ' Come along everyone into the car, we will be late for the train,' making Abigale jump and her ears ring.

Peter bounced through the hallway and bounded past Abigale knocking her into the door frame. Before she could steady herself, George came waddling forward, whose momentum increased as he reached Abigale. Smashing her into the door causing the Never-Believer door knocker to bang violently.

'Abigale Johnson!' Mrs Johnson chastised. 'Should that knocker break at your hands, I shall leave you in the care of Aunt Violet! Maybe then,' she paused, giving Abigale an icy death stare, 'You will respect other people's property.'

Abigale shuddered at these words. There was only one thing

worse than where Abigale was now, and that was staying at Aunt Violet's.

'Sorry ma'am, it won't happen again, ma'am,' Abigale's chin lowered nearly touching her chest. Peter and George laughed as they clambered into the back of Mr Johnson's black Ford Granada Estate.

The grey leather seats were icy cold making Abigale fidget, repetitiously pulling the back of her charcoal dress down under her legs protecting them from the cold. George kept elbowing her in the ribs every time the car turned a corner, making a red mark appear under the pleated panels of Abigale's dress.

Abigale stayed silent throughout the duration of the journey to the train station and once the seats had warmed up, she stayed stony still. The car hummed along and apart from the movement of Peter and George in the back, nudging and budging, you could almost mistake Abigale and Mr and Mrs Johnson as statues positioned in a travelling tableau.

The platform at the station was busy, full of Never-Believers. Abigale stood out amongst the sea of grey hair. Her hair seemed a richer caramel and her eyes more strikingly green than hazel, they dazzled like crystals staring back at you. She glowed against the gloom.

Many of the people standing around her, looked at her sideways in disgust. They gave that quick revolted look out of the corner of their eyes and then slowly edged away from Abigale like they would catch something. This being another reason Mrs Johnson had such disdain for Abigale. How could any child of hers bear such colour, there must be something wrong with her.

Peter and George were darting in between grey crowds,

much to Mr Johnson's displeasure. He tried in vain to reprimand them, flapping and floundering, the boys ignoring his plight for them to be still. Mr Johnson became flustered and in desperation he flicked the back of his hand and clipped Peter round the back of his head.

'BOYS!' Mrs Johnson yelled with venom through gritted teeth.

This caused not only Peter and George to stand deathly still, but also called Mr Johnson to attention. Abigale stood a distance away, close enough as to be with her family, but far enough away to not get caught in the commotion. She was of course standing absolutely still. This was the only thing Mrs Johnson vaguely admired about Abigale, not that she would ever say, but never had she known a Never-Believer stand so still.

The train appeared on the horizon coasting silently towards the station. As it pulled to a stop Abigale looked up at its enormity. The train was modern, shiny, and silver, with the Never-Believer emblem printed on its side. Five large, black circles with the cross across the top. Mr Johnson pressed the door release button and the people on the platform surged forward, all desperately trying to get a seat.

The seats were of course, a dull grey cotton material, rough and not at all comfortable, just as you might expect on a train. The seats felt too upright, giving you the impression that you're constantly leaning forwards. Abigale was wedged in-between Peter and George on a seat meant for two.

Peter started first, 'Get off me Guttergale!' he shoved Abigale closer to George.

George pushed back as bread spluttered into Abigale's plaits and crumbs stuck upon her cheek, 'Don't touch me with your Guttergale body!' George shoved Abigale again.

Abigale's head began to whirl, she felt locked in, she couldn't breathe, she was getting hurt and no one was helping.

Mrs Johnson spat at Abigale, 'Stop it you defiant, stupid girl! Aunt Violet will soon knock this out of you!'

Abigale's head span faster and faster, was this always the plan to leave her at Aunt Violet's. Heat began to rise within Abigale. She could feel it rush from her toes up through her legs, up her torso and igniting her face into a bright crimson. Before she knew it, and to the amazement of Mr and Mr Johnson, Peter, and George, Abigale has dislodged herself from between the boys, and was up into the middle of the train aisle and running towards the next carriage.

Chapter 3

Abigale ran towards each of the carriage's dividing doors as if her life depended on it. Upon each approach the doors opened for her to go through without stopping, the modern sensors anticipating her movement. Abigale began to fatigue and for the first time after passing through what she felt was her hundredth carriage, she finally tried to glance behind her to see if the coast was clear.

WALLOP! Abigale was propelled backwards and knocked clean out onto the compartment floor.

After what seemed like an age, Abigale's eyes strained as they finally began to open. Her hand reached automatically towards her head, where she felt a large bump forming with her skin feeling stretched and tender. Abigale began looking around, her eyes half open, dazed.

The heat of panic began rising again in her body as she remembered what she had done. She tried to clamber to her feet. To her amazement she heard a fluted whistle of a large steam engine, making her jump in shock with its high-pitched scream. Abigale couldn't stop her body bobbing gently from side to side.

What is happening? muddled in her mind. Then, in a moment of clarity, a realisation whizzed through her thoughts. *Electric trains don't have whistles.*

Looking ahead Abigale saw a different dividing door. Not silver, not metallic and modern, but this was a wooden door, surrounded by a wooden carriage. The wood was dark and shiny, a deep Victorian mahogany. The engrained swirls of colour made it feel alive and wise. At its side there were two cast-iron hinges that were so detailed and beautiful, they resembled butterfly wings that hugged the wood of the door in a supporting embrace.

Suddenly, without any warning, the mahogany door creeped open. Abigale rubbed her head again. *Surely this isn't real,* she thought.

She pinched herself firmly on the arm, 'Ouch!'

Abigale rubbed her arm where a small pink mark was forming from the disbelieving pinch. She looked around for a second time and then focused upon the door. The most brilliant light began to seep through the crack. It was dazzling. Abigale saw colours she never imagined truly existed.

Green flecks in Abigale's hazel eyes danced as the rainbow of light emerging from the door grew brighter. Her caramel plaits lifted from her shoulders appearing to float and pull her forward. Reds, oranges, pinks, purples, and blues sparkled and pulled Abigale closer towards the door. It was like Abigale no longer had control, the power of the colours took over and were drawing her in. Gone was any thought of Peter or George, Mr, or Mrs Johnson. Abigale was completely focused on following the light.

She clasped the door to open it a little wider, her touch caused the door to fling open and the light sucked her inside. She felt butterflies dance in her tummy as fireworks of bursting colours surrounded her. Abigale was drawn through the opening. Practically floating within the light, she never wanted this feeling to end, Abigale had never felt so alive. A solitary tear escaped one of her eyes which slowly trickled down her cheek. Embracing herself she allowed herself to be submerged by the joy of the light.

Opening her eyes Abigale walked forward, placing one black shoe slowly in front of the other. The light began to separate, and she unexpectedly felt the urge to look behind her. She found that the dark, shiny, Victorian mahogany door had shut behind her.

Abigale searched for a handle to pull the door open again. But all she could see were the cast-iron, winged-hinges, not a handle in sight. Tracing her fingers over them she was amazed at their intricacy and beauty.

Abigale felt an unfamiliar ache in her face, her fingers reached up and felt the firm bumps in her cheeks and the creases at the sides of her eyes. The corners of her mouth reached from ear to ear making the bumps glow a perfect rose pink. Her first real smile, Abigale felt amazing.

Swish... Swoosh... Whizz... Abigale saw three speeding figures fly past her head so fast she couldn't make out what they were. They bounced around the deep reds and browns of the mahogany train carriage like shooting stars of glitter. Upon each landing making the wood glisten and gleam that little bit more.

Abigale was utterly baffled because she thought she could hear talking. The rockets of light sounded like they were giggling and saying in a repetitively high-pitched tone, 'We have another one, another one we have.'

Abigale without realising had resumed her instinctive stillness while she gazed down the gangway of the mahogany carriage. It was beautifully crafted with tumbling archways every four feet, intricate curves and gouges mirrored either sided of the carriage, highlighting the richness of the browns and reds that engrained the wood.

The cast-iron, winged-hinges found on the door were also dotted around the carriages. Giving the perception that each hinge lead to a secret hidden compartment.

The shine of the wood was mirror-like as Abigale noticed her reflection in it. Abigale stood out even more in her charcoal pleated, pinafore dress. A dress that reached just above her knee a few inches from her grey knee-high socks, and plain black, patent, slip-on shoes. This was the first time she'd seen her reflection full length and her smile dropped as she noticed her dullness against her surroundings. Before the thought could resonate too long in her head, a small woman appeared before her.

'Name?' she asked inquisitively.

Abigale stood motionless and silent, shocked, and a little fearful. The small woman looked over her tiny, rounded spectacles and paused. Abigale had never seen a woman like it. Her hair was lilac and swept back from her face in a top knot which was encircled with tiny plaits, beads, and crystals, which made her hair shimmer like a star.

Her skin was pink, and her cheeks cherry rose. Her tiny round spectacles rested on the bridge of her petite, delicate nose, which still allowed you to see her oval, slightly large, turquoise eyes. Eyes that were full of kindness and yet, danced with mischievous spirit.

She was slight in build and wore a pale-blue satin, long-sleeved dress that pinched in and flared out. The sleeves of the dress hugged her elegant arms to her elbow and then cascaded out like a waterfall of textile colour. Diamante embellishments making them shimmer like sunbeams reflecting on water. The sleeves looked like she had sparkling wings. The dress glistened and gleamed with its effortless sway and swish. Abigale couldn't make out how her legs were sparkling, but they were. Finally, blue satin shoes with the small kitten heel that had a satin butterfly clasp holding them on. Stunningly beautiful.

'What's your name, Dear?' the small woman asked again, even softer, gentler than before.

Abigale snapped out of her stillness, 'A... A... Abigale,' she stuttered in an inaudible whisper.

The small woman looked Abigale up and down with a puzzled expression and leaning in for a closer look, she said, 'You're certainly not like the usual Believer trainees we get here.'

Snapping backwards she span around away from Abigale with an unbelievable swiftness. She ordered, 'Come along dear, let's get you settled.'

The small woman started to glide forwards along the carriage. Abigale followed as if on autopilot, distracted by her new environment. The mahogany floorboards creaked underfoot, and you could feel the vibrations of the train clickety, clacketing along the track. *Believer trainee?* thought Abigale, there must be some kind of serious mistake.

Abigale tried in vain to speak to the small woman, 'Er... Ma'am, ma'am, I... er... Ma'am?'

Abigale's voice still not strong enough to gain the small woman's attention. Abigale was at a near jog the woman was moving so quickly. All the while overhead, the *swish... swoosh... whizz* of the three speeding figures shot across the ceiling. They darted from side to side like shooting stars illuminating the mahogany as they go.

A high-pitched trio of voices mimicked the small woman's words, 'Not the usual Believer, the Believer's not usual,' which echoed down the carriage.

The small woman stopped abruptly outside a doorway to the right of the carriage. 'Here we are then.' The woman stood to one side, 'You will be sharing with Annie and Clara, your meeting with Professor Mortley is at...,' she pulled out a jewel-encrusted clipboard from one of her cascading blue sleeves. Abigale blinked hard in disbelief. The small woman flicked through the pages over and over, then frustratedly called, '3 T's, time please?'

The swishing, swooshing, and whizzing stopped, and the three tiny figures harmoniously sang, 'Six and ten and back again, six and ten and back again.'

'Thank you!' the small woman clipped in an ascending voice as if to make sure that the figures knew to then be quiet.

'Meeting with Professor Mortley at ten past six, any questions?' the woman asked kindly.

The figures began to dance again, swishing, swooshing, and whizzing across the ceiling. Before Abigale could even muster her voice, the small woman swiftly turned again and began to glide away from Abigale. If she didn't know better, she would swear she was flying. Abigale tried to look harder to see if the blue satin shoes met the boards of the mahogany gangway. The small woman raised her hand like she remembered something but didn't turn back, this redirected Abigale's attention upwards as the small woman called, 'Oh, I'm Mama Gilbert my dear, I'll see you in class tomorrow.'

Mama Gilbert? Class tomorrow? Abigale's head started to whirl again as she stood stagnant outside another mahogany, winged hinged door that seemed to be urging her to open it.

Chapter 4

Abigale's hand extended slowly, timidly forwards, ready to gently apply pressure to the mirrored door for it to open. Her pale perfectly groomed fingers were reflected, giving the appearance that she was about to touch fingertips with another person inside the door.

Before she could make contact, the door flung open with gusto, a swish, a swoosh, and a whizz flew past her head. The three figures zoomed into the room ahead of her and were darting around like uncontrollable fireworks.

Abigale's attention was quickly drawn to the excited squeals of two girls jumping in the centre of the surprisingly large, red cedar wood cabin. Lunging toward Abigale, the girls embraced her giggling and letting out tiny cries of over-excitement. Abigale had never been hugged before, or not that she could remember. Apart from the pushing and shoving of Peter and George she didn't remember any other physical contact. So, she froze in absolute stillness.

Their skin felt warm against hers. The warmth felt heartfelt as their hold tightened. It felt like something she had needed for a long time. Abigale knew instantly she already loved these two over-excited, animated girls.

'Hello! I'm Annie, and this is Clara!'

The two girls released their hold of Abigale and danced around in a circle holding hands like they had been friends forever. Annie who had spoken first, was the taller of the two.

She had black, thick flowing hair, that as the light caught it shined and shimmered. Her skin was a warm ebony and appeared silky smooth. Big, thick, black-rimmed glasses encased her giant, brown eyes, and her smile was so big and so bright the corners touched the arms of her glasses.

Annie wore an emerald-green, A-lined dress that came in an inch or two above her waist, and then flowed out to just above her knee. Emphasising the smallest part of her and disguising her slightly plump figure. Her feet were bare as Abigale watched them dance and glide over the smooth cedar flooring.

Suddenly, Annie slipped and landed abruptly on her bottom, on top of a circular rug, which was a patchwork tapestry of blues and golds with faint, silver threads to add a hint of shimmer. The rug was hemmed with tassels that had a knot at the hem and strands of blue, gold, and silver wavering from it.

With a roll of Clara's eyes both girls started to laugh again. Annie's laugh was infectious, loud, and so clear that lit up the room. Clara pulled Annie to her feet and hugged her.

Clara's hair was similar to that of Mama Gilbert's. Clara's, however, was blonde with a pink hue. Her hair was swept back into a high bun full of intricate plaits embedded with pink beads and crystals that seemed to release sparks of glitter as they caught the light. Odd, pink curls of varying lengths caressed Clara's heart-shaped face, enhancing her almond-shaped eyes. Her eyes were like the ocean, a deep blue with the odd fleck of green. They were utterly mesmerising.

Clara wore a pink and white lace choker around her neck which matched her baby-pink and white sleeveless dress. The neckline swept from shoulder to shoulder laying just below her collarbone, accentuating her slimline neck giving her an almost regal look. The dress had a white lace petticoat that flared out, swaying from side to side, bell-like, in unison with Clara's motion. Clara was also barefooted, gracefully gliding and spinning around the cabin like a beautiful prima ballerina. Annie sat watching, clapping, and gasping as Clara pirouetted over and over again.

'Annie fell down, down Annie fell,' the three mysterious figures sang as they laughed, they perched themselves on a shelf slightly adjacent from the top bunk.

Annie looked up at them over the top of her large, rimmed glasses and blew the biggest raspberry in their direction. Then she began to giggle again, without a care in the world.

The cabin had three beds, two of the beds were protruding from one wall, one on top of the other like free-standing bunkbeds, and then another coming from the opposite wall in line with the bottom bunk. The top bunk was covered in a bubble gum-pink duvet with a dainty, white-lace trim, obviously Clara's.

The shelf that the figures had taken to, was full of multiple shades of pink accessories, French rose ribbons, hot-pink hairties, watermelon, ruby, and pink lemonade lip glosses. Abigale was dazzled, intrigued, and dying to know what all these things were and what they did. She felt overloaded with information, her mind trying to process it all at super speed.

The bottom duvet was a satin emerald-green, so pristinely laid that the corners of the duvet looked almost sharp. So perfect in fact, that it looked like no one had slept there, ever.

Abigale immediately knew it was Annie's. She was the type who has a place for everything and everything in its place. Her little shelf at the bottom of the bed consisted of just books, organised in alphabetical, size and genre order. Perfect.

There was a window in between the beds, adorned with a matching blue, gold, silver curtain with tassels around the edging of bottom hem, the same as the rug.

The tassels were tied back tightly with a knotted, white rope, which had the same silver strands woven through, they were tied back to allow the natural light into the room.

The window was edged in same cast-iron used in the carriages, with winged handles. The light accentuated the varying levels of the red engrained into the wood, giving the cabin a warm, soft, country feel. Never had Abigale seen a room so flawless, simply perfect.

Annie and Clara stopped dancing and returned their interest to Abigale. Annie went first and introduced herself properly, 'I'm Annie Rainerly and I'm from Enchanted Island, I'm third generation Believer, and I'm just so excited to be here!' she ended in a speeded up, high-pitched squeal.

Clara then excitedly burst in, 'I'm Clara Gilbert and I'm from Utopian Bay, as you can tell by the name, I'm Mama Gilbert's granddaughter, and I too am so excited to be here!' the girls embraced and bounced up and down again.

'So, tell us everything!' Annie and Clara said in unison, eager to hear all about Abigale. They were dancing around waiting for Abigale to respond.

Abigale sat on the spare empty bed covered in a brilliant white-lace duvet, clearly waiting for someone to make it their home. 'Erm… I'm, I'm Abigale,' Abigale said timidly, barely looking up from hands folded on her charcoal-grey pleated lap. 'Abigale spelt with a G.A.L.E,' she continued in an embarrassed whisper.

Annie and Clara stopped for a second and looked at each other puzzled. Annie then laughed looking at Clara incredulously, 'What? Well, how else would spell Abigale?'

Abigale sat looking at her hands in utter disbelief while the girls continued dancing and laughing at each other.

'Where are you from Abs?' Annie asked, 'I can call you Abs, can't I?' she queried not wanting to offend. Abigale's head was still looking at her lap, but she was now smiling, she'd never had a nickname before.

'Yes, that's fine,' she said a little louder, a little more confident, 'I'm from Greystone Valley.'

The girls and the three figures that had also begun dancing around the cabin froze. The girls turned and looked again at Abigale, mouths ajar, eyes wide, faces a cross between astonished and alarmed.

'You're a Stoney!' Clara exclaimed in a soft disbelieving whisper, putting her hand over mouth as if she had said something forbidden.

Abigale looked up, confused, 'I don't know what a Stoney is, but my family are Never-Believers.'

'Oh! A Stoney on the fairy train, no Stoney's on the fairy train,' the three figures sang in panicked, high-pitched voices over and over again. The cabin door flung open, swish, swoosh, whizz and the three figures left in a blaze of light. The door slammed behind them, and the cabin fell silent.

Abigale thought she had blown it, how could these beautiful girls want to be friends with her now. Her head returned to looking down at the charcoal-grey nothingness of her lap. Her smile gone and a hard lump began to grow in her throat making it ache with tightness. Abigale fought back the tears that threatened to escape her eyes and run down her pale, smooth cheeks.

Annie and Clara look at each other, then looked at Abigale, then at each other again, in total silence. Without warning Annie and Clara charged towards Abigale, Annie jumping one side of her and Clara darting to the other. Their arms become entwined around Abigale's shoulders and Annie almost shouted with enthusiasm, 'You must tell us EVERYTHING! Everything about you!'

'Really?' Abigale asked, a tear escaping and trickling down her cheek.

'Really!' they both shouted back enthusiastically.

'Don't leave anything out!' Annie said, reaching for a green, glitter notebook as not to miss a single detail.

Before Abigale could respond, Clara lifted one of Abigale's shiny, caramel, brown plaits from her shoulder that were finished with a plain, dull, grey, elastic-tie. With a mischievous look on her face, she gracefully leaped up on to her top bunk and leaned over to her shelf full of pink accessories. She fumbled and jumbled for a second and then pirouetted down onto Annie's perfect, green bed. Grabbing something from Annie's shelf in transit and making the tiniest of indentations upon the emerald-green, satin duvet.

Clara elegantly sat back down next to Abigale. Annie shot up like lightening and corrected her bed back to precision whilst throwing Clara a playful daggered look. Clara smiled at Annie and waited patiently for her to return to Abigale's other side.

Clara passed a sparkly, emerald-green hair-tie to Annie, who instinctively knew what Clara was doing. Clara in her own beautifully manicured hand, held a matching fuchsia-pink, sparkly hair-tie. Both picked up one of Abigale's plaits, removed the plain, grey tie and replaced each one with their respective coloured hair-ties. Annie and Clara look at each other and then to Abigale and smiled triumphantly.

'There, much better,' Clara beamed, 'I now pronounce us best friends forever!'

Annie clapped, and Abigale finally had some colour, but best of all, she had friends.

Abigale lifted her head, took a deep breath, and commenced telling her newly best friends, Annie, and Clara, all about Mr and Mrs Johnson, Peter, and George, and how she was going to be left at icy Aunt Violet's.

Annie wrote everything down with such exceptional speed, occasionally looking up in surprise and disbelief. Clara gasped dramatically and held one hand over her heart while the other squeezed Abigale's hands giving her the courage to tell them everything. Clara shed a tiny glitter-filled tear as Abigale told them of the no birthdays, no Christmas, and no talk of magic, and then recited the Never-Believer vow.

Finishing her story with her running through the carriages of the silver, metallic train. Of being unable to stop until she hit the deep mahogany door with the prism of light that pulled her in. When Abigale had finished they all sat in silence. Annie and Clara absorbing her story.

Abigale asked Annie, 'Why did you call me a Stoney?'

Annie's ebony cheeks blushed a shade of crimson, 'That's what Believers call the Never-Believer's as a kind of,' she paused and looked up to the ceiling as if she were looking for a suitable explanation, 'Nickname, you know, because of the pale skin and standing still, like stone, ergo, Stoney.'

'Sorry Abs if I hurt your feelings,' continued Annie, taking Abigale's free hand to hold.

Abigale saw the logic in the name, 'I prefer "Abs" much more,' Abigale said with a smile, a smile that corners touched the tops of her cheeks making them glow subtly rose-pink.

Chapter 5

*B*ang! *Swish, swoosh, whizz*, the door flew open with a force that made the cedar wood tremor. The three figures' lights darted fiercely across the top of room.

'She's not supposed to be here, supposed to be here she is not!' they chanted repeatedly in a now annoying high-pitch melody.

'Why are they saying that?' Abigale asked Annie and Clara with a hint of rising panic.

Clara rolled her eyes, 'Oh, don't listen to them, they are always causing trouble!' she reached her hands up and tried to swot the figures out of the room.

'What even are they?' Abigale asked puzzled and wanting to know why they were saying she should not be with Annie and Clara.

The trio of figures paused all with their hands on their tiny hips. Abigale could see them now as they had finally stopped swishing and swooshing. They were mini people, with wings, small enough to fit in the palm of Abigale's hand. They looked childlike, maybe a bit older, like tiny teenagers. Their skin was a pastel green, their features were all identical, elfin, precise, and inherently beautiful.

Their hair was short and dishevelled and tucked behind tiny, pointy ears, it was much darker than their skin, more an olive green. All three were wearing matching forest-green rag dresses, with a roughly tied belt that appeared to have some kind of faded, brown, leather holster bag attached. Abigale wondered what such a tiny bag might hold.

The trio hovered, their hands on their hips, well-formed, tiny, pastel-green legs apart, with their velvet-green, ankle boots pointing firmly to the floor. The three perfect faces were aghast in indignation that Abigale had absolutely no idea who or what they were.

'They're the 3 T's,' Annie told Abigale, shocked herself that Abigale hadn't been told about them growing up.

'Tiana, Tamsin and Tatum,' Annie announced. As each of their names were spoken they took it in turns to make a grand, over the top bow. Each one trying to outdo the other, much to the annoyance of the one before.

'They are Pixie sisters, Time Pixies to be exact,' Clara continued, explaining to Abigale that they were how they kept track of time on the train. They were also responsible for keeping the train sparkling clean; and making sure we got to class on time and any meetings we might have to go to.

Clara headed a warning though, 'They are naughty and mischievous though Abs,' Clara gave the 3 T's a knowing angry look, 'Don't listen to everything they say!'

The trio in unison turned round and playfully blew a raspberry at Clara. They then began darting across the ceiling again, chanting, 'Stoney's got to go, bye, bye goes the Stoney!'

Annie thumbed through her collection of books on her perfectly organised shelf. Using one finger she selected a rather tatty, old, green book. The spine of the book looked broken, and the corners were frayed, separating its material cover from its cardboard edges. The pages inside had a gold-trim, Annie wiped her hands over it lovingly and passed it to Abigale.

Abigale read the title to herself, *Everything you need to know about Pixies, about Pixies everything you need to know. How fitting*, Abigale thought, as she caressed the book gently. She'd never read anything before that wasn't a boring old, grey school textbook.

'Wow, thank you, Annie,' Abigale whispered in wonderment. Annie and Clara caught each other's eyes and beamed.

'Abs,' Annie said, 'We are going to teach you all you need to know about being a Believer, you're one of us now.' Annie and Clara exchanged a nod, accepting their task at hand.

Even though this made Abigale happier than she had ever possibly been, her heart paused for a second as her family flicked through her mind. After all, they were all she had ever known. This is the longest she had ever been apart from them, there was a tiny part of her that missed them, wondered if they were ok. What do they think has happened to her? Are they worried? Mrs Johnson come to the forefront of her mind, *probably not*, Abigale thought, feeling a sadness engulf her heart.

Unexpectedly, Mama Gilbert appeared in the doorway of the cabin, looking worried and flustered. The 3 T's started to chant louder, 'Stoney's got to go, bye, bye Stoney!'

'Abigale dear,' she said in an anxious, hushed tone, 'Can you come with me, you must see Professor Mortley right away.'

Annie and Clara clambered to their feet, 'Mama, everything's ok, isn't it?' Clara questioned her grandmother with a hint of worry.

'I... I... I can't quite say my dear,' Mama Gilbert stuttered, not knowing how to reply.

Mama Gilbert was making sure she avoided any eye contact with her granddaughter, looking everywhere she possibly could, ringing her hands repeatedly.

The three girls hugged each other tight. Annie and Clara tried to reassure Abigale, whispering quiet promises before they released her to face Mama Gilbert. Abigale was still in the charcoal pleated dress from this morning with the black-patent shoes and knee-high socks. The only difference being the sparkly green and pink hair-ties that adorned her caramel plaits. Which looked even more vibrant against the charcoal of her dress.

Smoothing down her dress with the palms of her hands she looked up at Mama Gilbert's kind waiting face. Abigale nodded in her direction in silent affirmation that she was ready to meet her fate. Abigale knew, all this was too good to last for long.

Clara flicked Abigale's pink hair-tie and whispered with a wink and a smile, 'We are with you, Abs.'

Abigale gave a crooked half-smile, lacking the confidence to agree. But she stepped forward towards the doorway. Mama Gilbert turned and glided away swiftly, muttering to herself as she went. Abigale couldn't make out what Mama Gilbert was saying, but she was guessing it wasn't good. The 3 T's were darting overhead, chanting their Stoney prophesy.

Abigale followed Mama Gilbert as quickly as she could down the mahogany aisle, noticing all the cast-iron, winged-hinges dotted along the way and the possibly hidden hideaways.

Maybe I could hide somewhere? Abigale thought hopefully.

More cast-iron-rimmed windows, the same as in their cabin, with the ornate-winged handles that matched the hinges. Abigale looked through the windows as they hurried along the aisle. She noticed passing clouds and brightly coloured birds, blinking hard as she looked again.

How could this true? Her mind was buzzing. Abigale was trying to keep up with Mama Gilbert, but also wanting to investigate what she was seeing out of the window. Abigale was virtually leaning back as she walked. *How can we be passing through clouds?* Abigale felt puzzled, looking down at her feet still feeling the vibration of the train clicketing and clacketing underfoot on the mahogany floorboards. Her eyes defying all that she had been brought up to be true.

Mama Gilbert stopped suddenly. Another mirrored mahogany door. Abigale could see Mama Gilbert's worried reflection, her prefect lilac hair looking a little ruffled. Her hands wavered nervously before she knocked loudly on the door.

Not waiting for a response Mama Gilbert pushed the door open with her palm, the winged-hinges creaking slightly, she stood aside holding open the door for Abigale to enter the room first.

Fear gripped Abigale as she apprehensively allowed her black-patent shoes to walk her into the large, dome-like room. The deep red and brown mahogany filled the room's every angle. The room had the highest ceiling Abigale had ever seen. The panelling walls rose to at least twenty feet before the arch took over. The boards of swirling deep browns and reds arched high from right to left, almost giving a church altar effect. Abigale couldn't comprehend how this room could be part of the train as her eyes traced over its every inch.

In the dead centre was large mahogany desk with stacks, upon stacks of papers and scrolls. The paper and scrolls were a mixture of old and new, some that had a torn, teabag, stain effect, making them look old. Whereas others had a gold and silver edging and were brilliantly white, looking new and untouched.

The desk was surround by filing cabinets, which were also mahogany, that seamlessly rose up from the polished floorboards. Abigale couldn't decide if they were decorative or actually functional in purpose, either way they look magnificent.

Behind the desk was a row of three large, rectangle windows, with an elliptical window at the top, a kind of half semi-circle. The elliptical window reached from the top-left corner of the first rectangle window to the top-right of the last rectangle window, like a top hat. The light beaming through sporadically as the fluffy, white clouds intermittently blocked the rainbow rays that lit up the room.

Pictures and tapestries adorned the walls which all seemed to depict the same story. A long line of young children following what looked like a flying boy. The boy held a small dagger in one hand and the other was in a clenched fist, placed just above his waist. Flying alongside the boy, Abigale could only now describe as what looked like a Pixie, like one of the 3 T's. But it looked surprisingly like Mama Gilbert and Clara. Abigale was transfixed by everything inside the room. The room however, appeared empty.

'HER... HUMMMMMMMM!' Mama Gilbert cleared her throat loudly.

The mahogany desk vibrated with a bonk! And out sprung a curious looking half-man, half-boy. Abigale couldn't make out if he were a middle-aged man or a young boy. His face was holographic in appearance, depending on how the rainbow of light hit him streaming in through the windows.

The holographic face had pink skin and dusty-brown hair, that seemed to have a life all of its own. His face was rounded with bright, red cheeks that bulged out, covering part of the bottom of his soft, hazel eyes. This aided the illusion of his changing appearance. He had bold, fleshy lips, where the top lip appeared glazed in something green, sparkly, and sticky. He had a shocked, bewildered look on his face, resembling a little boy having been caught red handed with his hands in the cookie jar.

'Miss Abigale, Professor Mortley,' Mama Gilbert introduced.

Professor Mortley quickly tried to correct himself, pulling down a too small tangerine-orange waistcoat, and hoisting up his chocolate-brown trousers. He wore a matching chocolate-brown, short-sleeved shirt under the tangerine waistcoat, which had become unreachable as it had somehow managed to rise up too far, leaving a forever gap between his garments. Everything had a tad too small look.

'Well, my dear, we seem to have a problem,' Professor Mortley addressed Abigale, rather flustered and fumbling through papers on the giant desk. 'I have been through all my files, and I have found no trace of you,' he paused and ruffled a hand through his dusty-brown hair. 'Can you tell me your full family name and address please.'

Professor Mortley pick up a bright orange quill and dipped it in what looked like a tub of ink, he shook off the excess and looked up at Abigale expectantly.

'Ermmm… Well…' Abigale's hands reached up to the pink and green hair-ties and squeezed them quickly before continuing. 'I'm Abigale Johnson, of the family Johnson,' she waited for Professor Mortley to look up a signal for her to continue. 'I live at 126, Grey Road, Greystone Valley, NB.'

Professor Mortley looked up, 'NB?' he quizzed with doubt.

The Professor glanced at Mama Gilbert, and she stared right back at him. He looked like he was beginning to sweat with worry, the hologram of his face looking more and more boylike, he looked like he didn't exactly know what to do. Mama Gilbert rushed over to the giant mahogany desk as if to give him counsel.

She repeated, 'N.B?' concern written all over her face.

'Yes, Never-Believer, ma'am,' Abigale strained as the throat tightening returned and her eyes glazed over with tears.

Professor Mortley and Mama Gilbert span around and began to talk animatedly, each one seemly taking their turn in throwing their hands into the air. They were speaking in such hushed and rushed tones, which were completely inaudible to Abigale, it was like they were speaking another language.

'Must I go home?' Abigale asked sadly, unable to wait any longer, yet not wanting to know the answer.

Abigale had reverted to her stillness, so still in fact you couldn't even make out if she were even breathing. She wasn't even vibrating with the humming and clickety clacking of the movement of the train beneath her feet.

Her head was low, her hands clasped together in front of her, resting on the pleats of her charcoal-grey dress.

Professor Mortley looked at her stillness and thought he remembered something for a moment, but then it was gone, and he darted beneath the giant mahogany desk. Mama Gilbert was staring at Abigale with a lost look on her face, but you could tell her mind was racing. She was clearly unaware of Professor Mortley's swift disappearance. Mama Gilbert turned to speak to him but wasn't shocked when he wasn't there, she seemed to automatically know where he had gone. Looking down, she grabbed with one hand and pulled Professor Mortley up to his feet.

Professor Mortley's, green, sparkly, sticky moustache had been renewed along with a guilty smile that he gave Mama Gilbert. The light faded over his face and Abigale could make out fine lines around his eyes now making him look much older and as if he should know better.

'Well, the problem is Abigale, you, er, er, can't go home,' Professor Mortley mumbled apologetically, 'Not until the train decides.'

The train's vibrations increased, the deep red and brown swirls of the mahogany wood turned as if the train were speaking. Professor Mortley and Mama Gilbert patted the giant mahogany desk as if they were reassuring it. Abigale couldn't believe her eyes or her ears. Her stillness finally broke as she steadied herself against the shaking of the train.

'The train collects the chosen Believers in, those who are meant to graduate to fairies,' Mama Gilbert explained.

'The train? That's impossible!' Abigale exclaimed. The train shook again, this time even more violently.

Chapter 6

Annie was laying on the floor on top of the blue and gold circular rug surrounded with old books, multi-coloured, sticky notepads, and a selection of illuminous-green highlighters. She was flicking through the pages frantically.

Clara was pacing the floor in front of her, occasionally stopping and pirouetting round to face Annie as if she had come up with whatever answer Annie was looking for, then stopping again and returning to her pacing.

'It's no good!' Annie cried, picking up yet another book to look through off her meticulously laid piles, 'I can't find anything about Stoney's being on the train before!'

Clara span dramatically, one hand palm facing outward resting on her forehead, falling backwards onto the white-lace duvet of the spare bed in their room. Which they both hoped would soon be Abigale's. Clara let out an even more theatrical sigh, before rolling over on the bed and turning to Annie.

'What are we going to do, Annie? She has never even had a birthday party, or collected Easter eggs, or had a Christmas tree,' a realisation hit Clara, 'Annie! Abigale has never had a Christmas! It's just all too heart-breaking!' Clara's voice full of melodrama.

Annie looked over at Clara, 'We shall not give up!' she declared with determination.

Annie's head lowered again, she engrossed herself in her next book and Clara bounced back to her feet and began pacing the floor again with matching determination. Her elegant steps turned into a stomping march as if the increased power would somehow unleash the information they needed. Not that it was helping. Neither Clara or Annie knew much about Stoney's, only the stories their parents had told them, and now Abigale.

'Surely, someone must know something?' Annie thought aloud in and incredulous tone.

Annie and Clara felt the first angered shake of the train. Unaware of what was occurring in Professor Mortley's office. Clara took this shaking as a confirmation of Annie's question.

'That's it Annie! Someone does know something!'

The only problem was, how on earth were they going to figure out who. They decided to make a list of all possible candidates that might know anything. Then the cabin shook again, this time more violently. Annie's reached out instinctively and placed a hand on her tower of books to stop them falling. Clara lost her footing and preforming a grand jeté, a long balletic horizontal jump, leapt gracefully over Annie and her books and landed with ease cross-legged next to Annie. Annie was still totally astounded that someone existed with such beauty and grace, feeling the tiniest, tinge of envy.

The cabin continued to shake, light beamed in through the window almost blinding Annie and Clara. Annie clambered to her knees and grabbed Clara. They began to hug each other tight, burying their heads into each other's shoulder at the nape of the neck, trying to protect their eyes from the unrelenting light.

They started to panic and let out little screams of fear as the light radiated powerfully through the cabin for what they thought was an age. Then, as quickly as it began the light disappeared, just like a switch, the power vanished. Just like that. Clara raised her head first looking over Annie's shoulder.

'Oh no!' Clara said in a low hushed tone with a mixture of dread and disgust.

'What?' Annie snapped her head up.

Turning round Annie laid eyes on what the light had done. Gone was the soft, white-lace duvet that covered the spare bed. Instead, an iron-grey, rough mottled blanket, and steely-grey sheets. A metal trunk had appeared at the base of the bed, Annie reached out and felt its coldness, she shivered in reaction.

Clara ran her hand over the iron-grey, mottled blanket and stood up angrily. Clara's hands formed perfect little fists, which she placed on each side of her tiny waist, in her most powerful cross stance. She began to shout at the walls of the train.

'This isn't staying here!' she yelled defiantly.

Clara attempted to pull back the covers of the bed. Annie stood up to help, both of them pulling at the steely grey sheets. They didn't budge. Undeterred and still as cross as cross can be, Clara turned away and walked towards the bunk she shared with Annie. Then, she spun abruptly and ran towards the grey bed, pouncing on it as if to trick the train. Pulling and tugging frantically, letting out little grunts of effort.

Clara appeared unrelenting until she fell spent and motion-less upon the iron-grey blankets. Annie thought Clara was done and moved towards her friend. Before Annie could get there Clara sprang to her feet again with a new lease of life and crazed and determined glint in her eye.

Annie had never seen Clara like this, the green took over the blue of her oceanic eyes. Clara jumped onto her bed and lent over and pulled out a hot-pink satin basket. She brought it to the ground where she placed it on the floor. Annie moved closer to see what Clara was doing. There were words embroidered in black italics on the top of the hot-pink basket, 'Beading, bedazzling and beautifying.'

Clara flipped open the lid and started to pull out her arsenal. Ribbons, lace, chiffon, and pink gingham. Pulling out a variety of needles and thread she began to attempt to sew onto the iron-grey blanket.

Every time Clara's needle hit the iron-grey blanket it made a little *ding* like metal were hitting metal. Clara tried over and over again, *ding, ding, ding*, but couldn't get the need to go through the blanket. She returned to her basket, Annie watching in utter bewilderment. This time pulling out her ultimate weapons, she had a glue gun in one hand and Bedazzler in the other. Annie knew she meant business.

Time after time Clara tried to adhere patch after patch of either satin, silk, or suede. They slipped off as quickly as a mischievous Pixie gliding down an unguarded banister. Clara's movements became more and more hysterical, she started throwing the pillows and cushions that adorned hers and Annie's bed at the greyness. Each pillow bouncing back from where it came from after hitting the iron-grey sheets.

Exhausted, Clara fell to her knees. Annie silently went over and kneeled beside her and placed a comforting arm around her neck. Glistening tears streamed down Clara's cheeks, leaving wet sparkly pathways.

'She can't come back to the grey, Annie,' Clara sobbed into her friend's shoulder.

Before Annie could say anything, the jangling and jolting of the door alerted them that they had company. Abigale walked into the room and Annie and Clara instinctively jumped up and tried to stand in front of the bed, desperately trying to hide the greyness.

Abigale was brighter than expected, 'What are you two trying to hide?' she asked, raising up onto her tippy toes trying to peer over them to see what they were trying to hide.

With expressions of sadness and guilt all over their faces, Annie and Clara parted and stood to one side, exposing the iron-grey, mottled blankets and steely sheets.

'I'm sorry Abs, I've been trying to fix them,' Clara said throwing clumps of pink material into the air, 'But it won't let me do it!' Clara let out a huge, defeated sigh.

'But don't you see Clara,' Abigale said smiling, 'This means I'm staying… for now, at least.'

Annie and Clara let out two very loud squeals of shocked excitement. The three of them hugged, and jumped, and danced around in their cabin. The 3 T's filled the ceiling with fireworks and vaulted across the room causing the most amazing light display. The three girls collapsed onto the floor laying in a circle, on top of the blue and gold rug, with their heads together at the centre and bodies pointing outward. Their legs fanned out just like the white and silver tassels at the rug's hem.

'Wow!' Abigale said in amazement.

They lay silently, holding hands, watching the 3 T's indoor fireworks display. Catherine Wheels span with flicking speckles of pink from their centres; rockets flew across the room with tails of vivid white and blue screeching to a magnificent explosion; bright, purple showers of light in the shape of the leaves of willow trees trickled from the ceiling, and bursts of brilliant, yellow chrysanthemums dripped like diamonds from the sky.

It was like nothing Abigale had ever seen before. Once the mischievous Pixies brought their display to a close Annie and Clara turned towards Abigale, propping their heads up on their hands.

Clara reached across and playfully flicked the pink hair-tie, 'So, what did they say?' she asked Abigale, eager to find out all the details.

Just as Abigale opened her mouth to start talking, Annie shouted, 'Stop!' she jumped up and ran over to her bed, grabbed her emerald-green sparkly notepad and pen, and rushed back. Now crossed-legged, next to Abigale and Clara.

'OK, GO!' Annie ordered, her eyes wide and dazzling and pen poised, ready to write down every detail.

Abigale told them all about the problem of the train deciding who comes onto the train and who leaves, and that the train had chosen her. Abigale told them that this had never happened before, neither Professor Mortley nor Mama Gilbert knew what to do, they would have to contact the Fairy Council.

'Whatever that is?' Abigale said blankly, looking at her friends for more information.

Clara looked at Annie to answer knowing this was Annie's area of expertise. Annie explained that the Fairy Council consisted of the residing Fairy Queen, and the four heads of the four fairy magical bloodlines.

'The Pixies,' Annie motioned towards the 3 T's now laying exhausted from their light show on Clara's shelf.

Tiana was laying with one arm and one leg hanging of the shelf with a little green towel over her forehead; Tamsin dramatically fanning herself with one of Clara's pastel pink hair feathers; and Tatum making minute exaggerated snoring movements, covered over in a small piece of cherry pink gingham.

Annie continued to explain, 'The Elves are tricky some are lovely but others not so much.'

Clara and Annie exchanged eye contact giving each other exaggerated looks of concern. To which Abigale just looked at them blank-faced, as if she had no idea what an Elf could possibly be.

Annie paused for effect, unfolded her hand in a motion of introduction towards Clara.

'And my personal favourites, The Personal and/or Tooth Fairies,' she announced with an air of grandeur.

Clara jumped into the air and pirouetted with elegance and precision, landing in a graceful curtsy, Clara acted like she was being introduced to Abigale for the first time. Abigale smiled, this suited Clara perfectly.

'Last and by no means least,' Annie proclaimed, she stood up and taking a rather clumsy curtsy announced, 'The Fairy Godmothers.'

Annie fell down to the floor giggling. Abigale looked at both of them utterly astounded.

'You're both fairies!' she said shocked, 'Like, real-life fairies?' Abigale's mouth ajar, her eyes bursting out of their sockets, speechless amazement was taut across her face as she looked from Annie to Clara.

In Abigale's heart she always believed this was true, it was taking her mind a minute to get around it. 'Can you do magic?'

'Not yet!' Annie answered in a giggle.

'But soon!' Clara continued, whirling around the room, 'When our powers come in, any day now.'

Abigale was utterly amazed and wanted to know every single, teeny, tiny, microscopic detail about both of them. Then, a thought hit her.

'Then how am I here?' Abigale said, a little dejected, 'I'm a Never-Believer, there's definitely no fairies in the Johnson family,' she finished sadly.

'That's exactly what we need to find out, Abs!' Annie said holding her emerald-green, glitter pen in the air, as if making a proclamation. 'Maybe we will find out more tomorrow in class,' Annie suggested.

'I'm not allowed to go to class, I have to be kept hidden,' Abigale admitted looking dejected. All the girls fell silent.

'Let's sleep on it then,' said Annie, feeling the enormity of the day take hold of her.

Clara spun over to Abigale and took hold of her hand, 'You are meant to be here, I can feel it.' She glanced around the cabin and the train shook gently like it was agreeing with her. 'Have a little faith, believe it,' Clara's eyes sparkled like diamonds.

Annie came over and grabbed Abigale's other hand squeezing it and lifting up her chin to meet her determined stare, 'Clara's right Abs, believe it.'

Clara looked again sadly at Abigale's iron-grey bedding. Abigale gave Clara a reassuring hug that the bedding didn't matter, after all, that was what she was used to.

Strangely enough, as Abigale put on the pearl-grey cotton nightdress, which had appeared at the end of the iron-grey bed, she felt the roughness of its hem graze the underside of her ankle and was reassured by the familiarity of the greyness. The iron-grey blanket gave her a modicum of comfort as she thought about what might happen tomorrow.

As the girls wished each other good night, Annie affirmed, 'Don't worry, Abs, we will find out why you're here.' Then yawning and stretching widely, she proclaimed, 'I have a plan.'

Chapter 7

Mrs Johnson stood over the hospital bed with a bored and impatient look on her face. The heating was making Mrs Johnson's oddly rounded nose run, much to her annoyance. She held her grey leather, snakeskin bag in front of her with both hands clasped closely together on the handle. The longer shoulder strap hanging down to just below the hemline of her grey-mink fur coat.

The walls of the hospital room were a stark white, very clinical. There was shiny, silver, metal machinery surrounding the bed, beeping, and giving off huffs and puffs of mechanical workings. The only beacon of colour was a red light flashing in unison with the continuous beeping sound.

Only Abigale could make such a drama out of head injury, thought Mrs Johnson. She was winding herself up more and more as Abigale lay unconscious in the bed before her. How could she cause us such embarrassment? Mrs Johnson's foot began to tap as her thoughts were making her anger boil up inside her.

Mrs Johnson had never been more embarrassed than she was today, being asked to leave the train and escort Abigale in the ambulance to the hospital. Mr Johnson, Peter, and George had to return home in their black, Ford Granada Estate, causing their trip to Aunt Violet's to be aborted.

If the truth be told, all the Johnson men where a tad thankful to Abigale for creating such a stunt, for they got to forgo the torture of the annual Aunt Violet visit.

Mrs Johnson's dark-grey, murky bob began to stick to her jawline as she continued to perspire in the unrelenting heat of the hospital room. Pulling out a steely-grey, monogrammed handkerchief, with the Never-Believe symbol on one corner and her initials M.J. on the other. She began patting her face to absorb some of the moisture, refusing to take off the grey-mink coat. Deluding herself that she would not be staying long at all.

After what seemed like forever to Mrs Johnson, a doctor entered to speak with her.

'It's about time, I've been waiting in here for the longest time, when can we leave?' Mrs Johnson snapped, checking her watch for the umpteenth time.

'Err, well,' the doctor said, shocked at how uncaring Mrs Johnson actually was.

Gathering himself he retorted, 'Mrs Johnson, we don't actually know what is wrong with the young Miss Johnson yet,' the doctor then sternly eyeballed Mrs Johnson. He was considerably shorter than her and looked almost boylike, Mrs Johnson was incensed by his bold-faced comments.

'Well, I can't stay here much longer I have a family to attend to,' Mrs Johnson asserted, ice dripping from every syllable.

The doctor unflinching and keeping her gaze retorted, 'Miss Johnson is in a self-induced coma, Mrs Johnson.'

'So, she is asleep,' Mrs Johnson continued with her cold, dismissive tone.

The doctor hung his head unable to comprehend the meanness of the woman in front of him. His uncontrollable dusty-brown hair flopping into a middle parting.

'Mrs Johnson, I am admitting Miss Johnson to stay at

Greystone Valley Hospital until she awakes from her coma.'

Mrs Johnson marched towards him menacingly, towering over him she bent forward peering down to his eye level. The doctor's courage now diminishing with Mrs Johnson in such close proximity. His head was sinking into his tangerine and brown garments that poked out of the doctoral, white blazer.

He was now looking much older as Mrs Johnson got up close and personal, she began to feel her power increase over him. Leaning back, she stuck out her hand sharply towards the doctor.

'Thank you for your time, Doctor,' Mrs Johnson said flatly waiting for the doctor to shake her outstretched hand. The doctor, confused, hesitantly shook Mrs Johnson's hand. She then headed towards the door, opened it, and as she walked out called back, 'Call me when she wakes up!'

Mrs Johnson headed down the hospital corridors trying to avoid any contact with anyone else. Passing through the long white halls that looked like a rat maze, each turn looking like the next, with the odd red cross or hospital bed number dotted along the route. She reached the grey doors of the elevator and outstretched her hand again to press the button. She noticed her finger almost stuck to the button, actually all of her fingers were sticky.

She ruffled through her leather snakeskin bag to find her monogrammed handkerchief, but she just couldn't find it. Realising she must have left it in the hospital room, she further investigated the substance now on her fingers as she entered the lift. Never before had she seen such a sticky, green, and sparkly substance.

Mrs Johnson returned home via the Greydog buses, the

Never-Believer bus service. A fleet of shiny, metallic buses with a dark-grey bulldog plastered on the side. The bus dropped her a stone's throw from the Johnson bungalow on Grey Road. She walked up the winding concrete pathway edged with the alternating black and white roses until she reached the black front door. Still unable to get the sticky residue off the fingers of her right hand. Placing her left hand on the Never-Believer knocker, she knocked sharply three times, then waited tapping her toe hard and fast.

The door opened slowly; George poked his chubby, spectacled head around the doorway to see who it was. When he saw it was Mrs Johnson, he jumped to attention, breadcrumbs tumbling everywhere and stood aside so she could come through.

Mrs Johnson walked through the house to the cupboard under the stairs, where she finally took off her mink, fur coat and hung it away, together with the matching hat and scarf, that she had been keeping in her grey snakeskin bag.

George bounded back up the stairs to continue his munch-a-thon in his bedroom. Peter didn't even acknowledge his mother's arrival and stayed in his room with the door firmly shut. Mr Johnson was sitting at the table reading the *Never Gazette*, his rounded glasses so far down his rounded nose it was a miracle they stayed on. His short, crisp-grey hair seemed to darken as Mrs Johnson entered the room. His cold, steel eyes stayed fixed on the text of the paper.

Without looking up he said blankly, devoid of emotion, 'Hello, dear.'

'Dear,' Mrs Johnson replied in a clipped monotone acknowledgment walking towards the Dove grey, speckled kitchen counter to make herself a cup of tea.

Not one mention of Abigale, not one family member asked, not one thought, not one care, not in the Johnson house. It was like Abigale was never there in the first place.

***

The doctor placed a hand over Abigale's as she slept peacefully in the cold hospital room. Abigale's cheeks had a rosy, pink glow against her pale skin, her caramel hair seemed richer somehow. The doctor hovered for a moment, thinking that there was something about her that felt familiar. The door opened and a head popped round the corner.

'There's a tonsillectomy that needs checking in room 3, Doctor,' said a pretty, grey-tinged, brunette nurse in haste.

The thought was then gone, he patted Abigale on the hand, 'I'll see you soon, Miss Johnson,' he whispered pulling out a green, sticky, sparkly marshmallow Christmas tree from his doctoral, white coat. Taking a large bite and leaving behind the tell-tale, green, sparkly, sticky moustache, he strode towards the door.

Chapter 8

Abigale sat on the edge of her iron-grey bed, in her pearl-grey cotton nightdress watching Annie and Clara get ready for their first class. She could hardly make out what they were saying as they were speaking so quickly and their voices an unusual high-pitched babble. Every sentence was accompanied by a jump or overanimated movement.

Abigale, however, was still, statue-like, disguising the torrent of emotions she was feeling inside. Annie and Clara were mesmerising. Never had Abigale seen such enthusiasm in people, nor the colours that swirled around the room while they were deciding which dresses to wear.

Abigale hadn't noticed them before, but under both of the lower beds in their room were the cast-iron fairy wings, hiding hidden cupboards that were to be filled with clothes and other personal items she guessed.

Annie and Clara were both bent over in the cupboard under Annie's bed. They were pulling out garment after garment holding it up to themselves while the other one examined it. Then, they gave a nod or a shake of their head if they thought it might be a possible option for the day.

Abigale had never seen anything like it and so wanted to join in. But all she had were four charcoal-grey, pleated, pinafore dresses, all carbon copies of each other, folded at the end of her bed. One pair of black-patent shoes, a selection of grey and white undergarments and six, black hair-ties. Which, she had already decided she would never wear again. Abigale was keeping the sparkly emerald-green and hot-pink hair-ties in that Annie and Clara gave her. They were special, they were her colour.

Annie and Clara finally decided on a fitting outfit for the day. Annie wore a jade-green wrap-dress, which again pulled in at all the right places, flattering her shape. The hem and neckline were trimmed in green glitter, diamantes were dotted here and there, adding just enough bling. Annie's hair was so shiny it was virtually reflective, the light rebounded of its jet-blackness, making it gleam. Her ebony skin was flawless. Abigale looked down at her own pale, translucent skin wishing it could be more like Annie's.

Clara was spinning around in a circle, high up on the point of her tippy toes, creating the perfect pirouette position. This was emphasizing the pouffiness in her skirt. The cream-pink dress nipped in at the waist and then the large pleats made a full skirt creating its pouffiness. A thick belt fastened around her waist and a chic ring of pearls encircled her slimline neck. Clara enhanced the pink hue in her blonde hair by adding matching pearls to her high bun. A criss-cross plait design also covered the bun, which was just stunning. Clara practically twinkled as she spun.

Abigale so wanted to go with them today, to be part of whatever they were going to experience, but she was under strict instructions, that Never-Believer's cannot be allowed to be part of Fae teachings. She must not go anywhere unless accompanied by either Mama Gilbert or Professor Mortley. Abigale understood, but she couldn't shake her longing to be part of this wonderful world.

'I hope you two have the very best day,' Abigale said with all the positivity she could muster.

Abigale noticed that even within one day of being here, smiling didn't hurt as much, it was getting easier and easier. Annie and Clara immediately stopped what they were doing and took their self-appointed places either side of Abigale. Annie scooped up one of Abigale's free hands, giving it a heartfelt squeeze and Clara playfully flicked Abigale's pink hair-tie.

'We're sorry Abs, we wish you were coming too,' Annie said trying to comfort Abigale, 'Don't forget we have our plan of action!' she added firmly.

Abigale nodded now thinking more positively. Yes the plan, Abigale remembered it to herself.

Annie was going to go the train library after class and look for anything about Never-Believers and the Fairy Train. Clara was going to go for afternoon tea with Mama Gilbert and see what she could find out from her, and her job was to read as many of Annie's books as possible. To learn about the Fae and Believers and see if anything clicks. Abigale didn't exactly know what 'clicks' meant, but Annie seemed sure something would. Still, she was excited to learn about all things Fae and Believers anyway.

The cabin door flung open, and three rockets of light flew into the room, the 3 T's had come to tell Annie and Clara it was time for class.

'It's class time, time for class!' they chanted annoyingly.

Abigale felt they were rubbing it in a bit as they were encircling Abigale's head as they rhymed. Clara came over and swatted them away tutting at them with a cross face, her perfect little nose all scrunched up as if she meant business.

The 3 T's just giggled and continued to fly and zoom around the room, swishing, swooshing, whizzing, rhyming, and giggling.

Annie and Clara gathered their bags. Annie had a jade-green rucksack, matching her dress which was full to the brim, bursting full of books. The green ribbon-tie holding the bag closed was beginning to fray a little under the weight of all the books.

Clara had an oversized lemonade-pink shoulder bag that matched her cute pumps completing her outfit. Clara reached into the oversized bag, which appeared to be empty, and rumbled around until she pulled out a pink glitter lip gloss achieving her goal. Clara applied it expertly arching it over her top lip. Annie and Abigale gawped as she did so, straightening her shoulders Clara announced with a showman's curtsy, 'Ready!'

Annie rolled her eyes and giggled. They both ran over to Abigale and hugged her tightly. As they released their hug, they both simultaneously flicked their correspondingly-coloured hair-ties on Abigale's plaits, giving her their version of a high five. Abigale couldn't help but smile.

Walking towards the doorway, Annie leaned over and grabbed a book from her shelf. She straightened her duvet, making sure it looked absolutely pristine. Then, nodding with affirmation, she tossed the book at Abigale and asserted under her breath, 'Ready.'

Abigale broke her stillness and caught the book in mid-air, frightened it could get damaged. Looking up towards the door, Annie and Clara had disappeared. Abigale just caught a glimpse of one of the T's taillights as the door closed gently behind them.

ale's, Annie's, and Clara's beds. Bedding of luxurious red ... blankets trimmed with a white fluffy hem, like the suit ...e man in red. The blue, in the blue and gold carpet is ...aced with a deep red and the silver thread replaced with ..., giving the finishing Christmassy touches, to the most ...fect Christmas room.

Abigale's eyes squeezed tight as she tried to keep the image ...her mind of their Christmas-themed cabin. Feeling how it ...uld feel to lay in it, be in it, live in it. Unable to keep her ...es squeezed closed any longer as her lids started to ache, she ...egan to open them slowly. She had given herself tunnel vision ...where her eyes had been closed for so long.

Abigale raised her hands up to give her eyes a rub, rubbing away the light and the dark spherical pathway. Actuality then made her jump to her feet in astonishment. Her hands went to her mouth covering it as not to let out a squeal. Blinking repeatedly, she turned around the room slowly, never had she, could she have ever thought... it was just so utterly amazing!

Opening her arms widely she spun around quicker in the centre of the room taking in every minute detail that had come to life. The colours, the feelings, and the magic. Abigale fell to the floor on the red and gold circular carpet.

Laying on her back looking up in wonderful admiration at the feathered fir from the real Norwegian, green, spruce tree that had appeared, identical to the one in her imagination. A sparkly, happy tear glistened as it rolled down her cheek.

Abigale gasped in astonishment and in the loudest stage whisper said, 'Oh No! I've... I've Christmassed the room!'

Abigale was finally alone. But for the first time, Abigale didn't feel lonely. Looking down at the brown leather book, it looked so old, the edges of the leather were faded in comparison to the centre of the book. On the front cover the emblem of the Believers was embossed into leather. Abigale ran her finger over the circles, liking the way the edges of the circles caressed each other without the big cross of the Never-Believers over the top. She loved the feel of the leather, so soft against her fingertips. Turning the book to see the edges of the pages Abigale felt a shiver of excitement run up her back. Hugging the book close to her body Abigale embraced its feeling of warmth.

Sitting on the edge of her iron-grey bed her eyes began to caress the red cedar room and she drank in every detail of the surroundings. Opening up the leather cover Abigale read aloud, 'A History of Believers.' Her tummy started to feel funny, a little queasy and bubbly, but in a good way. It felt like tiny little fireworks had begun popping in her stomach.

Abigale began to read, her eye dissecting and absorbing every single word. Her eyes were transfixed to the page, turning every page with utmost care as she read. *So, Believers are just like me?* Abigale thought.

Abigale had thought that Believers must be wicked or inhuman from the way Mr and Mrs Johnson used to speak about them. Well, the hushed whispers she sometimes overheard anyway.

Abigale began to read about the Believers traditions, the birthdays, and Christmases. How parents of young Believer children celebrate the day their children were born. She tried hard to imagine what that must be like, what it must be like to have coloured balloons and gifts each year on her birthday.

But most of all she wondered what it must be like to have a mother who celebrated her, fussed over her, hugged her.

Abigale's thoughts again wandered to Mrs Johnson and if her mother was missing her. Strangely, at that moment Abigale had an odd pulling on her heart, she wanted to see Mrs Johnson.

Trying to push the feeling deep down to the pit of her stomach, Abigale read on. She adored that they kept using the word, 'Family'. How they all got together and shared the most amazing magic of a time they called, 'Christmas'.

They told stories of a magical man in a bright-red suit with a long, bushy white beard, who lived at a place called the North Pole. He would spend all year-round making presents for all the good boys and girls with his army of Elf helpers. Then, on one night he would fly around the world delivering all the presents to all the good children. He would fly on his red and gold encrusted sleigh, pulled along by nine flying reindeer.

'Amazing…' Abigale breathed aloud dreamily. Abigale thought that it must be the most wonderful thing in all the world to be a Believer.

Rolling over onto her back, on her iron-grey bed, folding her arms across her charcoal-grey, pleated dress. She quickly closed her eyes causing creases to form on her temple and tried to picture what it would be like to wake up on Christmas day and find presents under a tree.

It was the most incomprehensible thing to Abigale, putting a tree up and decorating it in your house. Abigale laid there and thought about what decorations she would put on the tree. Her tree would be the greenest of greens, slightly bushy, and tall. It would fill the room with a pine smell that lingered around the tip of your nose.

I'll place it just by the window, she thou[ght]

Abigale pictured in her mind the greenes[t] tree she could ever imagine. It would sta[nd by the] window in between Annie's, Clara's, and her b[...] ing light could make the tree shine just as m[uch as it] did at night. The branches separating exactly r[...] each ornament perfectly.

Abigale dreamt she would pick the Believe[rs'] Christmas colours of red and gold. Enhancing the [...] life of the green and highlighting the red in the c[...] room. The tree ornaments would be stars, reinde[er] and fairies. All glittering around their edges swingi[ng] showing the innate life of the tree within its gentle [...]

The tinsel would flicker red and gold as the ligh[t lit] up the ornaments colour. Twinkle lights would wind[...] the tree from the base of the fir all the way to the v[...] twinkling brightly. Just like the picture in the Believers' [...] the tree would sit in a big red box, full of fresh, damp, b[...] earth, giving lots of room for the magical appearance of [...] from the man in red.

Crowning the tree would be a beautiful golden fairy, po[sed] in mid-flight offering comfort and protection as she watche[d] over the room while you slept. Abigale would hang red an[d] gold tinsel across the room, that would zigzag from one corner of the ceiling to the other.

The tinsel would twinkle and glimmer and fill the room with excitement, and hope. There would be little figurines of Snowmen and Christmas Elves dotted around the room together discussing the excitement to come. Tiny lights that twinkled intermittently in differing patterns, surrounding

Chapter 9

Annie and Clara sat at their mahogany desks waiting for the rest of their classmates to join them. Clara looks at Annie and rolled her eyes, she knew they were going to be too early, but she listened to Annie and there they were, first ones seated. Annie was paying no notice to Clara as she was nervously and meticulously placing and replacing her highlighters, pens, pencils, and notepads to figure out what layout would be most helpful when class began.

'Do you think there will be any boys?' Clara asked excitedly, leaning over into Annie.

'Do you think we will have a test today?' Annie replied worriedly.

They both looked at each other and laughed, grabbing each other's hands, squeezing them in between the desks.

'There's sure to be at least one boy!' Annie squeaked excitedly to Clara.

'You're going to be cleverest here, Annie,' Clara gave Annie's hand another reassuring squeeze.

The door swung open and in walked the most handsome boy they had ever seen, both their mouths dropped open a little bit in awe. His hair was dark, nearly jet-black. It spiked over to one side at the front and was sharply shaved in around his pointy long ears. His face was diamond-shaped, and his eyes were like two dazzling, green sapphires, encased in a perfect almond shape that were almost hypnotic.

His nose was long, narrow, and ever so slightly pointed. His face was uncannily symmetrical. He wore a short-sleeved shirt, printed with a surfer riding the crest of a wave and blue, crisp, denim jeans. Bright white trainers that seemed too big but somehow set off his look. A look that Annie and Clara would say looked 'Dreamy'.

He carried an assortment of books under one arm, walking with confidence, his shoulders back and head up straight.

'Ok if I sit here?' he asked Annie, looking straight at her with those sparkly sapphire-green eyes.

Annie looked up to meet them, unable to talk, her cheek-bones blushing crimson against her ebony skin, her lips moving but absolutely no words coming out.

'Of course, it is! I'm Clara and this silent goddess is Annie,' Clara said with a winning confident smile. 'Annie!' she called in a stage whisper trying to shock her out of her trance.

'Hi,' Annie finally managed weakly, pushing her glasses up the bridge of her nose, slowly dying inside from embarrassment.

'I'm Elliot, great to meet you,' he said with self-assurance, and yet, soft and kind his eyes flickering over to Annie's direction and then flashing Clara a half-crooked smile, that even made Clara swoon a little. Before Elliot could even touch his seat at his desk behind Annie, a rocket of light flew into the room.

Fireworks erupted from this circular blazing ball of light. A tiny piece of ember fell down onto one of the pleats of Clara's pink pouf-dress, burning a small, black-rimmed hole. Clara started to pat her dress frantically, the blood rushing to her face as she got angrier and angrier.

The light stopped and laughter started. Tiny, little, belly-hugging laughter. Annie, Clara, and Elliot looked around the room, and then there, on top of the teacher's enormous mahogany desk, in front of the large blackboard sat, cross-legged, holding his belly, laughing, was a mischievous Pixie.

His skin was the same pastel-green as the 3 T's. The same olive dishevelled hair and forest-green rag shorts and t-shirt. His features small and elfin with tiny pointy ears. His confidence though, was bigger than the desk he perched on. His eyes danced with mischievousness and fun. For someone so small, he seemed to fill up the entire room.

'I'm Tyson!' he exclaimed, as if everyone should know exactly who he was, 'But, most Fae call me "Little T".'

'Nice to meet you Little T, I'm Elliot,' Elliot said laughing at the chaos Little T had already created. Little T rocketed over and gave Elliot a tiny, little fist punch.

Little T laid on Elliot's desk, one arm propping up his head and then crossing one leg over the other. Looking back and forth from Annie to Clara, 'And who are you two crazy chicks'?' he said coolly, acting like the king of room.

'I'm Annie and this is Clara,' Annie said softly, finally finding her voice. It was now Clara's turn to be unable to speak. This time though, in anger.

Clara span around and folded her arms abruptly across her chest. A fire burning in her oceanic eyes and her heart-shaped lips pursed together so tightly Annie thought it must be quite painful.

Clara let out a tiny, little cross sound, 'Humph!'

'Annie… and… Clara,' Little T said, pretending like he was thinking deeply about their names. 'My sisters talk about you two all the time!' he finished with a half laugh, like he knew their deepest darkest secrets.

Clara's head spun round and her usually beautiful eyes, shot daggers at the little Pixie. Annie rolled her eyes and turned to face the front of the class, it made total sense that this was what the 3 T's little brother was like. Little T took the seat behind Elliot, both boys still laughing at Clara's dramatic upset.

The boys started to chatter in muffled tones so Annie and Clara couldn't hear them, but their faces and the way Little T kept pointing over and looking at them, gave the distinct impression they were talking about them.

This seemed to add to Clara's annoyance, as she began to shuffle in her seat, the frustration bubbling away inside her. Annie just sat facing forwards trying to block everything out, she started to silently recite the Fairy Magical Words Alphabet, 'A is for abracadabra, B is for believer, C is for conjure'. This had always helped Annie calm down, even as a toddler she would recite the Magical Words Alphabet to stop her freaking out in new situations. Before Annie could get to H is for Hocus Pocus, Mama Gilbert glided into the room.

Without looking at any of the children she went straight to the blackboard and wrote in large, white-chalk italics, *Mama Gilbert's introduction into Fairydom.* Mama Gilbert managed to fill the room with calmness and reassurance, even though she herself, appeared flustered and unorganised.

Annie instantly relaxed.

Turning towards the class, Mama Gilbert began hunting for her glasses to take the register. She started to look on the large mahogany table, then in the draws, patting down all the pockets in her dress, nothing. Mama Gilbert looked absolutely perplexed as to where her glasses could be.

Clara then, faked a loud cough, 'Akem, Akem!' catching Mama Gilbert's attention.

Clara patted the top of her head signalling the whereabouts of Mama Gilbert's glasses. Mama Gilbert gave out a loud sigh of relief, patting herself on her head she located her tiny, rounded glasses. Which, much to her amusement were perched upon her lilac hair, just where she left them. Giggling still, she placed them upon her nose, her turquoise eyes dancing with joviality.

After a further fumble through an exceptionally large, lavender satin bag, matching her outfit. Which was in her usual style, sleeves cascading out, trimmed in glitter and diamante, and shimmering like lavender waterfalls. Mama Gilbert leaped elegantly onto the edge of the desk, crossed her sparkling legs, clicked her kitten heals together and started to take the register.

'Annie Rainerly,' Mama Gilbert called first, peering over her spectacles, and looking at Annie with a warm knowing smile.

Annie's arm shot up over excitedly together with a shout of, 'HERE! Mama Gilbert,' nearly scaring Mama Gilbert half to death with her eagerness.

'Good morning, Annie dear, loving the enthusiasm,' she sparkled, adoring the excitement. 'Elliot Carstina?' Mama continued.

'Yes, Mama Gilbert, here,' Elliot replied confidently, just raising his arm slightly off the desk. It was actually more of a flick of the wrist, a smooth motion just to signal where he was.

'My you're a handsome one, aren't you, Elliot. Good morning,' Elliot bowed his head a little as his face flashed red. Clara began to sink lower into her seat from embarrassment.

'Now then, who's next, ah yes, the magnificently beautiful, most scrum-diddly-um-shous, perfect prima ballerina, my fluffy princess… Clara Gilbert,' said Mama Gilbert proudly.

Clara buried her head in her hands, cringing at her grandmother's every word before raising her hand and meekly saying, 'Here, Mama.'

She knew it was going to be excruciating but nothing had quite prepared her for the full weight that was now hanging on her shoulders. She could hear Little T sniggering in the back which just added to her pain.

'Come along dear, sit up straight,' Mama Gilbert corrected Clara, reaching out her arm and signalling with her hand for Clara to raise herself up. 'Ok, now let me get this name right,' she looked down at her register a little closer, 'Tyson Glitterfluff Thunderlily?'

The class erupted in little giggles, Clara turned and flashed a smile of pure delight at Little T, beaming like she had just won the lottery. Looking at Annie, Clara then mouthed the words silently and slowly, 'Glitterfluff Thunderlily!' Annie couldn't help but giggle and bowed her head to hide her sniggers.

Little T blushed, trying desperately to act unaffected by his family name, he attempted to say confidently, 'That's just Little T, Mama Gilbert, if you don't mind.'

'Of course, dear… Mr…er… Glitterfluff Thunderlily.'

Mama Gilbert pulled an enormous lavender quill from the cascade of material in her right sleeve and appeared to scrub out what was written.

Then said loudly, 'No more, Glitterfluff Thunderlily, just Little T, done. Thank you, My Littlest T,' she emphasised.

Little T shuddered twice as Mama Gilbert said his name aloud again. Much to his embarrassment he noticed Clara's tiny shoulders going up and down as she was trying to suppress her giggles. He straightened his back and flicked the collar of his ragged forest-green shirt, as if dusting the comments and giggles away. Then, holding his finger in the shape of a gun he shot a little firework in Clara's direction. Which just diffused before reaching the hem of her pouf dress.

Clara shoulders stopped instantly, spinning her head around she glared at Little T. Little T gave her a playful wink and giggled at her, regaining back his confidence and perceived upper hand.

'And last but by no means least, Freddie Wildthorn,' the whole class looked around stunned, no one had even noticed another kid come in.

But there, sat behind Clara, Freddie had appeared like some kind of black-feathered Thistle Goose. Freddie sat with his back straight, firmly to attention, shoulders back, head up, face forwards.

Freddie was lean, not thin, but muscularly lean. His hair was cut into an army crop, where you could see hints of blonde seep through, brushing the tips at the top. He didn't make eye contact or look around at anybody. He stayed still, focused. He had a pile of books upon his desk and an array of markers and pens just like Annie.

'Here,' Freddie asserted, short, sharp and to the point.

'Hello, Freddie, such a pleasure to have you all in my class,' Mama Gilbert gushed.

Freddie just nodded in acknowledgment. Mama Gilbert put down her register and quill.

'Welcome to The Faedora Fairy Train Academy, and this is an introduction into Fairydom,' Mama Gilbert announced, perfectly overpronouncing every syllable whilst taking a bow as if she were on stage giving a performance. 'First things first, types of Fae and what can they do?'

Annie and Freddie's hands shot up in unison both eager to answer.

Chapter 10

Sitting with his feet up on his giant desk, leaning way back and slightly rocking from side to side, Professor Mortley was slowly and lovingly starting to peel off the shiny, green foil of his beloved sparkly, green, Christmas tree marshmallow.

He was still surrounded by stacks of papers, but he was oblivious to potential work piling up in front of him. Professor Mortley was wholeheartedly concentrating on the direction of the marshmallow Christmas tree, making sure it reached his bulging, fleshly lips. Taking the largest bite which obviously left the tell-tale sparkly, green, sticky residue across his top lip. He closed his eyes letting the taste wash over him, allowing the sugar rush to flow through his body. Professor Mortley had absolutely and completely gone into his happy place.

'Looks like some things never change, ah Pockets?'

Professor Mortley flung himself up, virtually choking on his beloved marshmallow. Upon hearing the voice, he stood to attention. Desperately trying to smooth down his tangerine waistcoat to meet the pulling-up of his chocolate, brown trousers in an attempt to cover the forever gap. Trying frantically to lick off his green, sparkly, sticky moustache.

The owner of the voice appeared, gliding around the room looking at, and overturning objects as she came to them, touching things and inspecting them like she was looking for hidden clues.

'We seem to have a slight predicament here, don't we Pockets?'

'Your Majesty,' Professor Mortley said awkwardly, apologetically, whilst attempting a half-bow, half-curtsy. 'I... I... wasn't expecting you,' he was bumbling his words as he became increasingly more nervous and uncomfortable. His holographic face was boylike and innocent. 'Queen Noralynn, I have been looking into why the train brought the Stoney on, but I've been unable to find anything.' Professor Mortley rambled off quickly.

'Never-Believer, Pockets, Never-Believer,' Queen Noralynn corrected.

'There is something oddly familiar about her though...' Professor Mortley looked older again, his facial hologram in overdrive. His voice trailed off whilst his mind went into deep thought, he looked off into space as if the answer were somehow within the air.

'Pockets!' Queen Noralynn snapped, purposely breaking his train of thought regaining his attention, 'Take a seat, we need to talk,' she commanded.

Professor Mortley sat back in his seat behind his desk, sitting upright this time, waiting for instruction. The light flashing in through the window created by the passing clouds was making his holographic face flicker from frightened little boy to perplexed and worried middle-aged man. He ran his hand through his dusty-brown hair nervously, making it look even more messy and unkept.

Queen Noralynn continued her walk around the room. She was wearing a long, white gown which was cut into a fishtail design, that silhouetted her long, slender figure. Her hair was platinum-blonde and reached just below her waistline and shone like a disco ball in the light. Her small, pointy ears parted her hair either side of her head, leaving two thick, platinum-blonde strands framing her face.

Her skin was porcelain, her face was entirely symmetrical. Queen Noralynn's almond-shaped eyes were bright green and gave the appearance of being too large for her elfin face. They were striking and hypnotic. She had a perfect elfin nose and beautifully formed heart-shaped lips.

Placed flawlessly upon her head was the Fae Crown, an embodiment of all of nature's elements, earth, wind, fire, and water. Entwined ancient twigs that were said to be from the Royal Bellflower trees, which were the same deep reds and browns as the mahogany of the train. Wildflowers woven through in varying shades of blue that gently swayed and bobbed as the Queen moved. Red rubies dotted around the edges of the crown that as the light touched dazzled red and orange. Finally, two lines of tiny blue sapphires that dangled down at each side of her face, all depicting the power of elements.

'You know we have to get her off the train, Pockets,' the Queen continued in a sing-song deliberate voice, 'A Never-Believer cannot be privy to our ways and teachings,' she picked up an old wooden thimble and twirled it around her finger.

Professor Mortley nearly jumped out of his skin and hurried over to where she was standing. Taking the thimble preciously from a wicked smiling Queen, he placed the thimble delicately back in its glass case.

'Your Highness, I haven't been able to find a way as yet.' Professor Mortley gathered up some courage and said more confidently, 'You know as well as I, it's the train that decides.'

Queen Noralynn sighed with menace, 'Oh, Pockets, Pockets, Pockets,' she chuckled to herself.

Professor Mortley's shoulders tightened with anxiety every time she called him by this name. He was now following her around the room trying to create a barrier between her and his precious possessions whilst trying to pay attention to what she was saying.

'The Fairy Council and I have come up with a rather ingenious way of shall we say…' Noralynn pretended to think for a moment, 'Of overriding the train.'

The train shook slightly as if protesting. Noralynn was weighing up Professor Mortley's reactions as she spoke. 'How much do you actually know about the girl?' she finally asked, probing the professor.

'Abigale?' Professor Mortley enquired, the mischievous boy back in charge.

'Do you have more than one Never-Believer on board, Pockets?' quipped Noralynn.

'Sorry, Your Highness, I seem to be all of a muddle,' Professor Mortley replied practically bowing every time he addresses her.

He licked his lips and found an odd piece of marshmallow left in the corner, pleasantly surprised he tried frantically to lick it off, taking his mind away again from the task at hand. Noralynn passed him a white hanky impatiently with a look of utter disgust.

'Thank you, Your Highness,' he bowed and nodded smiling into the hanky.

'This Never-Believer, Abigale, you say?' Noralynn said dismissively, she was beginning to tire of the communicative dance they were doing. 'Well, we have found a way for her to leave the train, without the train's magic.' The train began to shake harder objecting to what Noralynn was saying.

'Shhhhhh, Shhhhhh, my old friend,' Professor Mortley whispered under his breath to the train patting it gently, turning his back on Noralynn to hide his actions.

Noralynn smiled at Professor Mortley's back, 'The Fairy Godmother Cindercrest has advised that we can use the power of the Pink Moon at the end of the month,' there was a finality to the statement. 'That is all I'm permitted to say at the moment,' Noralynn teased.

The train shook harder. Professor Mortley, with more vigour than expected, bounded on top of his desk, and sat cross-legged on its edge. He folded one arm across his chest and the other arm was half-crossed with his finger posed on his lips, giving an appearance of fake concentration, combined with over-exaggerated nodding like he was somehow mocking her.

'Interesting,' he said through his finger, his voice vibrating with the train's continuous unhappy shaking. The steady rays of light now showing his boyish looks and making his reply seemingly satirical.

'ArrrrArrrrArrrrArrrrArrrArrrrrrrrr,' Professor Mortley's voice vibrated, 'PaaaPaaaPaaaPaaaPaaa,' he went again, 'Try it, it's fun, Haahaaaahaaaahaaahaaaaa,' he encouraged Noralynn, with a cheeky glint in his eyes.

Noralynn's patience was wearing thin, 'We don't have much time,' she snapped looking down her perfectly formed nose at him. 'I'll now be staying here in my suite at the back of the train, until the transfer is done.'

'OOOOOOOOOOOOOOOOooooooooookkkkkk…' the train stopped vibrating. 'Oh, it stopped,' Professor Mortley said with disappointment. Looking up at Noralynn he jumped off his desk, still showing the embodiment of a boy. 'As you wish Your Highness-es-es,' he finished making the most theatrical bow.

Noralynn had had enough, she headed towards the door which the train opened for her to glide through uninterrupted.

'Always a pleasure Pockets,' she called back to Professor Mortley, giving the distinct impression that it wasn't a pleasure at all.

Professor Mortley's eyes followed her out giving her a hard, unforgiving glare. She always seemed to bring out the worse in him. He collapsed back into his chair exasperated. Opening his top draw, he pulled out another green, sparkly, sticky, Christmas tree marshmallow. Peeling it back slowly he took a large bite, letting his teeth glide through the soft, sweet, doughy sugar mixture. His eyes began to close again as the sugar swept over him hoping the pleasure of the marshmallow would irradicate the pain of having to deal with Noralynn. He didn't hear the door open and close again.

'Professor Mortley! What are you doing? It's the middle of the afternoon!' the sweet voice chastised.

Professor Mortley again nearly choked on his sparkles at the shock of someone sneaking into his office again. This time though he wasn't alarmed as he knew he loved this voice.

'Mama Gilbert,' he said with his mouth full off green stickiness, 'You almost killed me!'

'Oh, my sweet boy, you'd know if I were going to kill you,' Mama Gilbert giggled at Professor Mortley her eyes filled with mischief. He smiled back, a smile that only two of the oldest friends could share, knowing each other inside and out. 'Now my boy, what is her royal nastiness doing here?' Mama Gilbert probed.

Professor Mortley hung his head dramatically, 'She was here about Abigale and getting her off the train.'

'Hmmmmm,' Mama Gilbert thought for a moment. 'Has she told you how? The train decides who stays and who goes.'

'That's what I said!' the train shook gently in agreement with Professor Mortley. 'But, she then said something about the Fairy Godmother and a Pink Moon.' He looked up as if trying to remember, 'At the end of the month, NoraBora is staying here till it's done.'

Mama Gilbert began to pace the room, mumbling to herself, her head was down, asking herself questions. 'I've never known the Queen to stay until the council's wishes are carried out, have you?'

'Nope, and she was nicer to me than normal,' Professor Mortley pointed out, 'There is definitely something fishy going on.'

'Have you been back to the hospital?' Mama Gilbert asked hopefully. Professor Mortley just shook his head. 'I think you need to go back, see if anything changed,' Mama Gilbert suggested.

'I keep getting the feeling I know her, Mama,' Professor Mortley confessed. 'I just can't put my finger on it,' Professor Mortley held his finger up in the air as if by doing so he would magically remember.

'Have another meeting with Abigale, get to know her a little and then return to the hospital,' Mama Gilbert advised. Professor Mortley nodded agreeing a plan of action. 'Did Noralynn say anything else?' Mama Gilbert enquired.

'Yes,' Professor Mortley moaned in annoyance, 'She kept calling me Pockets!'

Chapter 11

The 3 T's were darting across the ceiling of the carriage swishing, swooshing, and whizzing.

'The Queen is here, here is the Queen!' their usual high-pitched, melodic voices echoing each other's mischievously. This time though, there was a fourth light, lower following the four children as they returned to their rooms.

'Hey guys wait up!' Little T yelled in his biggest voice.

Giggling the 3 T's chimed, 'He can't keep up, up he can't keep.'

Clara looked up at the 3 T's and stopped, arms folded and waited. Annie, Elliot, and Freddie also stood waiting for Little T.

'Thanks Clara,' Little T panted, giving her a little embarrassed look.

Clara's face softened slightly, she almost gave him a smile, before spinning on her toes and starting to walk again.

Elliot patted his shoulder, 'Hitch a ride, T,' he called out and Little T took his place on Elliot's shoulder. Smiling from ear to ear at his newfound friends.

'We must get back to our room!' Annie said sideways to Clara, giving her a secret look, trying to surreptitiously remind her about Abigale. Annie grabbed her arm and tried to hurry Clara along attempting to separate her from the group.

'Hey guys, why don't we all go back to my cabin, and we can try and figure out why the Queen is here!' Elliot said trying to encourage the group to stay together, 'I have snacks!' he bribed.

'Sounds great, I'm in,' Little T said pretty much immediately, holding out a tiny hand for Elliot to fist pump in conformation. Elliot looked up to Freddie who towered over him.

'How about you, big guy?' Elliot asked, Freddie didn't say anything and just nodded in agreement to the invitation. 'Annie? Clara?'

'Errrrrr, Errrrr, We, erm…' Elliot looked Annie straight in the eyes rendering her speechless, Annie turned to Clara, her eyes bulging, silently pleading with Clara to help her answer the question. Fairies are totally and utterly forbidden to lie.

'We have another pressing engagement this afternoon,' which was the truth as they had planned to help Abigale, 'Another time maybe,' Clara replied, her voice filled with confidence and a purposely implied air of self-importance. Clara began to drag Annie away from the boys, picking up the pace.

The boys looked on after them.

'I don't trust those two,' Little T said suspiciously, 'They know something!'

'Maybe,' Elliot agreed unsure, he stopped outside his cabin door, 'Let's talk about it inside.'

***

Annie and Clara stood outside their cabin door; their images reflected in the mirror shine.

'Right,' Annie said in a whisper to Clara, 'Let's not make a big deal about today, we don't want to upset Abs.'

Nodding Clara replied, 'I think the boys think we are hiding something though, we have to be careful.'

Clara leaned on the door pushing it open with her back, as

the door opened Annie dropped her books to the floor, her mouth opens in disbelief. Clara's head turned to look inside; she drew in the biggest gasp of air ready to explode in the biggest squeal of surprise.

Annie scrambled to pick up her books and promptly fell through the open-door landing on the newly changed red and gold Christmas carpet. Annie laid there, rendered yet again speechless for the third time that day.

Clara pirouetted with tremendous speed around the door and slammed it shut behind her. Standing with her arms and legs spread wide across the closed door behind her, stopping anyone from opening it ever again.

'What happened?!' Clara said in hushed amazement.

In a still bewildered and astonished voice Abigale answered, 'I kinda Christmas'd the room.'

Shocked into silence Annie arouse from the floor. Clara walked towards her, and they both started to turn around slowly, taking in every inch of their newly Christmassed cabin. Annie reached out and touch the green pine needles of the Norwegian Spruce tree. Then, she gently pushed a red star, so it swung back and forth, making the twinkling lights catch its glittered edges.

Clara ran her hand over the luxurious red velvet bedding with the fluffy white trim, feeling its softness she spun around to look at Abigale's bed.

'It didn't work on your bed, ah?' Clara asked rhetorically.

Sitting still on her iron-grey bed Abigale just shrugged her shoulders as if it were just one of those things. Rising she joined her friends in the centre of their room. 'It's just how I imagine it.'

Clara and Annie looked at each other, then back to Abigale, 'Abs,' Annie said finally, 'You did this?'

Abigale sat them both down and told them all about reading the Believer book, then, lying down and closing her eyes and imagining her most perfect Christmas.

And then when she opened her eyes, 'Ta dah!' Abigale reached out her arms and signalled to the room.

'It's truly amazing,' Clara said, 'I love it, Christmas is my favourite time of year!' Clara flicked Abigale's plait with the sparkly pink, hair-tie and winked.

Annie had gotten up and was rooting though her books.

'What's wrong, Annie?' Abigale asked, starting to get a little worried.

Annie turned and pushed her thick-rimmed glasses up the bridge of her nose, looking at Abigale puzzled. 'It's just,' she paused thinking, 'Never-Believers, don't have magic, have never had magic,' she looked at Abigale as if searching for an answer.

The train began to shake violently, Abigale and Clara hugged closing their eyes. Annie threw herself onto the bed, head down buried into the luxurious red blanket, covering her head with her hands. They had never felt the train shake like this before. It seemed cross.

After a few minutes, the shaking stopped. Abigale and Clara release their hold of each other. Annie lifted her head as she felt the material change beneath her. The soft fluffy feel of the luxurious red blankets had vanished, and the familiar feel of satin had replaced it. Annie looked over at Abigale and Clara, both were looking a little sad.

'It's gone,' Abigale said softly.

They all looked around the cabin, which now felt strangely

bare. Clara's bright-pink bed full of haberdashery and Annie's array of pristine green accesssories with bundles of books now looked sparse. An emptiness had filled the room, along with a heaviness of heart.

'It was pretty cool though,' Clara said nudging Abigale with a smile.

'It was amazing,' Abigale said a smile returning to her face as both her friends beamed at her.

'Ok,' Annie said firmly, getting up and pacing the room, 'We now have an added mystery to solve.' Annie looked at Abigale, 'Can a Stoney…' Annie corrected herself, 'A Never-Believer have magic?'

'I've got afternoon tea with Mama this afternoon, I'll ask her some questions,' Clara added.

'I'll make you a list,' Annie said reaching for a pen and paper. 'I'll go to the library and see what history I can dig up,' Annie concluded.

'What should I do?' Abigale asked, excitedly hoping to get a job.

The girls fell quiet again, they all tried desperately to think of a job for Abigale. Which was really hard as none of them knew to what extent Abigale should be kept hidden and hidden from who exactly.

'I think you need to speak to Professor Mortley again, Abs.' Annie said finally breaking the silence, 'Someone must know something as to why you're here.'

The three of them sat on Abigale's iron-grey bed, Annie, Abigale, then Clara. Holding hands, their fingers entwined. All contemplating the missions ahead of them.

'So, how was class?' Abigale asked with a quizzical lightness of tone.

Abigale hadn't realised until they returned how much she had missed them. The heaviness of chest that was left from the disappearing of Christmas had increased as her heart pounded against it. Shyly she wondered - what if they didn't feel the same?

'Oh, we met some boys,' Clara answered flatly, a tiny smile emerging.

'BOYS!' yelled Abigale in giggling surprise, 'Tell me everything!'

'We missed you though, Abs.' Annie squeezed her hand, while Clara nodded with vigour.

And just like that, the heaviness lifted.

Chapter 12

Mr and Mrs Johnson were sat opposite each other at their rounded grey marble table, which was off-set to the left in the kitchen. The kitchen was a contemporary L-shape with a mixture of greys and blacks, against stark white walls. Steel accessories and sharp lines, clean and clear, completely devoid of homeliness.

The Johnsons were sipping tea out of their dull ceramic stone-grey cups. Mr Johnson slurping loudly at each sip, making his small bulbous top lip vibrate. You could hear rumblings from the floorboards upstairs, along with the odd yell, or scream.

'Peter stop it!' followed by, 'That's my bread!' George was shouting in a whingy, whiney, annoying cry.

'Ha, ha, ha, Georgie Porgy, it's mine now!' Peter teased, holding the bread up in one hand and pointing his long bony finger at George, 'Come on, try to get it,' he challenged.

George's tiny little mouth turned up at the ends and kind of smiled at him. Then, an evil, knowing smirk appeared.

'No George don't do it, I'm only messing,' Peter started on the back foot. 'Here, have your bread back,' Peter offered apologetically.

Maybe it was because George's mouth was so small that he was able perform this horrid version of a smile without it hurting, maybe he practiced it too. But it seemed to get bigger the more horrible he was planning to be.

George leaned his head back and yelled at the top of his voice, 'MUUUMMMMMMMMM!'

Peter took his chance, leaned forward and with his bony, long fingers and creepy long nails, pinched George under the top of his arm. George practically hit the roof, his eyes bulging and real tears emerging. He frantically rubbed his under-arm jumping up and down like it was on fire. George was giving Peter daggers through his rimmed, circular glasses, his eyes wet and swollen.

'Well, if I'm going to get in trouble anyway,' Peter said, holding his hands up as if he just couldn't help himself. Meanness oozing from every pore. A moment of anger flashed through George's eyes, before he increased his whaling level to distraught.

Footsteps started to pound up the stairs, Peter's face turned from having a grey hue to pure white, he swallowed loudly as fear began to rise in his belly. George's cries got louder, playing up to his new approaching audience.

Mrs Johnson appeared at the top of the stairs on the steely-grey carpet. Peter's heart sank. Mrs Johnson was silent, she turned towards Peter. Gone were the purple flecks her eyes normally carried, instead icy, stone cold, greyness. The precision of the cut of her hair that followed her jawline made her murky, grey hair appear to have a razor-blade effect. She held out her hand.

'No, please, I'll be good, I'll leave him alone,' begged Peter. 'I promise… I… I… I'm sorry, George,' he stuttered in a desperate plea. Mrs Johnson stood deathly still, staring at Peter as if he weren't even speaking, as if his words were nothing.

Mrs Johnson leaned forwards looming over Peter, her face

inches away from his, she stayed perfectly clam and spitefully whispered, practically spitting in Peter's face with the venom in which she spoke, 'Now, Peter Johnson, NOW!'

All the while George stood behind Mrs Johnson, stuffing slice after slice of bread into his abnormally small mouth, filling his hamster-like cheeks to the brim. So much so, the crumbs were spilling out onto the steel-grey carpet forming a crumbed ring around him. George's eyes were dancing, revelling in getting Peter in trouble.

Peter's attempt to diffuse Mrs Johnson was pointless, his scrawny shoulders fell, his eyes dropped to the floor, and he turned on his heels and disappeared into his room.

Seconds later, he re-emerged and handed to Mrs Johnson's still outstretched hand, his Dantone 8th Edition Silver fox Phone and tablet. Mrs Johnson pulled out her own phone from her pocket, flicking the screen up swiftly with her thumb and then placing it on the fingerprint reader, she opened her apps.

Her thumb worked like lightening, settings, accounts, Wi Fi, and Internet, she paused and looked at Peter, enjoying his misery. Turning her phone towards Peter so he could see the 'Disable Peter's devices' option. Mrs Johnson then swiped her thumb slowly across the screen.

'Blip, Blip'

The devastating sound of both devices shutting down. Mrs Johnson checked that both devices we off and meanly tossed them at Peter's feet and put her phone back in her pocket. She looked down at him with pity as he scrambled to check the screens were ok. Peter stood in the black painted doorway of his room, head hanging down, his spirit a little broken, awaiting any further punishment.

Quickly turning an outstretched hand, Mrs Johnson managed to clip George at the side of the head, ruffling his mousy-brown, grey-tinged hair, and taking George totally by surprise. Peter's mouth dropped open as she struck George, partly shocked, partly jubilant. George coughed and spluttered on the chunks of bread in his mouth, holding his chubby hands to his chest; you could barely hear the doorbell ring over his exaggerated choking noises.

Before Mrs Johnson could being her torment of George, Mr Johnson called up the stairs. But not in his normal, cold, confident voice, but in a shaky, trembling overly nice voice, 'Dear, we have a guest, could you please come down.'

Mrs Johnson's back straightened, just like Peter, her normal grey-tinged skin turned white, and fear gripped her body. Peter froze, George stopped spluttering and his eyes went from side-to-side searching, not knowing how to react, he knew something was wrong but didn't know what. There was only one person that made Mr Johnson speak like that.

'Dear?!' Mr Johnson called up again, this time more forceful, impatient, and much louder. He was wondering what on earth was taking so long, he needed help.

'Coming dear, one moment!' Mrs Johnson finally responded, 'Take our guest to the sitting room.'

Mrs Johnson crossly smoothed down her grey tea-stained pinafore dress. She wasn't dressed for guests, but she couldn't refuse them, not these. Taking three deep breaths she turned to head back down the stairs, spinning her head back towards Peter and George she spoke in a hushed whisper and angrily ordered, 'Get washed up, and get downstairs, no messing!'

She grabbed the half-full bag of bread from George's chubby

hand, giving him a threatening, evil stare.

Mrs Johnson tried to walk down the stairs gracefully, slowly, trying to regain her composure before facing the sitting room. It had been thirteen years since they had been in this house, a trip Mrs Johnson thought they would never make again.

Mrs Johnson walked passed the kitchen doorway, where Mr Johnson was pacing between the table and the counter-top, waiting for the kettle to boil. He looked up and caught Mrs Johnson's eye before she entered the sitting room. Mr Johnson's eyes looked worried, he paused slightly looking at Mrs Johnson as if he were totally lost as to what would have prompted the visit.

Mrs Johnson entered her pride and joy room. Dolphin grey thick double twisted fibre carpet, with a Payton Silver three-piece suite, complete with standalone puffer. A luxury Cashmere charcoal throw, that was draped over the puffer perfectly. Dolphin Grey cushions fluffed and plumped to perfection with Luna Blush charcoal blackout-curtains, pulled open just enough to frame the large bay-window behind them.

The three-piece encircled the room with the three-seater running along one wall from one side of the bay-window to the doorway. The double-seater was in front of you as you walk in through the door and then, at the opposite side of the bay-window, a single seat, where sat Mrs Johnson's most feared guests.

'Aunt Violet,' Mrs Johnson said through gritted teeth, 'So lovely to see you, to what do we owe the pleasure?' Mrs Johnson's voice was dripping with insincere kindness.

'This room needs a bit of work,' Aunt Violet said spitefully, enjoying the look on the face of the horrible woman in front of her.

'Er, does it?' Mrs Johnson was now seething inside, she began physically shrinking under the strain of her contained hatred of this woman. 'We have been meaning to get it done,' the words struggling to come out of her mouth, making her look weak and nervous. 'You're looking well,' she tried to change the subject.

'I'm looking old, you silly woman,' Aunt Violet scolded.

Aunt Violet's hair was pulled back into a low bun at the base of neck, unlike other Never-Believers her hair was white, not a grey in sight. Her skin was freckled which made it look darker than the normal Never-Believer pale-grey. Her eyes were blue and had an unspeakable ferociousness about them, a fire which seemed to complement her mean words. Her features were well-proportioned. A dainty, small nose and although encrusted with wrinkles, she had lips that if weren't always pursed and saying something mean, could, maybe be, heart-shaped.

She wore a long-sleeved, grey-wrap dress, always long-sleeved, that reached the floor with a black wrap over her shoulders. Aunt Violet was always dressed the same, same style, same shade, same everything. Adding to the severity of her look. She held her black throw with one hand the whole time, as if she were hiding something under there and one foot continually tapped under the hem of her dress, giving the impression of being constantly impatient.

Peter and George appeared in the doorway. Speaking in unison the tone of their voices rose and fell as they greeted Aunt Violet, slowly, pronouncing every syllable, 'G-ood morn-ning Aun-tie, Vi-o-let!' dripping with the same false kindness and insincerity of Mrs Johnson. They walked into the living room and stood in front of the two-seater settee.

Aunt Violet turned up her nose and a tiny growl came out from under her skirt. Mitsey. The little grey and white Jack Russel showed its sharp, pointy teeth to the boys, they both took a step back closer to the edge settee.

'Sit!' Aunt Violet said sharply, so sharply that Mitsey, Peter and George sat simultaneously.

'So, Auntie, how long are you here for?' Mrs Johnson asked trying to get a feel for why she was here. Mrs Johnson called to the kitchen looking for back up, 'Dear? Are the teas ready yet? Aunt Violet's just about to tell us her plans,' Mrs Johnson nodded at Aunt Violet to speak.

'Did you come on the train, Aunt Violet?' George asked rubbing his hand across his mouth trying to eradicate any leftover crumbs. Which was followed by a swift elbow to his chubby ribs from Peter.

'You know Aunt Violet fears trains!' Mrs Jonson scolded, 'Think boy! Go and help your father.'

Mrs Johnson almost lunged at George for saying something that might set Aunt Violet off. But this time Aunt Violet stayed strangely quiet as George scurried out the room to help Mr Johnson. Aunt Violet leaned down and stroked Mitsey, Mitsey rubbed his head into her hand welcoming the fuss.

Mr Johnson came in with the tray of teas, the tray shaking and the grey-stone cups clattering. Similar to George, his large-ness made him awkward and uncoordinated. He handed Aunt Violet a cup which she took without even a look of gratitude. Mr Johnson now sat with Mrs Johnson at the edge of the three-seater, unable to relax until they knew the plans of the old lady in front of them.

'Aunt Violet, your plans?' Mrs Johnson pressed.

Aunt Violet paused and sipped her tea, screwing up her face as she did like she had just drunk some sort of putrid perfume.

'Where's the girl?' she asked, looking Mrs Johnson directly in the eyes.

'What girl?' Mrs Johnson looked confused, 'What? Abigale?' Mrs Johnson replied in astonishment.

'Yes, Abigale,' Aunt Violet pursed her lips and stared at Mrs Johnson, who looked completely baffled by the question.

'She is in the hospital, refusing to wake up,' Mrs Johnson complained, her voice cool, matter-of-fact, she was now returning Aunt Violet's hardened stare, perplexed as to why Aunt Violet would even care.

'Mitsey and I shall take the room to the left of the stairs,' Aunt Violet announced. Peter's shoulders collapsed, that was his room. 'Percy, you can take me to see the girl in the morning,' she ordered at Mr Johnson, who just nodded in feared agreement.

This day can't get any worse, thought Peter having lost all contact with the outside world only minutes before and now he has lost his bedroom.

'Peter, you share with George,' Mrs Johnson insisted.

Peter was wrong.

Chapter 13

Queen Noralynn sat at her vintage, white wood dressing table. The edges and legs of which were coated in gold-leaf, that reflected the light that came through a large porthole-style window. It had a matching seat where the ornate, curved legs were coated with the same gold-leaf at its edges and topped with a thick, white cushion trimmed with gold thread, totally fitting for a queen.

The rectangular mirror was huge, four-foot-deep, and nearly the same in width, reaching the entire length of the dressing table. It was curved at the corners and trimmed in the same white wood and gold-leaf decoration. Noralynn sat looking at her reflection.

The Fae Crown was resting upon the dressing table, the light from the circular window catching the rubies woven through the mahogany stems. Making the crown glow like kindling. Looking down at the crown and back to her reflection, Noralynn's hand came up to her cheek, making circular movements over her pale, porcelain skin. A skin that defied time, line-free and as clear as the day she passed through the Training Fae Chamber.

The person within the skin was not, however, so line-free. Noralynn looked harder at her reflection. The glow of her bright-green eyes seemed darker to her, but then it would be, she knew her truth. Placing both hands now on the Fae Crown she replaced it on her platinum-blonde hair, arranging the strands at the sides of each ear and made sure her appearance was perfect.

Noralynn began to chant, 'Mirror on the wall, dial it up and make me a call, make it speedy, make it travel, bring up the members of the Royal Fae Council.'

Noralynn waited. The mirror then split into four divisions. Flickering in the top right-hand corner before a man appeared, large in stature, muscular though not chubby. He gave the appearance that he was tall, although he was sitting. Dark, oak eyes that would melt the coldest of hearts, chiselled cheek bones and a strong jawline. He wore a dark, navy pinstripe suit with a white shirt and rose-blush tie. Smart, strong, and sophisticated.

'Alaris, thank you for attending,' Noralynn welcomed the handsome man.

'The TF colony and Personal Fairies at your service, my Queen,' he replied in a strong, deep voice. Noralynn nodded and smiled in appreciation.

The bottom right-hand corner started to flicker, like a TV trying to tune in. You could hear a woman's high-pitch well-spoken voice, crackling trying to get through. The section went black.

'Give the box a bang, will you honey!' said the voice behind the blank screen. With another flicker of the mirrored screen the woman appeared, 'Ah! There you are my lovelies, apologies for the box, technological problems,' the voice eloquent, soft, yet jovial.

'Godmother Tula Cindercrest, it is always a pleasure,' Noralynn replied, with a tense half-smile, finding her continuous struggle with the new mirrored-communication system amusing.

Godmother Cindercrest was full-figured and bubbled over with jolliness. Her head was full of ringlets that were a shade of punch-pink. Her cheeks were full and rosy, and her smile reached from ear to ear. Her eyes were dancing with life and fun, embodying all that Godmothers stand for: kindness, education, power, and fun.

Noralynn and Godmother Cindercrest's eyes locked in a moment, Godmother Cindercrest's smile seemed to light up even more revelling in the Queen's exasperation of her.

Noralynn bowed her head, thinking Godmother Cindercrest could be the most annoying woman amongst all Fae.

Godmother Cindercrest noticed Noralynn look away and noted it. How the stuck-up, know-it-all Elf ever became Queen she never knew. Continuing to smile without a care in the world the Godmother's attention turned to Alaris.

'Alaris,' she said practically drooling with a flirtatious smile, 'You're looking super handsome,' she giggled.

Blushing slightly, but enjoying every second Alaris replied, 'Tula, your smile dazzles as always.'

Noralynn rolled her eyes in disapproval as the bottom left-hand screen began to flicker, this time it was Troma, President of the Pixies. Troma appeared standing on top of a desk, poised as if she were about to lead an army into battle. Her legs wide, hands in little fist on her hips and a face of total concentration.

Emulating the 3 T's and Little T, her skin was pastel-green, with tiny elfin features, similar to that of Noralynn, only smaller. Short, dishevelled olive-green hair, with a fringe she had to keep flicking up off her face.

Troma however, wore a tailored forest-green shorts and waistcoat uniform, which was expertly cut to fit the intricacies of her tiny body, a far cry from the ragged clothes of the other Pixies. On the top pocket of her waistcoat were two strips of gold medals for her service to the Fae. Troma was well-respected by everyone and feared by many, ruthless to the core if it meant the survival or rise in power of her Pixie kin.

'Troma, thank you for coming, I know you are very busy,' Noralynn bowed her head as a mark of respect in welcoming her.

Troma just nodded back in response, adding arrogant and self-righteous to her list of credentials. The final screen began to flicker in the top-left, the final member of the council appeared.

A small, old, and bald man appeared. His ears were pointy and too large for his head, the pointy bits were bent over at the tip, drooping through old age. Like Noralynn's, his features elfin and small. But his too-large eyes and angular face made what should be a kind and welcoming face, look hard, straight, and emotionless.

'Chancellor Carstina, thank you for joining us,' Noralynn said extending eye contact and giving him an overly familiar nod.

'Shall we just get on with it, Your Highness,' Chancellor Carstina replied looking down impatiently, ruffling through some supposed papers that were below the screen.

'Certainly, Chancellor, would you like to start?' said Noralynn, offering the spotlight to this strange, angry-looking man.

'Yes, thank you,' he said quickly, his voice low and serious, 'As you all now know, we have a castaway in our ranks, a Never-Believer aboard the Faedora train.'

'Shall I take care of it, Chancellor?' Troma volunteered,

stepping forward and holding a tiny dagger up towards the sky.

'Oh,' Godmother Cindercrest gasped, 'She is but a little girl, no real threat, there is another way… Less violent on the child, if performed correctly of course, Chancellor,' Godmother Cindercrest concluded, much more forcefully waving her purple sparkling wand, making sure Chancellor Carstina heeded her warning.

Noralynn held up her hand as if to stop Godmother Cindercrest's thoughts going any further.

'Of course, we will not bring any harm to the girl, Cindercrest,' Noralynn assured giving a fleeting look to the Chancellor, 'But we need to assure our light and traditions, and our safety are not compromised.'

Godmother Cindercrest nodded along reluctantly.

'So, what do you propose?' Alaris asked short and sharp. 'We can't leave it too much longer before news trickles down to the Fae population, my Queen, my Tula…'

'Alaris, if I may, interject,' the Chancellor interrupted slightly, ruffling Alaris, 'We are aware this is a time-sensitive matter, we agree with Godmother Cindercrest's idea,' the Chancellor said with a hesitant air, pausing before carrying out the rest of his sentence.

Fairy Godmother Cindercrest fluffed and primmed herself ready to take the glory, 'But,' the Chancellor continued, 'There are some tweaks we would like to make.'

Chancellor Carstina said this a little kinder waving his hand towards Noralynn, to explain more. The Fairy Godmother's face dropped. Chancellor Carstina tried his hardest to appear charming, but he knew his efforts fell on deaf ears as it was almost certain Alaris would side with whatever way Godmother Cindercrest went.

Noralynn began to speak in an enchanting soft and melodic voice, 'I shall be performing the spell to extract the Never-Believer from the train, not Godmother Cindercrest.'

'But Your Highness, you are not powerful enough, you need Godmothers' magic,' Godmother Cindercrest said with a slightly smug giggle.

Noralynn expected this and countered holding up her hand overrulingly to quieten the Godmother, 'I have accounted for that with the Rainerly girl,' she explained.

'But you can't…' the Godmother's face flashed with disbelief, shock, and utter contempt.

'Let's put it to the Vote,' the Chancellor interjected quickly, 'All those for the Queen taking lead say "Aye", Aye!' the Chancellor raised his hand.

'Aye,' said Troma loyally.

'Not for all the sparkle dust in heaven,' Fairy Godmother Cindercrest sat back in her seat and sprayed glitter into the air.

Alaris came next now being much more formal, 'Fairy Godmother Cindercrest is correct, it is too dangerous not to let her perform the spell, I'm a Nay!'

The Chancellor then spoke with a calculating, proud smile, 'My Queen we have a tie, it is down to you to cast the deciding vote.'

Noralynn lifted her head and locked eyes with an enraged Fairy Godmother. With an air of superiority Noralynn simply said, 'Aye.'

Letting the word sink in for a second she then went on to explain Fairy Godmother's Cindercrest plan.

'Come the end of month, the Luna calendar predicts a Pink Moon. The Pink Moon should increase the power of the Fae, allowing it to then be focused. *I,*' she emphasized looking at Fairy Godmother Cindercrest, 'Will then harness the power of the Rainerly girl and be strong enough to overpower the train and send the Never-Believer back to the train she should have stayed on.'

'This is too dangerous for you, my Queen,' Alaris said in a fake concerned for her well-being voice, and a bid to get Godmother Cindercrest back to the fore.

'Alaris, the Chancellor and I have discussed the finer points and I have the approval for the help I need,' she looks directly at the Chancellor for conformation.

'Of course, Your Highness,' Chancellor Carstina said smugly, 'You take all the help you need, we all need to help each other.'

'How can the Pixies help?' Troma asked wanting to be part of such a historic venture.

'Well,' Noralynn said slowly looking down in sly anticipation, the conversation developing exactly as she had predicted, 'We, I mean, I, wondered if the 3 T's would be available to be my aids, we can't be everywhere all the time, I need eyes and ears everywhere making sure the Fae children are safe around the Never-Believer.'

'Of course, I shall tell them to report directly to you, and to you directly,' Troma said in a vow of allegiance, raising her tiny dagger to the sky again.

The Chancellor noticed Godmother Cindercrest was obviously disgruntled 'Godmother, I'm sure her highness has thought of every eventuality,' his voice dripping with insincere proclamation.

Noralynn then added, 'As Queen of the Fae and Believer realms I hope you believe wholeheartedly that I have only the best interests of our families at heart,' her voice became melodic again, 'I will see to it that we will thrive and prosper for your children and your children's children, they will have lives full of magic and light.' Noralynn place a hand over her heart as if sealing her promise.

All four of the council members placed their right hand on their chest, over their heart, and said together, 'Magic and light.'

'The proof will certainly be in the pudding, Your Highness, I trust you will keep us updated on any developments,' Godmother Cindercrest requested firmly, clearly not happy with what had transpired.

'Of course,' Noralynn confirmed with a smooth, cool smile.

'Good, in magic and light we trust,' she said begrudgingly, 'Alaris, the Magic Symposium this weekend?' she giggled, in a dramatic change of mood.

'Absolutely Tula,' Alaris replied jovially, giving her a playful wink, 'I'll bring the ivory if you bring the fairy dust,' he said dashingly, with a soppy giggle to himself.

Giggling uncontrollably now Godmother Cindercrest's screen went blank. Troma and the Chancellor looked on with unimpressed, hard expressions. Alaris's face then changed back to being a serious businessman, 'Please keep us updated if the TF colony and Personal Fairies can help in any way.'

Noralynn nodded her goodbye, and his screen went blank.

'We are action ready and ready for action, should you need, my Queen,' Troma gave a bow and was gone.

'You have to get the girl off the train, Nora,' the Chancellor hissed. 'By any means necessary, it will be bad for both of us,' he warned, his face turning menacing.

'I know, Uncle, but it means harnessing all the power of the strongest Fae on the train, a mere girl,' Noralynn warned back, 'I need to get her on side first.'

'Nora, remember the pain we have endured at the hands of Never-Believers, they are a threat to the Fae, to you, AND to you keeping the crown, the vultures are circling.' Chancellor Carstina eyes narrowed as he stared at Noralynn making sure she knew the gravity of his words.

'I shall not fail, Uncle,' she said with certainty tinged with a little sadness in her eyes.

'I know, Nora,' he said softer, then immediately corrected himself, 'Your Majesty,' he affirmed, perplexed by his words, his softness appeared to frighten him. With his hand on his heart and bowing his head, he said, 'Magic and Light.'

The screen went blank before Noralynn could respond. She was left looking at her reflection, the reflection of someone she didn't recognise anymore.

Chapter 14

'Maybe she is here to give me my first medal... most promising new student,' Little T bounded around Elliot's room like a little rocket, over-excited and utterly full of himself.

Elliot's room was the same cedar red as the girls, just much smaller. One bunk on the right-hand side with a cedar desk next to the head end of the bed, which was under a chamber-style window, not too dissimilar to the one in Professor Mortley's office, only smaller.

Elliot's duvet was royal blue with a golden edging with a matching pillowcase giving it a regal feel. Regal if it wasn't such a mess. The covers were all crumpled up in a heap on the bed showing the pale-blue, of a not-so-fitted bottom sheet. His shelf was curiously empty, nothing to show what he liked, where he was from or his family. It was like he hadn't emptied any of his things yet.

The window was surrounded with navy-blue, criss-cross, textured curtains with gold strands woven through. A rug similar to the one in the girls' room, circular, navy-blue and with gold strands tied the dishevelled room together.

'I don't think so T,' Elliot said with a smile.

'A Queen hasn't been on board the Faedora train in forty-two years,' Freddie piped up.

'What ARE you doing, Freddie?' Little T asked in amusement.

Freddie was laying on the floor pushing himself up and down with his hands.

'48, 49, 50, I'm training for the 36th Colony Test,' he said slightly breathless as he collapsed face-down onto the floor.

'Don't you need muscles for that?' Little T teased, pretending to flex his muscles in various mocking bodybuilding poses.

'Don't you need to be alive to be a Pixie?' Freddie threatened, pretending to get up in Little T's direction.

Little T darted onto Elliot's shoulder to safety, his little green gleeful face peeping out from behind Elliot's ear.

'Ok you two! Cool it,' Elliot said holding his hands out like a referee calling time. 'I think those two girls know a lot more than they were saying!' he suggested.

'Ohhhhhhhh, definitely! They know something,' Little T agreed, putting on a fake pair of glasses, trying to make himself look cleverer and nodding his head in agreement.

'Take those off, you look ridiculous,' said Freddie, laughing at Little T.

Little T pulled them off slowly actually feeling a little hurt by Freddie's words. Freddie noticed and not wanting to be a Molar Mouth said, 'Maybe a hat would suit you better.'

'What? Like this?'

Little T pulled out of his brown leather bag a forest-green pointy hat, in the shape of a paper sailboat, with a tiny feather hanging out the back. The feather fanning all the colours of the rainbow and within the blades a hidden eye, just like a miniature peacock feather.

Not wanting to hurt Little T's feelings again, Freddie agreed to the hat, 'Errm, yeah, just like that.'

Elliot smiled at Freddie and Freddie smiled back, they knew

then, they were cut from the same cloth. Little T puffed out his chest like he was king of the world, thrilled with the compliments of these two new friends.

'So, how are we going to get to the truth, we need to get Annie and Clara to talk,' Elliot queried, wanting to formulate a plan. 'We should split them up!' he suggested.

'I'll take Clara!' Little T said excitedly, 'I think she likes me!' he said confidently.

'Yeah, ok, T,' Elliot laughed at his confidence, 'If you're sure?'

'Of course, I'm sure,' Little T scoffed.

'Brilliant, ok then, Freddie you talk to Annie?' Elliot said.

Freddie began to choke on the air, redness began to rise from his lean neck, up his strong jawline and highlighted his long, oblong face. He started pushing his thin-rimmed rectangle glasses repeatedly up his strong, roman nose in a kind of physical stutter.

'Jeeze, you ok Fred?' Elliot asked concerned.

'Those push-ups have killed him!' Little T laughed.

Freddie whispered, slowly, full of embarrassment, 'I've never spoken to a girl before,' he looked down unable to look at the other boys.

'What?' Little T shouted, large belly laughs just beginning to emerge from his mouth.

Elliot's hand came up to his shoulder with the speed of light before Little T's laugh could escape. Elliot flicked him off his shoulder and sent him tumbling down on to the piled up royal-blue duvet, knocking the peacock-feather hat to cover his face, while he sat dazed, not quite knowing what had hit him.

Annie was seated at large desk that displayed the same mirror-finish as the rest of the train. She was always amazed by the train library. Firstly, by how such a massive area could fit onto a train and secondly, by its sheer beauty.

The library was cylindrical, with a large singular desk that went entirely around the whole ground floor. Little dividers emerged from the wall, creating cubicles and workstations. Then, there were the books. Books, as far as the eye could see, starting around the top of the cubicles and then going up for another four floors.

The first and second floors were full of Fae spell casting and illusion books, all looking relatively new. Although, some were hundreds of years old. The third floor was restricted to third year Fae students, including books on the history of fairy magic, necromancing and voodoo origin spells, and of course dark fairy magic spells.

Then, finally, the fourth floor, restricted access. Forbidden to all except, Professor Mortley, The Fae Council and Guardian of the Books.

From the ground floor the books looked so old and delicate, even the considered 'new' ones. Annie would give anything to be able to read one of those books on the fourth floor. She watched the unmanned sliding ladders that lay diagonally across the bookshelves. Sliding and moving to different sections of the bookcases waiting for a reader to hitch a ride.

Books magically flying from shelf to shelf as if in constant reorganisation.

In the middle of the room was a circular reception station, full of papers and scrolls and a little old lady Elf, that seemed to be lost in the chaos of the papers.

The Elf lady's hair was tied back loosely into two, sliver plaits on each side of her head. They started just above her tiny pointy ears and pinned back in a knot at the nape of her neck. The braids having two purposes, keeping the untamed stray locks away from her face and holding an array of pens and pencils that were wedged within the weave of the plaits.

She had two sets of glasses, the pair she was wearing, small and round, which perched on the end or her usually long elfin nose. The other pair were square and rested on top of her head waiting for her to use.

Miss Petula was the Guardian of the Books. Nothing or no one went in or out of the library without Miss Petula knowing. She opened scroll after scroll, appearing to read it at lightning speed and then placed it in another pile. A system that baffled Annie as each pile looked exactly the same.

'Miss Petula,' Annie asked is a soft whisper, 'Miss Petula, could you help me please?'

Miss Petula was engrossed in what she was doing and didn't even look up at Annie, 'Annie, I'm not sure I can, most of the books you want are on the fourth floor.'

Annie was taken a back, how did she know what she wanted to look at, 'But how…,' Annie began.

Interrupting Annie, Miss Petula spun her opal gaze on to Annie. Looking through her circular glasses her stare rendered Annie speechless. Totally stunned, Annie was unable to break from her stare.

Then, in an old vibrating, soft voice Miss Petula spoke, 'You search for Never-Believers, their history and relation to the train, yes?'

It was a rhetorical question, but Annie couldn't answer even if she wanted to.

'I cannot allow you to breach the fourth floor Annie, maybe there is someone, or *something,* else that can help you?'

Miss Petula gave Annie a look as if she should know what she was talking about, but Annie had absolutely no clue.

'You can go now, Annie, your cubical is ready.'

Miss Petula broke the gaze that had held Annie and pointed over to a cubicle. She then lowered her head returning to the sorting of her scrolls.

Wide-eyed behind her thick-rimmed glasses, Annie looked over in the direction of Miss Petula's hand. There, waiting for her was a cubical full of books.

Annie was utterly baffled, she covered her mouth with her hand and whispered secretly under her breath to make sure her voice had been restored. Plonking herself down she began to read the spines of the old leather-bound books she hadn't picked. *A History of Elves,* she read in her head. *What has Elf history got to do with Never-Believers?* Annie thought. Opening the book, she noticed a strange inscription on the very first page.

Amica mea V,
Qui annales referri facti sunt
Et magicae lucis
Vestra Dominicus xx

Annie wondered who the note was for and who Dominicus was, she had never heard the name before. *What did this mean?* Annie quietly contemplated, *Why had Miss Petula given her Elf history to read.* It made no sense to her at all.

Other books started to appear on Annie's desk, she read the spines of the new books, *Cloaking spells and casting, The Elfin language, Barrier spells, and Graduating Fae - Rules and Regulations.*

Annie untied the fraying green ribbon of her jade rucksack and pulled out a lined pad and glittery, green pen. She began making notes and lists, trying to make sense of the books she had been given. Annie knew she was in for a long night.

Feeling like she had been in the library for hours, Annie was ears deep in notes and theories when she heard the most enchanting voice. She lifted her head to see where it was coming from, she thought was the only person left in the library. The enchanting voice continued, she didn't recognise it, but it was calling her name, getting closer and closer.

Chapter 15

'Mama!' Clara called, 'I'm here!' Clara's voice was melodic entering Mama Gilbert's cabin.

Normally, when Clara visited her grandmother, everything was in its place and there was a place for everything. But today, her cabin was in total disarray. Mama Gilberts' cabin was an Aladdin's cave of magical objects. Full of what she called 'Her personal treasures'. Ornaments and knick-knacks that she had collected and loved over the years. Lamps, figurines, stones, runes, magical talismans, crystals, cups, and saucers. But none of these objects were where they normally lived.

Mama's cabin was red cedar like the other cabins on board the train. Not that you could see much of it today as there were dresses and materials strewn everywhere.

Her living room was odd, she had a large round table just to the right of the bedroom door. In the middle of the table was an enormous old-looking book, the pages were a tea-stained brown and the edges trimmed with gold. It was open somewhere in the middle as the pages looked equal on either side. The writing was swirly and joined together looking utterly unreadable to Clara.

There were two used giant purple candles on either side of the book, you could tell the candles had been used as you could see where the wax had dripped down their sides and onto the golden candelabras. Creating hardened road maps of wax, holding the secrets of spells cast as it cooled before it reached its table, hiding the ornate beauty of each of the golden candelabra.

There were, however, no chairs at this table. This table was not meant for sitting or dining at. In fact, there were only two chairs in the whole room. One little standalone stool, with a dark plum-coloured, puff top with three cedar legs coming out of it, this stood opposite the table next to a large bookcase. A bookcase that was stuffed full of books along with all kinds of trinkets in front of them making them challenging obstacles should you wish to see a book.

Clara would often just sit on the stool staring at the trinkets and wanting to know how Mama Gilbert had come to acquire them. Clara loved Mama's old stories and could listen to them for hours.

Mama Gilbert always sat in the other chair that was a large, oversized armchair. 'The comfy chair,' Mama Gilbert would call it. It was a vibrant boysenberry-purple, covered in a material with a twelve hundred Egyptian thread count, making it durable and ever so soft. Whenever Mama sat in the chair it would almost consume her it was so big in comparison. Her little feet would hang just off the end. This giving her the benefit of seeing her amethyst-encrusted kitten heels, that sparkled and twinkled as she pointed her toes backwards and forwards.

The room always smelled of lavender, which made Clara feel relaxed and a little sleepy. It felt like home. But today, there was a hint of sage, which was unusual as Mama Gilbert only used sage when she was worried about something.

'Mama!' Clara called again, 'Are you here?'

'Yes!' a distant voice called, 'I'm in the back, dear, I'm coming!'

The voice came from the bedroom, which you couldn't see from the doorway, only the end of her lavender bedspread. Mama Gilbert emerged looking red-faced and lost within her own thoughts.

'What's wrong, Mama?' Clara asked, holding her hands out pointing to everything that was not in its usual place.

'I've lost my memory stick, dear,' Mama Gilbert replied, still looking puzzled turning in circles around the room, the light catching her lilac hair and the stones and jewels that lay within. Mama always sparkled.

'Oh Mama, you can get another one of those from the library,' Clara said dismissively, plonking herself down on the little, dark plum stool.

'Not that kind of memory stick, dear, my Nephilim memory stick, the one that restores memories,' Mama sat down herself on the comfy chair, sinking into it slowly. 'If only I could remember where I put it!' Mama Gilbert giggled tiredly at the irony.

'Are you ok, Mama? I smell sage,' Clara inquired, remembering then why she was here; to complete her part of "The Plan".'

'Hmmm, yes dear, something's off, I just can't put my finger on it!' Mama said rubbing her tummy as if that's how she knew. 'The sage will help, it always does,' she said confidently.

'Mama?' Clara said slowly, raising the pitch of her voice as she finished the word. The tell-tale sign she wanted something.

'Yes, dear?' Mama waited, her eyes still darting around the room, forever seeking.

'Have there always just been the Fae on the train?'

'Ermmmm, yes dear,' she paused lifting up a crystal glass slipper on her square, metal, side-table, as if her stick would somehow be there, 'Well, and our dear Professor obviously.'

'Oh, ok, anyone else?' Clara persisted. Mama Gilbert started bouncing up and down slightly in her chair excited by the way her dress fluffed and floated, 'Mama?'

'Mmmmmm, hmmmm, hmmmm,' sang Mama Gilbert, her eyes back to scouring the room.

'Mama?!' Clara sighed laughing, falling forwards with mock frustration.

Mama Gilbert smiled, a warm, deliberate smile, 'Yes, my dear?'

Clara thought for a moment trying to think of the best way to put her question 'What do you know about Never-Believers, has there ever been one on the train before?' *Blatantly was the only way to go*, she thought.

Mama Gilbert sighed, she knew this question was coming, she didn't know how much to share with Clara, as it wasn't really her story to tell.

Mama Gilbert was contemplating how she should begin, she started to wriggle around in her normally very comfy chair, but something was poking her in the back. She wriggled and shuffled and then, 'Ah ha!' Mama Gilbert pulled out a long, brown downtrodden branch that was wedged deep down within the comfy chair.

'Professor Mortley *will* remember, hurrah!' Mama Gilbert giggled in celebration of finding the Nephilim memory stick.

***

Abigale jumped out of her skin as the cabin door exploded open and the 3 T's entered the room like rockets.

'Professor Mortley wants to see the Stoney, Stoney to

117

Professor Mortley,' it was haunting the way they chanted in unison.

Slight giggles behind their words as they criss-crossed around the ceiling of the cabin. They appeared to be enjoying the prospect of sending Abigale to an uncertain fate far too much.

Abigale smoothed down her charcoal-grey, pleated dress, pulled forward her caramel plaits, so that the pink and green sparkly hair-ties rested on either side of her collarbone. She took a deep breath and headed for the door. Pulling it wide-open with more force than she expected she unsteadied herself slightly, almost losing her footing.

Annie is rubbing off on me, she thought, smiling to herself as her friend crossed her mind. Regaining her composure, Abigale paused at the door, turned, and with all the confidence she could muster she asserted, 'Are we going then?'

The 3 T's stopped mid-flight and mid-chant and looked down at Abigale. Shock written all over their little faces. Abigale felt a moment of pride in herself. The 3 T's then started to laugh and giggle. Abigale's confidence took an immediate nosedive.

'Stoney's got lively, lively little Stoney,' they chanted as they flew a little too closely over Abigale's head, making Abigale duck for cover as they headed out the door.

Abigale was again fascinated by the beauty of the forever-changing swirls of reds and browns of the train wood as she followed the 3 T's down the carriage. Mirror-shine appeared as the 3 T's leaped across the panels. The trains vibration was more evident underfoot, it's rhythmical clickety, clacketing cast an unusual calmness over Abigale. It felt like the train was encouraging her, supporting her.

Abigale stopped outside of Professor Mortley's office door.

Her grey reflection peering back at her in the mirror-mahogany. Abigale gave her pink and green sparkly hair-ties a squeeze and knocked on the door.

She waited. And she waited.

'Go in Stoney, Stoney go in,' repeated the 3 T's, their little green bodies hovering over the doorway, their reflection making it seem like 6 T's. Abigale was pleased this wasn't the case. Abigale slowly pushed the door open, hearing it squeak and creak as she did.

'Hello… Professor Mortley?' Abigale enquired, her voice hushed and unsure.

She continued her entrance into the room, her steps gentle, tippy-toeing across the vibrating boards. Behind the giant mahogany desk was a rumbling and Abigale could just see the top of Professor Mortley's chocolate-brown trousers and the forever gap before the tangerine-orange waistcoat started. It was bobbing up and down as Abigale got closer and closer.

Reaching the giant desk and starting to rise up higher onto the very tip of her toes, Abigale tried to peer over to see more as she quizzed again, 'Professor Mortley?'

Thud. The Professor's head struck the underside of the desk. Abigale retreated from her tip-toes and took one step back from the desk with lightning speed, looking a little worried. This was the second time she had made him hit his head.

Slowly, Professor Mortley appeared from behind the desk one hand rubbing where he had struck he his head and looking puzzled as to who was here. As he focused on Abigale, both his hands sprung to his waistcoat pulling it down swiftly over his little, round belly to meet chocolate-brown trousers. He then patted himself down, straightening himself in an attempt to look more professional, or to at least look a little more Professor-like.

'Abigale, Ermmmm,' Professor Mortley seemed utterly lost as to why she was there.

The 3 T's interjected, 'Stoney's got to go Professor, remember Professor, Stoney's got to go!'

They giggled and laughed as they gave the news reminding the Professor. The 3 T's shot around the room dancing like they were celebrating. The Professor noticed Abigale's face fall. A sadness he remembered all too well.

'That's quite enough Tiana, Tamsin, and Tatum!' The Professor said crossly, the older side of his holographic appearance taking over, 'You can go,' Professor Mortley snapped motioning towards the door.

'The Queen told us to stay, to stay said the Queen,' they recited with indignation and a spiteful inflection.

Professor Mortley's face turned nearly as red as the wood in his desk, the light struck his face from a different angle and there was the image of a cross little boy. The disarray of the Professor's dusty, brown hair now framed the face of a furious young boy that looked intent on causing trouble.

The Professor leaned back and reached under the desk, he pulled out a large Y-shaped piece of wood. With what looked like a thick rubber band attached to each tip of the Y. He leaned forward and out of a little jar hidden behind the bundles of papers on his desk he pulled out a little, opaque marble. Placing the marble in the rubber band and pulling it backwards as far as the elastic tension would allow, he took aim at the 3 T's.

Pop! The marble hurtled toward the 3 T's just missing Tiana. They all stopped and stared at Profession Mortley, shocked and angry. But Professor Mortley wasn't finished there.

Pop! Pop! Pop! Never had Abigale seen anyone move so quick, marble after marble flew through the air. The 3 T's ducked and dived and tried to hide. The Professor, however, was too quick for them and an expert Marbleman.

The 3 T's charged towards the door hoping to escape unscathed. Just as the door opened, the Professor closed one eye and aimed. *Pop!* With expert precision the marble flew through the air hitting Tatum on the bottom.

'Ha!' Professor Mortley exclaimed, with pure joy written all over his face.

'Ouch!' Tatum squeaked, throwing Professor Mortley the angriest look for such a tiny little face.

'Croooooooowooooochoow! Chrooooooooruch!' Professor Mortley let off the biggest crowing sound in victory.

The door slammed shut and Professor Mortley collapsed onto his large red leather chair, exhausted. He was laughing hard, just as a mischievous little boy would do after winning a battle against their arch enemy. He was lost in his laugher, his boyish joy, the presence of Abigale totally lost.

Abigale was standing back in her stillness. It was easy to forget she was there, nothing on her body moved, she became virtually transparent as she stood there faded and camouflaged. Professor Mortley's laughter started to quieten, his face changed back to being slightly older. He looked around the room nearly missing Abigale completely. Doing a double-take he looked again and there she was, and his purpose was renewed.

'Abigale, I'm afraid I have some sad news for you,' Professor Mortley began to deliver the news that she was going to be made to leave the train. 'This is very unusual my dear, usually the train decides who stays and when they go,' the train shook in recognition.

'Oh,' Abigale replied, stroking her foot slowly from side to side against the decking floor. The train shook harder.

Placing a hand on his desk in acknowledgement he continued, 'They haven't told me much, but you need to be ready by the Pink Moon.'

Professor Mortley began to fumble through papers on his desk, the ache in his chest increasing, his shoulders lowered with the weight of the news. 'At least the Pink will bring out the colour in your eyes!' he babbled trying to fill the silence.

Abigale lifted her head catching the hopeful gaze of the Professor, she managed a half-smile, 'Can I ask?' she said finally, Professor Mortley nodding quickly eager to fill the room with anything other than his own thoughts, 'Why a Pink Moon?'

Professor Mortley didn't expect that question, he didn't want that question, as for that question he didn't know the answer. Breathing out loudly, pulling out a sparkly, green, Christmas tree marshmallow. Taking a large mouthful, the boyish man offered Abigale a bite. Shaking her head in polite refusal, Professor Mortley's chomping and munching took a deliberately long time.

'Ermmmm, Wellllll,' he began, his mind racing to give a justifiable answer, 'You see, Abigale, Moons and colours and rainbows fly around the Fae and the train causing biddety-bob's and thingemy-jigs to happen, and errrr, then, errrmmmm...' The train shook causing a top hat to fall from one of the filing cabinets and bonk him on the head. Grabbing it he whispered, 'Michael.'

'Michael?' Abigale repeated.

'Err no,' Professor Mortley blushed and cleared his throat.

Throwing the hat so it landed perfectly on a waiting hat stand in the corner of the room, he looked into Abigale's eyes and as he did he couldn't continue, 'I'm sorry Abigale, I really don't know,' he admitted.

Abigale's head looked as if it had sunken even lower. Looking down at her black, patent shoes she spoke in a quiet sombre voice, 'Do I really have to go, Professor?' practically pleading as she spoke.

Professor Mortley hated what he had to say, 'I'm sorry my dear, but it is against the Council's rules to have anyone that isn't of a Believer decedent or of the Fae, on board the train,' Professor Mortley's tone echoed the sombreness of Abigale's.

The train then shook hard and sharp in continuing disagreement with the Professor. Professor Mortley gently stroked his desk acknowledging the feeling of the train.

Abigale's voice began to crack, 'But my friends…' her voice broke as a single tear escaped her eye and slowly began to run down her cheek. Her hands gravitated towards her hair-ties, holding them tightly as if her life depended on it. 'I can't go back to the grey…'

Little sobs began to escape from her body and the Professors face changed back to the mischievous little boy who had battled the 3 T's. This time though, the boy's face was tear stained and soft.

'I remember the grey, all too well,' the boylike Professor admitted.

Abigale looked up a little surprised, trying to wipe away the tears, 'How could you know?' Abigale tried to regain a little composure as she questioned Professor Mortley, 'You're a Believer, you're Fae.'

'Well, actually, dear,' Professor Mortley confessed, looking slightly embarrassed, 'I'm neither.'

'Neither?' Abigale looked bewildered and a little hurt, 'Then what are you?'

Professor Mortley saddened at the question. Abigale realised how rude she must have sounded. Stepping forwards she wanted to speak again, to apologise. Professor Mortley held up his hand to stop her, waving off what she had said showing her no offence was taken.

'I, Abigale dear,' the Professor paused for effect 'I am Lost Boy.' The Professor did an elaborate bow, 'Or Lost Man sometimes,' a quizzical, puzzled look appeared on his face briefly before he chuckled to himself.

'Lost Boy? I've never heard of one of those, you must be very magical to be the Professor of the train,' Abigale surmised.

The Professor looked up with a look of incredulousness. *Maybe there were some things he didn't have to tell Abigale,* he thought to himself cheekily.

The Professor signalled to Abigale to sit on a little, red-leather pouf at the side of his desk, nestled next to the large filing cabinets. He began to tell her animatedly of being a Lost Boy and his adventures with his friends. Standing, jumping, and leaping on to his desk as he told of the battles he fought alongside and for the boy named Peter. He pointed to the paintings and tapestries around the room as he told story after story.

After what seemed like a while of battles, triumphs and woes, his face turned sombre as he showed Abigale a thimble, delicately calling it, 'A Kiss.'

'And then, Peter decided to grow up and join a family, so we all did too,' he said sadly.

'I don't' understand, why is being part of a family of Believers sad?' Abigale was totally lost as to what the story had to do with her and being a Never-Believer or why he looked so incredibly sad.

Professor Mortley continued, 'Everyone else was sent to Believer families, but one of the Elves got my paperwork wrong and I was sent to a Never-Believer family,' he paused and shivered as he said their names, 'The Turners.'

Professor Mortley reached into his desk and pulled out a giant, sparkly, green marshmallow Christmas tree and took the largest bite Abigale had ever seen.

Abigale's mouth dropped opened, shocked that Professor Mortley had been part of a Never-Believer family. She edged herself towards the edge of the pouf, intent on listening to every syllable of Professor Mortley's story.

'I still have nightmares I'm back in my tiny, grey room, in my iron-grey bed, wearing a holey stone-grey, nightshirt, on Christmas eve,' Professor Mortley took another large bite of his Christmas tree as if it were giving him the strength to carry on his story. 'Christmases with Peter were always full of colour, and laughter, and gifts…,' his voice trailed off as he remembered, 'And then nothing but grey.'

'Wow, so you really do know how I feel?!' Abigale said in wonder.

'Yeah, I do dear,' he said his face looking older and older as the light faded from his face.

'But how did you end up here then?' Abigale asked puzzled.

'I was rescued,' he said happily, 'By a fairy…' he stopped short. Then repeated, 'By fairy…' he was looking around the room rubbing his head, why couldn't he remember. The most important day of his life and he had no memory of who saved him. He began to pace the room troubled by the knowledge he could not remember the fairy who saved him.

'3 T's!' Professor Mortley shouted, making Abigale jump.

In flew the three pixies like lightening, swishing, swooshing, and whizzing. All three crossed their arms and turned their back on him, still cross from being hit by marbles.

'Get me Mama Gilbert!' he boomed. The 3 T's hesitated in their actions.

'Presmartisan!' Professor Mortley shouted at them.

Abigale had no clue what he said but it seemed to be a word the Pixies knew as they darted out the door quicker than she had ever seen them move before.

The Professor regained some composure and went over to Abigale, 'I'm sorry dear, this is not how I wanted this meeting to end, but I'm afraid the date is set,' the train began to shake unhappily. 'We will be transporting you back on the Pink Moon at the end of the month.'

Professor Mortley reached his hand towards the door and tried to usher Abigale out. As his hand connected with her shoulder a blue spark shocked his finger making him draw his hand back quickly.

'I... I... I'm sorry,' Abigale said instinctively, apologising for something she had no clue how it happened. This spark seems to re-ignite the Professor's anger.

The Professor shouted again pushing Abigale out the door, '3 T's! Mama Gilbert... Presmartisan!' he bellowed.

Chapter 16

Elliot, Freddie, and Little T hoovered nervously outside Annie and Clara's cabin 'Go on then,' Little T urged, 'Knock!'

'I'm not knocking,' Freddie said, his oblong face looking directly down to the floor, a pinkish-hue beginning to rise as the blood rushed to his face, 'You do it!' Freddie nudged Elliot with his elbow. Not knowing his own strength nearly knocking Elliot to the floor.

'Whoooaaa, OK Big fella,' Elliot laughed, steading himself.

Elliot began to straighten his clothes. He had on a pair of stone-washed, dark-blue baggy denim jeans, fastened at the top with a dark-brown leather belt, the buckle having some kind of engraving on.

It looked like the Believer sign with the five circles, but one of the circles was missing and a clasp was there instead. He had on a plain-blue, light cotton T-shirt that seemed to fit his shoulders perfectly. This, paired with his jet-black hair enhanced his hypnotic piercing-green eyes. No blemishes, no spots, just pure teenage perfection.

Freddie pushed his rectangular, thin-rimmed spectacles up his roman nose. The light just catching a slight twinkle from his blue eyes. His cropped blonde hair looked even shorter than it did in class, cut with military precision. He tried to regain his authoritarian stature, but the thought of talking to actual girls made his normally ridged and firm posture buckle under the social pressure.

He was wearing khaki trousers that looked tough and uncomfortable; his matching shirt was perfectly ironed, not a crease in sight. He was rubbing his hands together nervously worrying and they were beginning to sweat.

'OK, then,' Elliot said taking a deep breath himself, 'Freddie you talk to Annie and Little T, you've got Clara, I'll snoop around a bit,' Elliot's voice had the slightest wobble as he began to raise his hand to knock on the mahogany mirrored door.

BANG! BANG! BANG! 'It's the boys, can we come in?' Little T swooped in and pounded on the door before Elliot could reach it, 'I couldn't wait for you two waffles to knock, we'd have been here all day!' Little T looked at Elliot and Freddie with a confident and cocky smile.

***

Annie and Clara were sitting on the blue and gold circular embroidered rug in the middle of the room. Their hands entwined in worried unity, Abigale had been gone for ages.

'Do you think something has happened, Annie?' Clara asked Annie, her voice trembling and strained, 'The trains vibrations didn't seem very happy.'

'I don't know, I hope she comes back,' Annie replied he voice also tight, strained with anxiety. Behind her thick-framed glasses, her giant brown eyes started to moisten.

'I have so much to tell you,' Clara said unable to hold it in anymore, 'Mama said tha…'

'Not yet!' Annie scolded, 'Not until Abigale's back, we said we would do it together,' she continued trying to insert some confidence and hope into her tone. 'She *will* come back,' Annie emphasized in a vow, pushing her glasses back up her nose and looking straight into Clara's oceanic eyes. A look that hopefully sealed Abigale's fate.

There was a scuffling sound. Both girls turned towards the door looking even more worried. And again, like someone was outside the door. Abigale would have just walked in not just stood outside. Annie and Clara were still holding onto each other when they moved closer towards the door. Fear beginning to rise and the hairs on their arms beginning to spike. As they reached the door, they could see two sets of foot shadows under the door's ridge. They hugged each other closer.

BANG! BANG! BANG! Annie and Clara very nearly jumped out of their skin.

'What do you want?' Annie yelled, squeezing Clara tight and shutting her eyes.

They waited.

'To come in would be nice!' A tiny familiar, arrogant voice yelled back.

Annie and Clara looked at each other still unsure what to think, but both gave each other a crooked smile as they began to relax a little. 'How do we know it's you?' Annie replied with caution.

A kinder and more hesitant voice then spoke, 'Errmm Annie, Clara, it's us,' Elliot said trying his best to sound smooth and confident, 'We've come to talk about class today.'

A wave of new panic came over Annie and Clara as it dawned on them that *the boys* were at *their* door. Clara ran to the mirrored door to check her appearance and smooth over her clothes and her hair. Annie just stood there motionless.

'Annie!' Clara whispered in a panicked and excited voice, 'Pick your stuff up, the boys are outside!'

'Clara,' Annie forced out, 'Clara!' she said again.

Clara stopped and looked at her friend shocked into stillness, 'What Annie, what's the matter?'

'I can't talk to them! I... I... I... don't know what to say,' Annie said nervously, tears dampening her eyes this time for a different reason.

Clara grabbed hold of Annie's shoulders and squared up to her, 'Annie Rainerly, you have got this, you can do whatever you set your mind to...'

'Are we coming in or not?'

Clara annoyed now that she didn't recognise Little T's annoying voice straight away, kept hold of Annie's shoulders.

'Just a minute!' Clara yelled with vigour to quieten Little T's impatience, not taking her eyes off Annie's. 'Annie, you good?' Annie nodded in reply, 'Good, you're amazing, just relax and take a deep breath!'

Annie started to move like lightening tidying the room then stopped, 'This is all your stuff Clara!' she panted.

'Shhhhhh!' Clara hissed, smiling through a finger pursed at her lips. And with that, Clara swung open their cabin door and with a biggest smile said, 'Come on in boys.'

Little T's rocketed in with a blaze of light at his tail, Elliot and Freddie then followed slowly and slightly more unsure.

'Hey Annie,' Elliot said, slightly nudging Freddie in her direction.

Annie attempted a smile but couldn't meet his gaze so spun around quickly picking up a few clothes that were strewn over her bed and tucked them quickly under Clara's pink duvet.

'Soooo,' Elliot said slowly, 'This is your cabin, ah?' even as he said it he could feel his confident exterior melt away.

'Yep,' Clara said with a dramatic spin, 'This is our little cabin.'

Silence fell over the room. Annie sat on the edge of her bed, her mind racing trying to think of something to say. Freddie plonked his large frame down on the floor at the base of Annie's bed, close to her feet. Elliot went and stood next to him trying to nudge him with his leg closer to Annie. Unfortunately for Elliot, Freddie was a dead weight and Elliot was fighting a losing battle. Everything was quiet as they all waited for someone to speak.

Little T couldn't take it any longer, 'Look,' he said impatiently, 'Clara, Annie, we know something is going on,' he continued.

Elliot made his way over to Little T and whispered, 'What about the mission?'

Little T whispered loudly out the corner of his mouth, 'It was a rubbish mission!' Motioning over to Freddie, 'Look at him, he can hardly move.'

Clara came raging up to where Little T was hovering 'Mission! What mission?' she said angrily, the heat rising up her ballerina body from her demi-pointe to the crystals embedded in her perfectly groomed hair.

Elliot tried to diffuse the situation, he smiled a soft handsome smile, 'Hey Clara, we just wanted to come talk to you guys,' he said softly, eyes sparkling with sincerity.

Little T zoomed past Elliot's face and hovered in front of Clara's, squaring up to her. He tried to make his little voice sound as big as he could, 'We wanted to find out what you two are hiding!' he accused Clara, first pointing a little green finger at her, and then turning it towards Annie. Little T knew fairies were unable to lie so he folded his arms and waited for the words to flow.

'The Queen is here because…' Annie began to ramble.

'No Annie,' Clara shouted, 'We don't have to tell them anything, we are not supposed to!' Clara walked over to where Annie sat on the bed, 'We mustn't!'

'See! I told you they were hiding something!' Little T boasted as if he had just uncovered the biggest secret in Faedom.

Picking up one of Clara's pink pillows Little T threw it across the room. Clara ran to pick it up in temper, she pirouetted quickly giving the pillow extra gusto as it flew through the air at Little T. He ducked and the pillow caught Elliot hard on the shoulder. Without thinking Elliot picked up a green cushion from Annie's bed, it was embroidered, much harder than the other pillows. He threw the cushion at Clara. She twirled out the way laughing, deflecting the throw.

Thud.

'OW!' Abigale yelled.

Everyone turned towards the door to see Abigale knocked on the floor rubbing her head.

'Oh my god I'm so sorry,' Elliot came rushing over offering his hand out to help Abigale up.

Abigale looked up and locked eyes with Elliot as he came towards her, she couldn't stop her hand reaching out for his. In one swift movement he pulled her to her feet and grabbed her waist to steady her. Abigale and Elliot stared at each other.

'Hey,' Elliot said shyly.

'Hey,' Abigale echoed, quickly looking to the floor as her cheeks began to glow.

Chapter 17

Mama Gilbert burst into Professor Mortley's office, 'I came as fast as I could,' she pushed her flowing sleeves up her arm as if she were meaning to get down to some serious work. Mama Gilbert looked stern, 'Right then, where is the heathen?'

Professor Mortley was pacing the room his holographic face flickering at such speed you couldn't make out what form he was, boy or man, he was just a blur. Mama Gilbert look around the room and realised there was just the two of them, confused she watched Professor Mortley.

'What's the emergency?' she asked hastily, 'Why did you use the under-attack code word?'

'Wefec arc underk attfrac! Mec Fae isc ink Dangek. Presmartisan!' Professor Mortley exclaimed like lightening, his words streaming together in panic.

'Whooooa, slow down,' Mama Gilbert said in a calming tone, 'My Lost Boy gibberish is a little rusty!' she half-giggled trying to gage the seriousness of the situation.

'I'm just,' Professor Mortley cut himself off as his pacing continued. He tried again, 'I'm just in such a state,' he exclaimed to Mama Gilbert, his voice wavering, slightly cracking as his holographic face steadied on the face of a heartbroken little boy.

Mama Gilbert walk round the giant mahogany desk and reached into the bottom draw and pulled out a sparkly, green, Christmas tree marshmallow and handed it to Professor Mortley.

'Now my dear,' Mama Gilbert said, placing his hand in hers and giving it a motherly squeeze, 'Start at the beginning and calmly tell me what's happened.'

Professor Mortley had taken a big bite of the sparkly, green, Christmas tree marshmallow. His mouth now encrusted with green, sticky sparkles.

With his mouth full of sticky greenness he said, 'My memories have been stolen.'

'Stolen!' Mama Gilbert gasped a little alarmed.

Taking another big bite of his marshmallow the Professor mumbled, 'It's not just the forgetfulness we thought, my memories are gone!'

Professor Mortley started pacing again his holographic face beginning to flicker. Mama Gilbert was silent. Thinking. 'What specifically can't you remember, dear?'

'I can't remember how or who saved me from the Turners!' Professor Mortley threw his hands up into the air in frustration, 'I remember the grey, I remember the horrible, little room. I remember not being allowed to talk about Peter or Michael, or Christmas, or having a birthday,' he was frantically listing everything, 'but the most important, the most important thing who I owe my everything to,' his voice broke and the little boy appeared again, bottom lip quivering, 'I can't remember who they are or how I got here!'

He walked round to the back of the desk, leaned down, and pulled out two sparkly, green marshmallow Christmas trees, then collapsed into his red, leather chair.

'Well, I can tell you who saved you, see if it jogs your memory?' Mama Gilbert offered hoping this would help, 'It was…' she paused in thought.

'It was…' again she thought, 'Oh, it's on the tip of my tongue.'

Mama began to pace, stopping and then pacing again as she racked her brain. Her sleeves had fallen back down her arm and instead of looking like waterfalls, they looked like fluttering wings that seemed to propel her backwards and forwards as she too began to pace.

Suddenly, she stamped her foot and stopped. Professor Mortley leaned forward, his face now pretty much covered in in sticky, green, sparkly Christmas marshmallow, he hoped she had remembered.

'It's gone!' Mama Gilbert exclaimed finally. 'I have no recollection of that day and other days,' Mama Gilbert continued, 'I have more missing, I can see the events but there are time gaps!' her face full of unusual tense lines.

'Who could have done such a thing?' the Professor bellowed out like he was asking the universe for answers. The train began to shake violently, 'We both need to use the memory stick!' he confirmed.

'But it doesn't work like that dear,' Mama Gilbert explained, 'The Nephilim memory stick will only restore your memory if you encounter someone or something from the time forgot.'

'It's still worth a try, could you?' Professor Mortley's little boy eyes pleaded with Mama Gilbert.

Mama Gilbert hesitated, but she wanted her memories back just as much as Professor Mortley, 'Ok dear, come close.'

The Professor bounded off his chair and wiped his green, sticky, sparkly face with the bottom of his tangerine waistcoat. Mama Gilbert held out her hands for him to take and warned him to stay extremely still. She let go of one of his hands and reach up her opposite sleeve and pulled out the long, brown, downtrodden branch. Holding it above her head she began to twirl it slowly.

'Close your eyes, dear and think about what it is your trying to remember,' she coached. Then she began to swing the branch harder and faster as she chanted, 'It's a time to remember, a spell we must cast, let the light help you remember what was lost in the past.'

A bright light began to illuminate at the end of the branch. Mama Gilbert brought it down gently and placed the light onto Professor Mortley's hair, causing a rainbow of light to encircle his head and make his dusty-brown hair stand up on end.

Mama Gilbert raised the Nephilim memory stick again and repeated the spell, 'It's a time to remember, a spell we must cast, let the light help you remember what was lost in the past.'

The light turned white again and she lowered it down onto her own lilac-tinged hair. As it made contact the rainbow of light again encircled her head. Mama Gilbert lowered the stick to the floor and took Professor Mortley's hands and they chanted together, 'Magic and light, magic and light, magic and light.'

***

Aunt Violet pulled her black wrap tighter around her shoulders, hiding the dreary, rough dress beneath. Her foot was tapping constantly, an unusual look of concern was plastered across her face. She felt so cold, which was a complete anomaly as hospital rooms were kept hot to help the pale Never-Believer blood flow.

Aunt Violet's bones felt icy, like an icy electric current were flowing through her old, tired veins. She looked down at her great-niece and felt a forgotten ache in her chest. She straightened her back and pushed the ache in her chest way down into the pit of her stomach, knowing this feeling was why she was here and half of her wished she weren't.

Her foot-tapping increased as she edged her chair a little closer to the bed, intently watching every aspect of Abigale. Aunt Violet watched her chest rising and falling as Abigale stayed deep within her mysterious slumber.

Having noticed Abigale's exposed hand from the white and grey cotton hospital sheets. Aunt Violet reached out with an unconscious instinct and touched Abigale's hand. No quicker than she had made contact with Abigale's skin than a blue spark sent Aunt Violet's hand instantly back to the safety of under her black wrap.

The hospital room door swung open with force that made Aunt Violet jump again. Aunt Violet knew who had come through the door before the door had even fully opened. The sweet smell of marshmallow was all-consuming. Aunt Violet looked down and raised her wrap higher as the impersonated doctor walked towards the bed.

Professor Mortley straightened his white doctoral coat as he stood by the bed, he was desperately hoping that seeing this Abigale would ignite his memories. He looked up and noticed the old woman sitting at her bedside. He took a step back in surprise as Abigale never had visitors.

'Good afternoon Mrs…' Professor Mortley voice trailed off and paused as he tried to address the old women searching for a name, he held out his hand for her to shake.

Aunt Violet kept her head down avoiding any kind of eye contact.

'I'm Doctor Mortley, I'm taking care of Abigale,' he continued returning his hand back to his side, he tilted his head slightly trying to get a look at the old woman's face.

'Mrs Johnson,' Aunt Violet said harshly with an unusual, scared quiver to her voice. Her hands began to shake, terror rising within her as Professor Mortley was getting closer.

Oh no! another Mrs Johnson, Professor Mortley thought, 'Do you mind if I examine Abigale?' he asked warily not wanting another encounter like the time before.

Waving her hand dismissively towards Abigale, signalling her consent, Aunt Violet tried to turn her body away from the hospital bed creating more distance between her and Professor Mortley.

Professor Mortley got closer to Abigale and began taking her pulse. He pulled a stethoscope out of his white coat pocket and began listening to her breathing. Nodding and mumbling to himself he was doing the best affirming doctorly actions as he could. Aunt Violet's fear was turning to anger, out of the corner of her eye she watched this display of idiocy.

Professor Mortley tried his hardest to ignite some kind of memory from Abigale, but every time he touched her, nothing. The hospital door opened again, a nurse came through the door and awaited instruction from Professor Mortley.

'Please bring me some blood vials,' Professor Mortley ordered in the best grown up doctor's voice. It was his last resort, maybe testing the blood back on the train would give some answers. Disappointment grew as he remembered absolutely nothing.

Aunt Violet's head lifted in sheer panic; she couldn't let Professor Mortley take her blood. The iciness in her blood had gone and heat began to rise, catastrophic scenarios ran through

Aunt Violet's mind of what could happen should Professor Mortley see Abigale's blood. She should never have agreed to the tests. The nurse was back with the vials before Aunt Violet could think of an excuse or an escape plan. She was too old now to run, she'd been hidden for so long, she couldn't do it again.

The nurse left the room and the sound of the door shutting echoed, it felt deafening to Aunt Violet. Her heart was pounding, she could feel the thud, thud, thud against the ache in her chest. Aunt Violet was struggling to control her breathing as the panic set in deeper.

It felt like it was all happening in slow motion. The thud in her chest becoming harder and faster, she dropped her protective black wrap to the floor. Aunt Violet's ferocious blue eyes glazed over with wet salty tears and Professor Mortley rested the needle on Abigale's skin.

'Nooooooooooooooooooooo!' Aunt Violet screamed and grabbed Professor Mortley's arm causing a blue electric current to catapult him into the corner of the hospital room.

Aunt Violet frantically check Abigale's skin to see if Professor Mortley had punctured it. Relived she sat back down and held her hands to her chest, eyes closed, rocking in silent prayer. Aunt Violet was taking deep breaths, she tried to regain her breathing, she was completely unaware of Professor Mortley gazing at her in total astonishment. The room was deathly silent and finally after what seemed eternity, Aunt Violet turned her gaze away from Abigale and inevitably made eye contact with Professor Mortley.

'*Viola?*' Professor Mortley had no words, tears began to stream down his face as his memories came flooding back.

Chapter 18

Annie, Clara, Abigale, Elliot, Freddie, and Little T, all sat on the floor in the girls' cabin in silence, looking at each other waiting for someone to speak. Elliot turned to Abigale and looked into her eyes, smiling gently he cleared his throat ready to ask a question.

'So,' Little T chimed in first, 'Who and what are you?'

Elliot's head spun around in annoyance and glared at Little T. Little T smiled wickedly and shrugged his shoulders flying closer to Abigale.

'You know what?' Clara butted in, 'Maybe it's time for you boys to go and we will see you in class tomorrow.'

'Yes, good idea, Clara,' Annie began to stand up awkwardly, Freddie jumped up and stood next to Annie as if she had called him to attention. Clara gave a little smile in their direction.

'Guys, it's ok,' Abigale eventually spoke, she didn't know why but she glanced up at Elliot, who gave an encouraging, friendly smile back, 'They can stay, I'm going to be leaving soon anyway,' she remarked, resigned and sad, she looked down and began to fiddle with the tassels of the blue and gold circular rug. Elliot's face dropped.

'What do you mean you'll be leaving soon?' Clara said shuffling over to sit nearer to Abigale. Annie sat back down with a plonk and Freddie followed suit.

'Well, I'm not sure, but Professor Mortley said I have to leave at the Pink Moon,' Abigale shrugged her shoulders and look around the group of faces, looking for any glimpse that they knew what a Pink Moon was.

Annie jumped up again and like he was joined at her hip, Freddie shadowed her. He followed her over to her bookshelf and Annie began piling books onto his already outstretched arms. Annie looked up at Freddie and gave him a frustrated glance, but Freddie's face stayed firm as if he knew Annie would find something.

'Ah ha!' Annie held up a navy book, with what looked like a witches pentagram embossed on it in gold. Symbols of the elements earth, wind, fire, water, and spirit were spread around the pentagram. Freddie took a sharp intake of breath, his face hardened.

'Where did you get that?' A look of concern was now planted on his face, 'That shouldn't be messed with!' he warned.

'Oh, don't be silly, my Nana gave it to me years ago and I'm perfectly fine!' Annie said with an unusual air of arrogance.

Clara and Abigale exchanged baffled looks. Neither of them had seen this side of her before. Annie and Freddie came back to group and this time Freddie edge himself away from Annie slightly. Annie rolled her eyes at his movements and began flicking through the pages of the ancient-looking book. She stopped and pushed her thick-rimmed glasses up the bridge of her nose as she bent her face in closer to the pages.

Muttering as she read to herself, she finally stopped and read aloud, 'Found it!' she pointed out, 'The Pink Moon follows the last enchanted gibbous moon of the fallen summer months.' Annie muttered to herself again for a few lines and then carried on, 'Should the Pink Moon fall on the same day as element equinox then it's energy can be harnessed to produce unrivalled power! And then there's something written I don't understand…' Annie looked harder, 'All I recognise is the 'Nisi Godmothers' which means "Godmothers only", but I can't make out the rest of the sentence.' Annie shrugged her shoulders and then shut the book triumphantly.

'So, do they fall on the same day?' Elliot asked shyly, unsure if this he this should be something he should already know.

Clara sprang elegantly up to her bed and reached for her diary. She gracefully floated back down to where she was sitting, and Little T flew over to read from behind her shoulder. Before Clara could answer, Little T inconsiderately exclaimed, 'Yep, looks like you're a goner in two days!'

Clara's hand flicked up swotting Little T into a backward somersault across Annie's bed.

'Two days!' Annie's voice cracked as she repeated the time frame.

Abigale lowered her head and the group fell silent. Clara then stood up and with determination addressed the group, 'Look, Mama Gilbert said to me this has never happened before, a Never-Believer has never been on the Faedora Train, EVER! There must be something about Abs that's different?' Clara fell quiet as she tried desperately to think of an answer.

Little T, Freddie, and Elliot were all sat with their mouths open in shock. Little T then rocketed towards Abigale's face and stopped inches away from her nose. Abigale flinched as he stopped.

Little T started to inspect her face, 'You're a Stoney,' he said with amazement, 'Wow, I've never seen a real-life Stoney before,' Little T continued.

Abigale felt the weight of everyone' eyes upon her and began to shrink back into her stillness.

'Do you have any sadness scars?' Freddie asked taking everyone by surprise, Abigale looked up as puzzled as everyone else. Freddie continued, 'Stoney's…' Annie elbowed Freddie in the ribs, 'Ouch! Sorry, Never-Believers,' he corrected himself giving Annie a harsh look while rubbing his side, 'Never-Believers are meant to have scars for every time the magic missed them, they are called sadness scars.'

Abigale looked up and was about to reply when the door flung open and the 3 T's burst into the room. Dancing and flying across the room like loose cannons, everyone's heads couldn't help but bob as they watched them criss-cross across the cabin ceiling.

'Annie to the Queen, the Queen wants to see Annie,' the 3 T's chanted over and over. Clara and Abigale shot each other another glance as they were taken by surprise. Annie jumped up knocking all her books onto the floor. Excitement now bursting out of her.

'This was what I wanted to tell you!' she almost shouted at the group excitedly, 'I met the Queen in the library, she is going to give me some private lessons!' The 3 T's tittered knowingly; Annie shot them a look full of daggers. Tiana and Tatum playfully pretended to die in mid-air, faking being stabbed with a knife through the heart.

'I've been bursting to tell you guys!' Annie continued in a high-pitch frenzy.

Clara and Abigale stood up and walked over to Annie, 'Wow, that's amazing Annie,' Abigale said giving her friend a hug.

'You're going now?' Clara was blunt and slightly peeved.

Annie was hurt by Clara's words, she hadn't heard why she was getting the lessons.

'Yes, I'm going now,' Annie retorted, her usually soft, giant brown eyes peering over her glasses into the fierceness of Clara's. Annie spun on her heels, her emerald-green dress swung clipping both Clara and Abigale, and she marched out the door.

The 3 T's continued to chant, 'Annie to the Queen, the Queen wants to see Annie.'

The door slammed behind them, Clara was fuming, 'How can she leave now?' Clara questioned, but not really wanting anyone to answer, she turned to Abigale, 'You're leaving in two days! *Two days* and Annie wants to go learn spells.' Clara sat herself down on Abigale's iron-grey bed, shocked at her friend's actions.

'Maybe we should go,' Elliot commented, shuffling from foot to foot, looking uncomfortable.

'I'm sorry,' Clara said, 'She's not normally like this,' she looked at Annie's bed and saw how all her books were left all strewn over her normally perfect bed. Clara felt a sadness, 'I wonder if I'm going to get a sadness scar,' she said starting to pick up the books from Annie's bed.

'Maybe we can help? Ay guys?' Elliot looked at both Freddie and Little T for encouragement.

Freddie jumped up and stood to attention, 'Yes sir!' he shouted. Abigale and Clara giggled.

'Little T, you in?' Elliot asked.

Little T pretended like he was mulling it over, like it was the most important decision he had ever made, 'Well,' he said, pausing for dramatic effect, 'I suppose I am the best man for the job,' he said with a wry smile on his face.

'Ok, great. Clara, Abs,' Elliot paused and caught Abigale's hazel eyes, the flecks of green against the brown were like fireworks, 'It's ok if I call you Abs, isn't it?' Elliot asked, his face a little flushed. Abigale nodded with her new smile brightening by the second. 'Clara,' Elliot continued, 'What are our orders?' Elliot went and stood to attention next to Freddie.

With a sarcastic roll of his eyes Little T flew to Freddie's other side and saluted the girls putting one hand up to his forehead and standing completely upright, 'Ready and willing Captains,' the group looked at each other and fell about laughing. Laughing like they had been friends for a lifetime.

'Let's give Abigale a tour of the train!' Clara suggested.

'But I'm not supposed to leave the cabin unless with Mama Gilbert or Professor Mortley!'

'Don't you worry about that,' Little T chimed in, 'We won't get caught!'

***

Annie heard the laughter from outside the cabin door. She couldn't help but think, were they laughing at her?

Her eye filled with tears, she felt a sickness in her stomach and an ache in her heart. They were supposed to be her friends. A tear escaped her eye, she wiped it away defiantly with the back of her hand. They didn't even give her a chance to explain.

Annie was hurt that not even Clara gave her a chance to tell them. *I'll show them*, she thought with resignation, *I know how to help Abigale*. Annie straightened her shoulders and followed the 3 T's down the gangway of the train, determined that she was doing what was best for her friend.

Lost within her thoughts of her friends, zombie-like she

followed the 3 T's to meet the Queen. They took her through a part of the train she had never seen before. The carriages seemed to be even more vibrant and alive as the wood markings swirled and twisted in their reds and browns.

The cast-iron, hinged-wings moved as if they were fluttering, teasing you to go over and look inside the boxes they guarded. The vibration of the train felt stronger under foot, the humming resonating through Annie's whole body. The 3 T's stopped outside a mirrored door that was totally out of place against the mahogany.

The three of them hovered there looking at themselves in the mirror, primping and preening each other to make sure they looked perfect before they entered. Annie looked at herself, her emerald dress was creased from the day and was now clinging to her larger frame showing her plumpness. Her warm ebony face had lost its shine beneath her glasses, her joy gone where she had been upset. Her nearly black hair, to her, had lost its sheen, she didn't sparkle. *Maybe she was something to be laughed at,* she thought sadly.

While she was lost in thought, the 3 T's pushed the door open taking Annie by surprise, the Queen was standing right in front of her.

The silver threads in her waist-length platinum-blonde hair made her glow and shimmer in the light. The glitter from her white fishtail dress was luminescent. To Annie she looked like she was surrounded by a magical ball of light. Annie was wholly captivated by her presence.

'Come in, my beautiful, talented Annie,' the Queen sang, enchanting and playing to Annie.

Annie entered the room and was floored by how beautiful

her cabin was. No cedar or mahogany, the walls were a warm sunshine colour and completely smooth. This made the beautiful vintage white furniture standout and look utterly dreamy. Everything was in its place, it looked spotlessly clean, Annie could not love it more. Beaming now from ear to ear she was drawn in by the Queen's complementary chants.

'I have something incredibly special for us to learn today, Annie,' the Queen voiced rhythmically. 'I'm taking you to the fourth floor.' Annie's mouth dropped open, the Queen forgot herself for a second dropping the enchantment from her voice, 'Our mouths should only be open when we speak, Annie,' she said sternly.

Annie shook her head for a second as if seeing the Queen for the first time. She looked older.

The Queen, realising her mistake, was quickly back on track, 'You see, my talented little Godmother-to-be, I have my own doorway to the fourth floor,'

The Queen sauntered over to a giant, white-vintage wardrobe trimmed in gold-leaf trim, the same as the rest of the white furniture and she waved her hand elegantly in a circular motion.

The wardrobe slid quickly over to one side, revealing a worn golden door. Annie stood gapping in absolute awe; this is a moment she had dreamed about all her life. Being taught by a Queen, not only was she going to save her friend but she was going to make her family so proud of her.

'Come, special child, come,' the Queen chanted, beckoning Annie forward, 'We have much to learn today,' the Queen stood to one side and let Annie pass her into the library opening.

The Queen quickly stepped behind Annie, stopping the 3

T's from following. She held up her hand making them stop quickly. The 3 T's looked puzzled - they were meant to be the Queen's most important soldiers.

'That's as far as you go,' the Queen said in a clipped voice, 'Go keep an eye on the others,' she ordered.

The 3 T's looked at each other shocked by her harsh tone.

'GO!' the Queen insisted more sternly, closing the door she pushed the 3 T's back into her cabin.

The door shut trapping the back of Tatum's shorts in its cracks. Tiana and Tamsin grab an arm each and start to pull Tatum free of the door. They tugged and tugged, then rolling up their imaginary sleeves they gave one almighty effort. As they pulled they heard a loud ripping sound as Tatum was finally freed from the enchanted door.

Tatum tumbled forward with Tasmin, and Tiana close behind her. The 3 T's hugged as they were reunited. All three turned and gave an angry, evil stare and blew the biggest raspberries they could muster at the door. Meant, obviously, for the benefit of the Queen. They flew closer to the door seeing a green piece of material flapping where Tatum had once been. Tatum looked behind her and found the hole in the back of her shorts. Her hands flew like lightening to cover her bare bottom. Tiana and Tamsin started to laugh hysterically, crossing their arms over their little bellies as if the force of the laughter were causing them pain.

Tatum's green cheeks glowed crimson and she flew out of the Queen's cabin furiously. Unable to stop their laughter, Tiana and Tamsin followed closely behind, leaving the Queen's door wide open.

Chapter 19

Abigale couldn't believe she was breaking the rules, her tummy fluttered with excitement and fear. She was desperate to see more of the train and their world. Burying her usual discipline, she decided to be spontaneous, to be brave.

'Where do you want to go first?' Clara asked in an excited, hushed voice.

'I really don't think we should be doing this!' Freddie interjected in a warned whisper.

'Come on Fred, you only live once!' Elliot joined in.

Abigale was feeling adventurous for the first time in her life, 'Some place magical,' she replied.

'You're on board the Faedora, everywhere is magical,' Elliot winked at her and touched one of the cast-iron winged clasps.

To Abigale's amazement the wings began to flutter and lift of from where they sat. Delicately the iron butterfly flew over to Abigale and fluttered around her head for a moment, and then rested back down on the ledge next to her in the carriage, returning to its ridged form.

Abigale looked at Elliot enchanted at her amazement.

He must think I'm such an idiot, she thought to herself, *of course everything is magical.* Abigale tried to explain herself, 'Sorry I'm just not used…'

'The first time I saw the train move,' Elliot interrupted, 'I touched everything in sight thinking it would come alive.'

Abigale could see that Elliot was trying to make her feel better.

'The first time I saw the train move I didn't sleep for a week!' Freddie admitted without thinking.

They all laughed finding comradery in sharing their firsts.

'I know!' Little T chimed in, 'Let's take her to the potion room!'

'I'm already hating myself for saying this…' Clara mouthed just to Abigale. 'That is a great idea, T!' Clara confirmed to the group.

Little T beamed with Clara's words, he perched on Elliot's shoulder and whispered, 'Did you hear that, she called me T!'

Elliot and Abigale smiled as they followed Clara down the carriage to the potion room.

Abigale felt like her head was spinning as they walked along carriage after carriage. They waited at the end of each one, making sure the coast was clear before darting forwards onto the next. They turned left, and then right, then headed up two flights of stairs.

Stairs! On a train! Abigale's mind boggled, even more so that this all was perfectly normal to her newly found friends, who didn't even bat an eye lid.

Every now and again Elliot would touch one of the wings and it would flutter up to Abigale. With newfound bravery, she held out a finger and the butterfly perched on it. As it landed the wings began to glow a shimmering blue.

'Wow, I've never seen that before!' Elliot nudged Freddie to look at Abigale.

Freddie was keeping lookout from behind and turned to see what the elbow in the ribs was all about.

Freddie looked curiously at Abigale, 'You sure you're a Never-Believer?'

'Yep, totally,' Abigale replied without looking at him transfixed by the blue glowing butterfly on her finger.

'We're here!' Clara said excitedly, reaching down to try the door.

Nothing. She tried the door again and pushed her small frame against it. It just wouldn't budge.

'Hey, big fella!' Little T called to Freddie in a hushed shout, 'We need your help.' Little T motioned animatedly towards the door.

'It's never locked,' Clara pondered.

Freddie reluctantly walked to the front of the line, taking hold of handle he braced himself to give it one almighty budge. Just before he made contact with the door it flew open causing Freddie to ungracefully fall through the door and face-plant the floor.

Little T hovered in the doorway, 'I done it!' he shouted with a victorious grin, 'What you are doing down there Fred?'

Abigale tried to hold in her giggle. Freddie clambered to his feet giving Little T a look that would make a Flounder Lilly wilt.

'Come on,' Elliot held out his hand for Abigale, pulling her inside the room.

Abigale entered and was taken aback by the beautiful music she heard. The room was full of glass shelves, upon each shelf were rows and rows of bottles and tubes, all of varying size and colour. The gentle rhythm of the train causing them to clink and chime in a melodic choir.

Absolutely breath-taking, Abigale thought, closing her eyes to listen to the glass *ping* and *peel*, swearing they were singing to her.

As Abigale opened her eyes she noticed Elliot was watching her, her cheeks flushed and she looked away, not understanding this strange feeling and pull towards him. Or the fact that every time she spoke to him she felt she had said something monumentally stupid. Noticing Clara hovering over a large, glass-stand in the corner of the room, which held a large open book, Abigale rushed over burying her confusing feelings. Clara was flicking through the pages with an intent look.

'Hey,' Abigale said to her.

'Hey, just give me one ickle second,' Clara flicked through a little bit more, 'Aaaa Ha!' she stopped on the page she wanted.

'What you got there?' Elliot came over with Little T and Freddie.

'It's a *Partt Crepitus* - party potion, I think,' Clara said, 'Freddie what do you think?'

'Party potion!' Little T exclaimed, 'Let's do it!'

Little T peered over Freddie's shoulder while he was examining the ingredients in the potion, and then flew off around the room beginning to mix and stir it all together.

'Hold on Little T, I don't think this is what we think it is!' Freddie called out in caution. He looked up to the sky repeating the words over and over again, '*Partt Crepitus, Partt Crepitus,*' trying to remember their meaning.

Abigale and Clara gave each other a now unsure look. *I wish Annie were here, she'd know what it said,* thought Abigale.

Little T flew up to the top row of bottles and tubes and gently tapped his finger on each glass as he read the labels aloud, looking for the last ingredient. 'Tonic of intellect, Potion of storms, Brew of luck... ah, here we are, flask of lighting, two drops.'

'Little T! NO!' shouted Freddie as the translation finally came to him, 'Partt Crepitus is Party EXPLOSION!' Freddie took cover crouching down behind the book-stand.

'Don't be silly Fred, look nothing is even happening,' Little T chuckled. The mixture in the tube then began to stir itself and Little T noticed tiny flickers of lighting within the mixture.

'Errrrrr, guys...' Little T stammered his voice wavering.

Everyone exchanged a look of fear and the glass tube that Little T was holding started to smoke. Smoke of red, blue, green, and yellow began to churn out of tube. Little T then dropped the tube shattering it over the floor. The floor started to smoke, then they heard a *pop, crackle,* and *fizz.* The sounds began to get louder and louder.

Pinneoooooooowwww! A firework flew across the room.

Pinneow! Pinneow! Pinneow! The soft music of chime was now gone, and a panicked, *Chinkety-clink* had replaced it, like the glass were crying out for help.

'Let's get out of here!' Freddie called, 'Keep down.'

They all stayed low to the ground following Freddie in an army-style crawl round the outside of the room, heading towards the door. Freddie stood up and peeked round the corner to check to see if the coast was clear. He ducked down quickly, sweat now dripping down his brow.

'What's wrong?' asked Elliot.

'Mama Gilbert!' Freddie shouted, she is on her way down the carriages.

'Oh no, she can't find me here!' Clara's voice began to wobble.

Abigale hated seeing the upset on her friend's face, no one seemed to know what to do. She had to do something, she couldn't let her new friends be found out. 'Freddie, can you stop the fireworks?' Abigale asked ducking her head down as one came flying over her head.

'I think so I just need to get back to the book and get the right potion to stop it.'

'Little T, I need a distraction for Mama Gilbert, to make her turn around,' Abigale suggested knowing he would be up for the job.

'One distraction coming up!' Little T sneaked out the door.

'I'll help Freddie, don't do anything dangerous!' Elliot warned.

Is he worried about me? Abigale's train of thought was suddenly distracted by Elliot.

Pinneow!

Abigale ducked and gave Freddie a nod. He started mixing up a new potion with Elliot fetching the ingredients. Clara looked frozen in fear of being caught.

'Clara,' Abigale called over the fireworks, 'I got this,' not knowing at all what she was doing.

Abigale peeked out the window into the carriage and waited for Little T's distraction.

BANG!

Mama Gilbert jumped and turned round to see where the sound was coming from. Abigale seized her opportunity and exited the potion cabin straight into Mama Gilbert's path.

Mama Gilbert turned back looking puzzled and confused, only to jump again at the appearance of Abigale.

'Oh! Abigale dear, you did give me a fright,' Mama Gilbert chuckled. Turning a little more serious and looking around cautiously Mama Gilbert continued, 'Abigale, you know you're not supposed to be wandering the carriage alone.'

'I know,' Abigale looked down to floor feeling guilty, 'I just… everything looks so…' The train was shaking as if trying to stop Abigale from speaking.

'Tut, tut!' Mama Gilbert tapped the wood of train in gentle reprimand, 'You are being naughty today,' Mama told the train.

Abigale stood lost for words, she didn't actually know what she was going to do to help her friends.

'It's OK dear, I understand,' Mama Gilbert smiled warmly at Abigale, 'We all need our little adventures.'

There was a little *pinneow* in the distance that grabbed Mama Gilbert's attention.

'Did you hear that, Dear? I need to investigate.'

'Errr Mama, I don't know my way back to the cabin, could you take me please?'

This wasn't a lie as Abigale had absolutely no clue on how to get back to the girls' cabin.

Mama Gilbert frowned looking in the direction of the suspicious noises, which had suddenly come to stop. Abigale thought quickly in a bid to nudge Mama Gilbert into helping her back to the cabin.

'What would happen if anyone else knew I was on the train?'

'Oh, Abigale dear, there's no need to fret, I will take you back this very moment,' Mama Gilbert then quickly spun on her heels, apparently now distracted with the task at hand, 'Come along Dear, we must get you back.'

Relieved, Abigale followed Mama Gilbert down the carriage and just as she turned the corner, she looked back over her shoulder and saw Clara, Elliot, Freddie, and Little T silently celebrating, jumping up and down in silent cheer of Abigale's bravery.

Abigale felt the warmest glow within her heart, her tummy tickled, and she felt light all over. For the first time she felt proud of herself.

Bravery suits me, she thought.

Chapter 20

Annie walked over to the silver railings and placed both her hands on the cold metal. Peering down she couldn't believe that in her first week on the Faedora Train she was already on the fourth floor of the library.

The Queen really must see something special in me, she thought to herself as she took in the wonder of the library from this momentous perspective.

Annie could see Miss Petula's large cubicle in the centre of the ground floor, still stacked high with scrolls and books. Annie peered over further, looking for Miss Petula but she couldn't see her anywhere.

The captivating voice started again, 'Annie?' the Queen charmed, 'Are you ready to start?'

Annie spun around quickly making eye contact with the Queen, giving her, her undivided attention. The Queen pretended to be looking for a specific book along the old and enchanted books. Annie tried with all her might, from where she was standing, to try and read the titles of the books from their spines. Alas, she was too far away. She edged her feet a little closer to try and get a better look while she waited for the Queen.

The Queen turned quickly as if she was trying to catch Annie out. But Annie snapped back to her upright position holding her breath while she waited for the Queen to speak again.

Turning back to the books the Queen found the book she had hidden earlier.

'Ah ha!' the Queen pulled a huge antique-looking book from the shelf, plastering a fake smile across her face, she turned and walked over to Annie. 'Take a seat child,' the Queen sang, smoothness and rhythm dripping from her plastered-on smile.

Annie looked from side to side confused, she hadn't seen anywhere to sit on the fourth floor. The Queen glided past Annie and as she turned a circular, silver table had appeared with two matching silver chairs.

The table and chairs sparkled along their edges as if they were trimmed in glitter. Annie, in her rush to please the Queen, pulled out one of the chairs a bit too quickly in her excitement, as she sat, landed a chair leg squarely on the Queen's foot.

'Oooooooooouch!' the Queen yelled and began frantically hopping around in a circle.

Annie was absolutely mortified. The Queen's enchanting voice was lost in pain, and she was unable to hold her temper, 'You stupid, stupid girl!' The Queen's pale, porcelain skin was the colour of beetroot, with her temper more than pain consuming her.

'I... I... I'm... I'm... I'm so deeply sorry,' Annie tried to apologise, her eyes beginning to fill with tears.

'How could you be so blundering?' the Queen spat nastily. Annie bowed her head as the Queen continued, 'How can such a clumsy oath of a child have enough pow...'

'Enough what? Noralynn?' Miss Petula came out of nowhere, addressing the Queen with firm informality.

The Queen looked up shocked to see Miss Petula, she composed herself immediately. Miss Petula was standing between the bookshelves, her silver hair tied back in the two plaits, both sets of glasses resting upon her head, one on her hair, and the other on the top of her creased forehead. Both her hands were wedged in the large pocket of her brown, suede pinafore. The creasing of her forehead made her look cross, yet her air eluded calmness.

Regaining her composure, the Queen finally spoke not looking happy at all.

'I think you're forgetting to whom you're addressing, Miss Petula,' the Queen said with sickly-sweet arrogance.

'No Noralynn, I haven't,' Miss Petula turned and faced the Queen full on, 'The day I address you as Queen will be the day I leave the library.'

Annie was absolutely astounded by what she was seeing, the Queen had taken on a mean almost frightening look she'd never seen before, she practically glowed red.

'Annie my lovely,' Miss Petula said kindly as she walked over to Annie, 'Are you ok?' she queried with a look of concern and sincerity.

Annie took and deep breath and nodded confidently. Annie had her own agenda - to help Abigale. When Miss Petula got close enough she lowered her voice to a whisper, 'You remember what I said, Annie?' Annie looked up at Miss Petula a little confused, 'It's not the someone that can help, but the something,' she gave Annie a gentle pat of her hand.

'What are you saying?' the Queen said crossly, 'The Council shall hear about this Miss Petula,' she said warning Miss Petula.

'I'm sure the Council would love to hear about a first-year being on the fourth floor too, Noralynn,' Miss Petula replied with her back to the Queen, she gave Annie a sly wink before she disappeared into the bookshelves.

Annie lowered her head to smile, she began to wonder what

she was even doing here. *What was so important?* Her mind felt groggy, and she raised a hand to her head.

The Queen was quick to notice and chanted Annie's name softly. Annie looked up at the Queen and she began to remember why she was so important. *The Queen needs me*, Annie thought.

'That's right Annie, I do,' the Queen replied, answering the implanted thought, captivating Annie once again.

Wow! Annie thought, *she can read minds too.*

The Queen began to flick swiftly through the pages of the ancient book. The gold edging of the pages dazzled as the light caught them. The dust from the pages hit the air and Annie could smell the history, musty and wondrous. The Queen finally stopped and rubbed her hands over the pages, caressing them as if she knew them. Annie noticed the Queen's smile grow wider, the corners rising up to meet her eyes, this time bright and proud.

'Is that the spell to help Abigale?' Annie questioned, eager to look at the book.

'Yes child, come take a look at the spell,' the Queen motioned with a delicate wave for Annie to come closer, 'You will need to practice this until you know it better than you know your own name,' the Queen forewarned.

Annie began to peer over the old, cracked pages. She breathed in slowly and let out the tiniest little squeal, not being able to hide her over excitement, giving a false grandeur to the occasion.

The Queen's fake smile resumed, trying to hide the tightening of her face in annoyance. Her mind boggled at such a girl. *How can this girl have the power of the Godmothers and why did she need this bumbling fairy?* thought the Queen.

Annie pushed her thick-rimmed glasses up the bridge of her nose and her brown eyes grew wide as she studied the page. Annie touched the book and withdrew her hand quickly as she was struck by a black spark. Annie took a step back from the book. She hadn't seen black sparks before. She looked up at the Queen for reassurance, her eyes filled with worry and confusion.

The Queen took Annie's hand in hers and then placed both their hands on the book as she spoke, 'Hoc donum lux tenebris,' Annie's hand could now touch the pages without the spark.

Darkness take this something of light, Annie read silently, translating the spell in her head. Her Latin spell-casting wasn't her strongest subject, but her Nana had taught her some. This book was giving her a bad feeling.

'You must not say the spell all at once,' the Queen warned, 'When the time is right we will say it together,' the Queen squeezed Annie's hand and gave her a huge fake smile. 'As a first-year I know the Latin is alien to you my child, so I shall go through it one word at time,' the Queen said encouragingly.

Annie looked down at the spell again and carried on translating the words she knew in her head, *Abalienare ne hic - Banish what shouldn't be here,'* she paused as she read, *Daemonum - Demon.*

Abalienare ne hic,
Per illud aere,
Includet eum sicut mortis,
Ita sinistra transferre nihil,

Elementis terra nostra pugna sentient,
Hanc noctem iter impostor,
Daemonum est aspectibus nostris minuit,
post finita obice claudunt atque conflatile.

Annie wanted to leave; something wasn't right, she felt sick to the pit of her stomach, she couldn't put a finger on what it was. Every fibre of her being felt like it was trying to warn her.

Annie had to say something, 'Excuse me, Your Majesty,' she said hesitantly, 'Daemonum – doesn't that mean demon?' she asked, 'Abigale isn't a demon she is my friend,' Annie voice was becoming slightly panicked.

The Queen flustered for a second, 'Er why, Annie, you are such clever girl,' the Queen's voice became rhythmical and chanting again, 'I knew you were the only one clever enough to help me.'

The Queen's words echoed around the fourth floor. Annie visibly calmed but her head became cloudy and muddled again. The Queen continued, 'Shall we begin?'

Annie nodded, but then said, 'This isn't going to hurt Abigale, is it? We will still be able to see her like you promised?'

The Queen broke eye contact with Annie and looked down at the book. Elves unlike Fairies do have the ability to lie, but this comes at a cost. The Queen forced the smile back upon her beautiful porcelain face and raised her hypnotic green eyes back to meet Annie's. With all the sincerity she could muster she replied, 'Of course child, Abigale will be perfectly fine.'

Annie then turned her full attention back to the book and the spell. The Queen turned away and grabbed the silver railing, her grip so tight the knuckles on her small, dainty hands were turning white. Pain ripped through her body like a lightning bolt. Taking a quick, deep breath, she tried to control the convulsion of her body as the fire of the lie-burn made its mark on her body.

'Are you ok, Your Majesty?' Annie turned and looked up from the book.

With her back still facing Annie, the Queen was quiet, silently trembling, her grasp still hard on the railings. She waited for final remnants of the dissipating agony from the lie to leave her body.

'Read child, read.'

Chapter 21

Little T was practicing his triple backflip summersault in the carriage on the way back to his cabin after his adventure with the girls. He was flipping and spinning and making the mahogany shine as he pushed off against it and projected himself through the carriages. Not taking any notice of what was going on around him or how far into the train he'd gone, he was suddenly struck hard and propelled into the archway of one of the carriage windows, banging his head on the cast-iron winged-handle.

A little dazed and a lot angry, Little T looked up to see what had hit him.

'Hey!' he shouted. A taillight flitted quickly out of sight.

Little T then heard giggling, familiar and mean giggling. Tiana and Tamsin, two of his older sisters hovered over staring at him, laughing at his misfortune. In the absence of Tatum, he knew instantly what had hit him with such force.

'Thunderlily got knocked down, knocked down is Thunderlily,' Tiana and Tamsin chanted in between their laughing.

'MY NAME IS TYSON!' Little T screamed at his sisters, gone was the pastel-green face, instead red rage now in its place.

The sisters laughed harder and began to fly in the direction of Tatum. 'Bye Thunderlily, Thunderlily bye, bye,' the Pixies picked up speed, they knew their little brother would come chasing if not.

Little T began to clumber to his feet ready to take on his sisters. Still a little dazed, he reached his feet only to fall back down again dizzily. He slapped both of his hands down on the edge of the windowsill in frustration, watching them disappear further down the train.

'I'll get you later!' he yelled after them, 'I'm telling Mum!' he finished a little half-heartedly, he knew they couldn't hear him anymore.

As he sat there waiting for the dizziness to pass, he began to take in his surroundings. He'd never been this far into the train before. It was different. The mahogany swirls in the walls were different, changing shape faster than normal.

Maybe it's because I've bumped my head, he thought as he rubbed a now-protruding green bump. Little T couldn't help but contemplate the swirls were beginning to look a little like arrows.

Little T got up slowly this time keeping his eyes all the time on the mahogany swirls of the train walls. Shrugging his little green shoulders, he decided to take a look in the direction of the presumed arrows. He was up for another adventure.

Bouncing of the carriage walls and leaving the Pixie mirror shine after each graceful contact, he continued to follow the swirly arrows. Four carriages later, the arrow swirls finally stopped. Little T stopped and looked around taking in his setting, he had come to a fork in the carriages. He looked down each row, both pathways looked the same, red and brown walls but with doors now adorning the carriages.

Then, Little T noticed one of the doors was open, a white light breaking up the monotony of the mahogany. He looked around him. He was totally alone.

I should go and check it out, he thought, *just in case it's dangerous, the Fae need protecting…* This train of thinking gave Little T the justification in letting him follow his curiosity. So, puffing up his tiny chest he began to boldly head towards the open door.

Listening at the doors opening, there was total silence, the train had even stopped humming. He decided to poke his head round the doorway and peer inside. It was beautiful, white-vintage wood and gold-leaf décor. As he entered the room, Little T couldn't help but think with a smile, *this is a little bit of me.*

The room was so smooth and pristine, sunshine walls appeared to have glitter flecks, making them sparkle. Little T flew in a little more. He saw the large white dressing table and huge mirror. He noticed the Fae Crown resting on the table and it dawned on him whose room this was.

One quick look around couldn't hurt, he reasoned, he couldn't help himself. He entered the empty room.

Boldly he flew across the room and picked up speed and launched himself onto the soft, white-lace of the elaborate bedspread. He sprung off and summersaulted across the room, landing on top of the wardrobe.

Sitting on top of the vintage, large white wardrobe he surveyed the room feeling like he was king of the world.

The wardrobe then shifted quickly, propelling Little T to the back where he hit the wall. He then heard a voice coming towards him, he didn't know what to do. He decided to stay in the shadows at the back of the wardrobe.

'Keep going Annie, remember to round R's on the "Elementis terra,"' the Queen made a purring sound over and over, 'I'll be back in a moment you're doing amazingly.' Little T could hear the Queen voice getting closer.

Creeping slowly towards the outer edge of the wardrobe, Little T made sure he was kept hidden. The Queen appeared below him, with her back to him she sauntered towards the large mirror and sat down on the white, pouf stool. Little T noticed how the Queen's hair shimmered as light reflected against each strand. She sat so upright and poised, looking elegant and regal.

Little T gazed at the Queen's reflection. To him she was beyond perfect. Her large, green almond-shaped eyes and flawlessly symmetrically-shaped face were hypnotic, he had never seen her in real-life before. He was in total awe of her.

The mirror started to flash and made a strange buzzing sound. The Queen's reflection disappeared, and lines of interference whirred across the face of the mirror. Little T watched, completely riveted.

A bald man appeared in the mirror reflection, he looked familiar to Little T, but he couldn't think how or where. His face was hard and stern devoid of emotion or spirit.

'Your Majesty,' the hardened, bald man half-bowed, 'Are the plans set to eradicate the problem?' he questioned the Queen.

'Everything is on schedule,' the Queen nodded. 'Are you sure we need this Rainerly girl for the spell?' the Queen queried in a drained and flippant tone, flicking part of the Fae Crown with her fingernail like a spoilt teenager.

'Noralynn,' the bald man chastised, 'The Rainerly Fairy Godmother bloodline is the strongest power source, second only to blue blood royalty,'

The Queen flinched, it was like he had just rubbed salt into her wounds, her green almond-shaped eyes flared with jealously and anger.

'I'm strong enough without her. Myself and Elliot will suffice,' the Queen sat bolt upright as if commanding her power. 'The stupid girl can't even recognise when she is being charmed into doing something,' the Queen almost spat the words at the bald man.

Little T felt his heart break, his respect for the Queen began to drip away as he watched what unfolded before him. *Elliot? What has Elliot got to do with this!* Little T thought.

'Noralynn, don't you forget how you got that crown,' the bald elf whispered menacingly, 'It can be taken away just a quick!' he threatened, staring the Queen straight in the eyes.

'Uncle,' the Queen said defeated, the realisation hitting her that she was always going to be trapped, she always going to be somebody's puppet.

'Do not address me as uncle,' the balding man spat at the Queen, you could see her shoulders physically shrink, 'Chancellor, and Chancellor only, Noralynn, do I make myself clear!' he said raising his voice to make sure the words impacted her.

Contrite, the Queen met the Chancellor's stare and responded quietly, 'As you wish, Chancellor.'

'I want that grey demon off my train before anyone finds out who she really is,' he continued, 'Get the Rainerly girl ready to annihilate the Never-Believer!'

Zap. The mirror went blank, and the Queen's reflection was back to looking back at her.

Little T saw someone different this time as he peered over the wardrobe hidden amongst the gold-leaf trim. The face was now devoid of some of its beauty with the bitter pout that was reflected in the mirror. What he had just witnessed had rocked his beliefs to the core. How could this be his Queen, he contemplated sadly.

Little T was lost in thought and didn't notice the Queen lift her hand and swipe it swiftly to one side. The wardrobe jolted and slid across the wall again, revealing the hidden doorway from which she came. Little T was catapulted back leaving him feeling winded with surprise for the second time. He could hear Annie's voice in the distance again practicing the purring of the 'R's.

The Queen looked at herself in the mirror and pinched her cheeks to give them a rosy glow, she turned to face the doorway and giving an irked roll of her eyes began to chant, 'Annie, my clever child, that sounds amazing, no one can help Abigale like you can.'

The Queen glided through the door and Little T could smell her intoxicating sweetness. He shook his head hard not allowing the aroma to penetrate his mind. He was not going to allow himself to be fooled or blinded by anything royal ever again. This time Little T held on tight to the wardrobe when it moved back to cover the hidden doorway. He froze for a moment with a heavy heart, taking in everything he had witnessed. He needed to do something, he needed to help Annie, he needed to tell Abigale and Clara.

Puffing out his little green chest with all his might, Little T knew there was only one Pixie for the job, one Pixie to save the girls, and that one Pixie was undoubtedly him. With a giant intake of breath and all the light speed he could muster he set his destination back to the girls' cabin.

Chapter 22

'*Viola?*' Professor Mortley said a little confused, he was a little dazed, but he would know that face anywhere, 'Viola,' he said again softly yet utterly astounded, 'It's me, P,' he said assuming she didn't know who he was.

Aunt Violet stepped back away from Professor Mortley, hugging her black-shawl tighter and tighter around her body. Her face was contorted with a mixture of fear and bitterness, 'I know who you are,' she spat.

Professor Mortley pressed off against the corners of the walls in the corner where he had been thrown, using them to stable himself as he got to his feet. Although not the image he remembered, he knew every inch of the old, haggard, tainted woman in front of him. But the words, the words coming out of her mouth, shocked him to the core. Professor Mortley began blinking furiously, the turmoil within him made it hard for him to hold off his holographic appearance outside the train.

'You won't be able to hold it for long, then you will be caught,' Aunt Violet spoke with a hidden threat.

'Viola, where have you been?' the Professor asked desperately needing answers, desperately trying to hold on, 'What happened to you?' the Professor was almost pleading.

Anger and bitterness filled Aunt Violet as she thought, *how could he be asking these questions?* She was beginning to get frantic as questions whirled through her mind - *After everyone failed her, how dare he ask her this? After all that they did? They made her leave.* Aunt Violet's body shook as she tried to control her emotions.

Professor Mortley held his hands up, 'I looked everywhere for you, we all did,' his eyes filling to a new level, sincere depth now embedded deep within his voice. He knew this could very quickly take a turn for the worse, this was not the Viola he remembered.

The words hit Aunt Violet with a force that left her unsteady on her feet and she faltered just for a second. Professor Mortley suddenly saw a fleeting glimpse of the Fairy Queen he once knew.

'How dare you, after what they did to us,' Aunt Violet resumed her hatred and bitterness as she remembered the hurt in her heart. Both of Aunt Violet's hands were now clenching beneath the black shawl, blue sparks were beginning to fire over her hands.

'Please Viola,' Professor Mortley begged, 'I have no idea what happened,' Professor Mortley was shocked at the venom coming out of the woman he idolised. He decided to keep talking, the sparks were beginning to get bigger, he needed to calm Aunt Violet down.

'Viola, Mama Gilbert and myself woke and you and Delphine were gone,' as the words left Professor Mortley's mouth a ball of blue kinetic energy escaped from Aunt Violet's hands. The Professor ducked as the ball flew towards him, missing him, it began rebounding off the hospital room walls.

Aunt Violet's legs buckled underneath her as the energy left her fingertips and the one word escaped her lips.

'Delphine,' she uttered, she reached out for the chair to steady her. She hadn't spoken her sister's name in years, grief gripped her body.

The blue ball of energy darted around the hospital room increasing its speed each time it reflected. Aunt Violet was momentarily lost in her memories and unresponsive to the danger. Professor Mortley tried calling her name to get her to stop the ball.

'Viola, Viola,' he yelled.

Everything felt like it was now in slow motion and the sound had been muted. Professor Mortley shouted and attempted to get closer to Aunt Violet whilst ducking out the way of the ball of light. The blue ball was getting quicker and quicker like it was being manipulated by a pinball wizard, the flippers being hit and controlled with lightning speed and pinpoint accuracy.

Professor Mortley knew he could be catapulted across the room again, but he needed to get Aunt Violet out of this trance. He placed a hand softly on the top of her arms and shook her and shouted for a final time, 'Viola, the light!'

Aunt Violet then looked into Professors Mortley's round, pink face and flushed cheeks; his messy, dusty-brown hair all over the place and remembered the little boy she brought back to the train all those years ago. Aunt Violet's mind cleared, she looked up and saw her ball of electric energy. Knocking Professor Mortley to one side, empowered by a newfound strength to stop its trajectory heading straight for Abigale's sleeping body.

The ball of energy struck Abigale with an almighty force, making her chest lift off of the bed and thud back down against the hard, grey hospital mattress. Aunt Violet gasped reaching Abigale's bedside.

Kneeling on the cold hospital floor without hesitation she grabbed Abigale's hand, encased it within hers, and brought it to her forehead. Instead of blue sparks, this time a blue fluid light began to encircle both their hands and Aunt Violet began to chant for the first time in years.

'Sorbere lux lucem erunt - absorb the light, the light be mine,' over and over again she chanted, the blue light swirling and a humming in rhythm to the soft-spoken words.

Professor Mortley's heart sored as he saw emerge the Fairy Queen he once knew, his boylike face beamed, 'There you are! I knew you were still in there!'

Professor Mortley walked round to the other side of the bed and knelt down, taking Abigale's other hand, and holding it to his forehead, he joined in Aunt Violet's chant. The pair locked eyes and Professor Mortley felt the warmth of the power he once knew.

After what seem like hours Aunt Violet finally spoke, 'That should be enough,' her voice was clipped but clam. Professor Mortley gently replaced Abigale's hand to her side, giving it a little caring pat as he did. This didn't go unnoticed by Aunt Violet.

Silence and tension refilled the room, 'I can't be found,' Aunt Violet finally said in the same clipped and cold manner as before, 'Explain what you are even doing here?'

Professor Mortley cleared his throat, 'I came to remember, Viola.' Aunt Violet looked confused, 'Remember what? What has this got to do with the girl?'

'Remember you,' he replied he eyes soft, staring at the woman in front of him, trying to find his queen again. Aunt Violet looked away and the room was silent. Professor Mortley was trying to piece everything together, but his mind was becoming fogged, his face began to holograph and Aunt Violet stared at the man/boy before her.

'Errrr, Ermmm,' Professor Mortley began to fumble.

'Spit it out!' Aunt Violet commanded.

'I… Errr… I think,' he paused, 'Abigale is in danger,' a worried look now plastered on the ever-changing face.

'Don't be ridiculous,' Aunt Violet turned away picking up her black shawl from the floor and wrapping it around her shoulders regaining the Aunt Violet imagery, 'The train will expel her at the end of term as a Never-Believer…'

'No, Viola,' Professor Mortley interjected, 'They are expelling her from the train in two days,' Aunt Violet turned back to face Professor Mortley, 'They are using the Pink Moon to overthrow the train,' Professor Mortley looked sadly at Abigale's sleeping body.

Aunt Violet's face dropped, drained of all colours, 'But she will die,' she said flatly, 'No one has survived leaving the train without the train's permission.'

The memory of her sister crossed her mind again. Professor Mortley looked helpless as he looked at the old woman before him. He couldn't believe how much the grey had affected her.

Professor Mortley said without a thought, 'We need your help,' he began to pace the floor, 'Yes, that's right, we need you, Viola,' his pacing got quicker, 'Your magic can stop Noralynn.'

'Noralynn?' Aunt Violet looked up with a new leaf of anger brimming to the surface.

Professor Mortley stopped pacing and looked down at his shoes nervously. 'Noralynn is the queen now, it's her decision to get Abigale off the train early,' he explained watching Aunt Violet's reaction carefully. She may have aged, but the fire and fight were still strong within her.

Aunt Violet's mind began to race again, 'I can't help you,

I'm not who I once was,' she said with finality.

'But Viola,' Professor Mortley tried to protest.

'No!' she shouted, making a fist and punching it into the side of her leg, 'I just can't, you don't know…,' her voice filled with a flatness of a foreordained defeat.

The hospital room door flung open with a bang. Aunt Violet and Professor Mortley turned towards the door.

'What the are you doing in my daughter's room?' Mrs Johnson said sternly. She was standing in the doorway, one hand on her hip and the other holding her large, grey snakeskin bag. Her grey, bobbed hair motionless as she commandeered the room.

'The doctor was just leaving,' Aunt Violet said matching her sternness.

'Good!' Mrs Johnson confirmed. 'I'd hoped my request for an alternative doctor would have been in place by now,' she added with a look of disgust at Professor Mortley.

Professor Mortley put his hands in his pockets and began to rock backwards and forwards on his toes, 'Would you like an update on Abigale, ma'am?' he asked Mrs Johnson matter-of-factly.

'She is still asleep, isn't she?' Mrs Johnson said with utter disdain. 'Are you ready?' she asked Aunt Violet, not even glancing in Abigale's direction.

Aunt Violet could see Professor Mortley was appalled by Mrs Johnson, she was appalled by her, never could she have imagined that the events of the past would have caused such coldness.

'I'll meet you in the car,' Aunt Violet ordered with contempt.

Mrs Johnson was horror-struck into silence that Aunt

Violet would speak to her like that in front of that doctor. Mrs Johnson hovered still in the doorway.

Gathering her things Aunt Violet looked up again with all the meanness she could muster she repeated herself slowly, 'I... shall... meet... you... in... the... car!'

Mrs Johnson found herself unable to answer as anger rose and steam felt like it was escaping through her ears.

Professor Mortley walked over and held out his hand, 'Goodbye Mrs Johnson, Doctor Pearce will be taking over from me.'

She shook his hand without thinking and again was covered in a sticky, green, sparkly residue. Professor Mortley smiled to himself as he turned away and picked up the chart at the end of Abigale's bed and pretended to check the information written down.

Mrs Johnson was fuming. She spun on her heels and stormed through the door and down the corridor. Professor Mortley looked after her in utter disbelief that people as mean as her actually existed.

'It's what happens,' Aunt Violet said as she walked towards the door answering the Professor's unasked question, 'When blue bloods don't transition to the Fae,' she looked sad, guilty, and old, 'Our hearts turn icy blue, the coldest of cold,' her voice trailed off as she reached the door.

Professor Mortley made one more last-ditch attempt, 'It's not too late, Viola, you can help Abigale.'

Aunt Violet looked over her shoulder at Professor Mortley passing through the doorway, 'No, P, I can't.'

Chapter 23

Abigale was sitting on the edge of her iron-grey bed watching Clara decide on which shade and style of pink pyjamas she should wear. Abigale loved watching all the colours and the happiness on Clara's face as she explained how, why, and when you should wear certain clothes. Abigale could listen to her talk forever.

'This is the kind of pink you should wear if you should have a gentleman caller,' Clara said trying to make her voice sound older and with an air of regal splendour.

Turning around slowly she held up her baby-pink silk nightie causing a look of mock shock to appear on Abigale's face. They both fell about giggling, laughing hard, in a way that girls that were best friends did, unbridled, cheeks hurting, belly-hugging, laughter.

Clara slumped herself down onto Annie's emerald-green bed, her tummy aching from the laughter. It was almost like a psychic connection as they both instantly stopped laughing at the same time and fell quiet, looking at Annie's empty bed. Clara, deep in thought, rubbed her hand over the green, satin cover, torment painted over her face.

'She'll be back soon,' Abigale reassured with a half-smile, not really knowing if she would be.

Clara looked up at Abigale and said sadly, 'I miss her.' Clara began to ruffle and crease Annie's pillows and rearranged the books on her shelf.

Abigale stood up and pulled Clara off Annie's bed, 'Clara!' Abigale chastised, trying to stop her muddling quest.

Just as they reached their feet they were startled by a *tap, tap, tap*.

'Can you hear that?' questioned Clara.

The tapping got louder. The girls turned around and started looking around their room for the source of the sound. The tapping seemed to get faster and more frequent. Clara began to fling her nighties and pyjamas around the room as if the tapping were coming from underneath them, Abigale headed towards the door.

Tap, Tap, Tap, Tap, TAP! It was getting louder as she reached the door. Abigale began to open the door when she was flung backwards as a rocket of light exploded through the doorway.

'Ahhhhhhhhhhhhh!' squealed Clara, trying to cover her pink satin nightdress with her arms. One arm flung across her chest the other trying to pull down the hem of her silk nightdress, trying to make it reach lower than the top of her thighs.

'I'VE BEEN KNOCKING FOR AGES!' yelled Little T before he realised what he had walked in on. Looking at Clara up and down he breathed out with a whistle, 'Nice.'

As soon the words had left his mouth he could feel his face burning red and buried them in the palms of his hands as he spun around facing away from Clara.

'Little T!' Clara yelled, 'Have you no manners!' she chastised.

Abigale had to put her head down to hide her smile. Clara reached for her fuchsia-pink silk dressing gown and dramatically spun around as she put it on. She tied it crossly in a double knot and placed her hands on her hips getting ready to let Little T have a piece of her mind. Abigale raised one of her plaits to her mouth in a last-ditch attempt to hide the amused smile she couldn't get rid of. She walked round to stand just behind Clara.

'Little T…' Clara began but was soon interrupted.

'Clara, just stop,' Little T said, spinning back around, holding out both of his hands. His face looked worried and a little scared. 'I've got something important to tell you both,' his voice wobbled and cracked a little, the enormity becoming all too much.

Abigale and Clara looked at each other and then back to Little T. They realised he was serious.

'What's wrong?' Abigale asked concerned.

Clara still had her hands on her hips, ready to give him a piece of her mind, already deciding what he was going to say was unimportant.

Little T took a deep breath.

'Spit it out, T!' Clara said impatiently.

'It's Annie,' he said looking deep into Clara's eyes, trying to express his absolute sincerity. 'She's in trouble,' he began to rant, flying from side to side, 'But I'm not sure you're going to believe me about how much trouble she is in, or, how we can help her,' he paused and looked up to the sky, 'Can we even help her?' he continued speaking in a high-pitched squeak. 'But she needs our, help!' Little T flew up closer to Abigale, 'AND you!' he screeched, now in a frantic twist pointing at Abigale, 'You need help too!'

'LITTLE T!' Clara shouted, he stopped mid-flight and just stared at Clara. Clara then changed her tone, soft and sing-song, smooth and comforting, 'Start from the beginning and tell us what's happened.'

Abigale and Clara sat down on Annie's bed. Little T calmed himself and began to tell of his summersaults and being nearly knocked out by Tatum and went off on a tangent of his mean sisters. Every time Little T went off track Clara flicked a green diamante at his head, which brought him back to the task at hand.

He finally explained about Annie being enchanted by the Queen to help cast the spell to get Abigale off the train and the strange bald man on the mirror call. He told them everything.

Everything, except about Elliot. Little T was planning on talking to him first as boy code was everything to him. Elliot was his friend, and he couldn't throw him to girls without good cause. His mind raced with thoughts of Elliot, *I thought I knew him? I thought we were friends. Bros*, he thought.

'...And then she went back through the doorway, and I barely escaped with my life,' Little T exaggerated as he finished.

Clara and Abigale were silent for a moment, taking it all in. Clara then bounced out of her seat, 'I knew something wasn't right with Annie!' she proclaimed, now beginning to pace the room beside Little T.

Abigale was stunned at all this and felt totally helpless and guilty, 'I have no clue what to do,' she said, 'Maybe we should get some help. Little T, maybe you should write it down before you forget?'

Little T nodded and looked around for something to write with.

'That's it!' said Clara, 'A Dear Diary spell,' grabbing Little T's small green hand and turning him to face her, 'A diary spell, T,' she said nodding to Little T in affirmation. Little T thought for a moment and then began to get excited.

'Have we got everything we need?' he asked Clara quizzically.

Clara went to Annie's bookshelf and grabbed one of the books. It looked new in a red leather hardcover, with a gold trim. Opening it a tiny cloud of sparkly dust escaped, like the book had taken its first breath. Clara flicked through until she found the right page.

'Ok,' Clara said reading the list of ingredients, 'We need, something that belongs to the writer,' Little T grabbed an emerald-green ceramic cup off Annie's bookshelf.

'Check!' he said.

Abigale watched in awe.

'Pureness of heart,' Clara continued, Little T stopped and looked at Clara puzzled as to what to get. Clara rolled her eyes over to Abigale, giving Little T a private signal. Little T thought for a moment and then realised. He flew over to Abigale.

Hovering by Abigale's head momentarily, 'Sorry Abs,' he said as he grabbed one strand of her caramel hair from the bottom of one of her plaits and pulled it out.

'Ouch!' Abigale said while rubbing her head, her gaze followed Little T as he darted off with one strand of hair in his hand.

He placed it inside the cup and the looked up at Clara, 'Two drops of fairy happy tears, one drop of sad.'

Clara pirouetted up to her top bunk and dug deep into one of her multi-coloured, sequined bags. She pulled out two little bottles of clear liquid, one labelled happy, one labelled sad. Pouring the required amount into the cup she stirred it whilst saying the magic words.

'Tell me your secrets I'm making an enquiry, tell all the details and write it in a dairy,' she looked at Little T and

Abigale, 'Now all we need is her favourite drink to mix with it and a blank book for her to write in.'

'Hold on,' Abigale said, 'You're going to put a spell on Annie?' questioning if what Clara was doing was right. 'She's our friend, that makes us no better than the Queen.'

Clara and Little T lowered their heads as the reality sank in. Abigale was right they shouldn't cast a spell on their friend. Clara sank back down to sitting on the bed looking a little deflated.

'Jeeze, for a minute there I actually thought you were going to poison me!' came a voice from the doorway.

Clara, Abigale, and Little T jumped up in surprise. Annie walked in looking sad.

'How long have you been standing there?' asked Clara, looking a little embarrassed.

Clara leaned forward awkwardly, crossing her legs, and stretching her arm over the side table, pushing the green mug out of sight. She then rested her head on her arm in an over-exaggerated stretch and yawned with a guilty smile as she attempted to hide the rest of the evidence.

Little T couldn't help himself and started rambling about her being in danger.

'Little T,' Annie held up her hand, 'I know,' she said sadly, 'I overheard her on the mirror call, the charm faded when she was consumed by herself.'

Annie tripped slightly on the blue and gold circular rug and toppled ungracefully onto to Abigale's iron-grey bed. But this time, it wasn't funny. Everyone then sat glumly.

'So, it turns out I'm not so special,' Annie stated looking down at her feet, 'Turns out I'm actually stupid, that I didn't even know she was charming me.' Her words were tainted with anger and hurt. Annie kicked the tassels of the carpet feeling utterly dejected.

'Hold on a fairy damn minute!' Clara rose to her feet, 'You, Annie Rainerly, are the smartest, kindest, bravest Fairy Godmother-to-be I know!' Clara walked over and sat next to Annie on the bed. Giving Annie a little nudge she said, 'Plus, your my bestest…' Clara paused, looked at Abigale as Abigale nudged up the other side of Annie, then corrected herself, 'Your OUR bestest friend,' they both put their arms around Annie and hugged her.

'Stop!' Annie shouted as they hugged her, Abigale and Clara edged back in shock, 'Who's been messing up my books and my bed!'

'She's back, she's back!' Clara squealed, hugging Annie tightly as if she were never going to let her go.

'OMG get me a bucket, bluh, bluh, bluh,' Little T was pretending to be sick everywhere in mock disgust at what he was witnessing, 'This is not helping! What are we going to do?'

Annie smiled a small smile as she stood, 'So what spell were you going to put on me?' she asked one hand on her hip and sass all over her face.

Clara lowered her head in shame, 'The Dear Diary spell.'

Annie lowered her head as if she were disappointed.

'I'm so sorry Annie, we just didn't know what to do, I didn't think you'd believe us about the Queen as she was training you.' Clara tried to make it up to Annie, her voice was soft, she was pleading as she explained.

Annie lifted her head, 'The Dear Diary spell, you say?' in hopeful reflection. Clara stopped talking and looked at Annie puzzled.

'Err… Yeah?' Clara confirmed, eyeing up the room, now not knowing what to think.

'Clara, you're a genius!' Annie yelled, beaming at a surprised Clara.

Little T was totally baffled, 'Wow!' he said, 'That's a quick emotional turnaround,' he laid himself down on top of Clara's top bunk watching the show below.

Annie shot Little T a wicked look and then turned to Abigale and Clara. 'You need to cast the spell on me,' the girls looked at each other, shocked by Annie's words. 'Abigale, we know you're in trouble, but we don't know how, why or what is going to happen.' The girls were all standing together now, the three of them in a circle holding hands. 'I can't remember any of the time I'm with *her*,' Annie over-pronounced the word with disgust. 'Or at least what I do remember doesn't make sense.'

Annie then continued to lay out her plan, 'We only have two days till the Pink Moon, if I can write down everything that actually happens when I'm with the Queen,' she took a deep breath, 'Then, maybe, just maybe, we will have a chance of saving Abigale from leaving.'

The three of them held hands tightly and the train began to shake in agreement, cementing their unity and joining together in a predestined power.

'So, you don't remember what you've been doing all this time?' Abigale asked wanting to know more. Annie sat down and thought about it.

'The only thing I remember for sure was seeing Miss Petula,' Annie said thinking back.

'Oohhh I like her,' Clara said excitedly, 'What did she say?'

'Well, it was the strangest thing,' Annie replied, 'She obviously doesn't like the Queen,' she scoffed.

'Who does?' Little T injected flippantly and with a little sorrow.

'But…' Annie flipped Little T another 'please shut up!' look and carried on, 'She kept saying I need to ask something and not someone for help?'

They all looked at each other blankly. The train began to shake, this time harder. The girls held on to each other as not to topple over. The shaking increased and was getting harder and more violent.

'Get on to the bed!' Clara shouted over the rattling of the train.

The three of them jumped onto Annie's bed, the shaking increased, the girls held on tightly to each other. Little T was shouting something, but the girls couldn't make out what it was over the noise of the train. He started acting out what he was trying to say, looking like he was the worst player ever in charades. He started pointing around at the train frantically.

'Ask something,' Annie repeated trying to make out Little T's actions. Then the three of them shouted in unison.

'Ask the train!' and with that the train stopped. Everything was still. Apart from Little T who was still playing his game of charades. The girls giggled at him.

'Ok, ask the train,' Annie said becoming serious again. The train hummed as if waiting.

'Can you help us, Train?' Annie asked out loud.
Nothing.
'How do we help Abigale, Train?' Clara asked this time.
Nothing.

'Train, can you give us a break and tell us the lotion, potion or spell we need to beat the wicked witch of the west?' Little T exclaimed, falling back on the bed in a flump.

'She's a Queen,' Annie corrected under her breath. Little T rolled his eyes at her, Annie was certainly back.

Then, taking everyone by surprise Abigale said in a delicate, heartfelt, and innocent voice, 'Train, please, can you help me?'

The train shook and an ancient, giant book flew across the cabin floor and stopped in the middle of the circular carpet. Opening by itself the pages flew erratically backwards and forwards until resting on the pages it wanted open.

The four of them crept near the book and looked down at the pages. There was a picture of a little girl, caramel-brown hair, with two cane roll plaits that hung either side of her head. Annie, Clara, and Little T all looked at Abigale with their mouths open in shock.

Annie read aloud the chapter heading, 'Blue Fairies – The Royal Bloodline.'

They all stared back to Abigale. Abigale's chest then convulsed violently, and a blue light flashed within her. Abigale collapsed and her lifeless body fell to the floor.

Chapter 24

Mrs Johnson was sitting in the passenger seat of Mr Johnson's black Granada Estate, her rounded little nose twitched with annoyance. The purple hue in her eyes had deepened giving her pointy face a demonic look as her temper bubbled within. Her murky, grey bob protruded out from mink hat that matched her coat like it had been put on without the normal care to attention. Her lower jaw seemed to be moving like she was chewing on something.

Aunt Violet was in the back seat looking vacantly out of the window, her normally upright rigidity was gone as she slumped against the grey, leather seats. Her black wrap hung around her shoulders and her normally ice-cold blue eyes dazzled in the reflection of the window. She watched expressionless as the grey Stepford houses of Greystone Valley passed by.

Mr Johnson could barely see over the steering wheel; he was leaning forwards as he drove, his chin practically touching the top of the smooth steering column. His rounded glasses resting on the very edge of his little, rounded nose as he navigated his way back to their house. The car jolted as he misjudged the curb on the driveway causing Mrs Johnson to let out a groan of infuriation at Mr Johnson's driving. She began to get out of the car before it had even come to a complete stop.

Slamming the door behind her making the whole car shudder, Mrs Johnson stomped up the winding pathway so quickly she even caused the black and white roses to sway as she passed.

She burst through the front door causing the door to shake as she did and the Never-Believer knocker to bang furiously.

Mrs Johnson yelled as she passed through the door like a hurricane, 'Peter!, George! Come here now!'

Mr Johnson straighten his back as he opened his car door, his rounded face stern as he turned to open the passenger door for Aunt Violet. Noticing Aunt Violet was out of sorts he had a rare moment of bravery.

'I hope your pleased with yourself,' he commented with an air of indignation.

Breaking Aunt Violet from her trance, she questioned, 'What did you say?' with a coolness that made a shiver rundown the back of Mr Johnson's spine. The hairs on his arms stood up on end. He began to fumble with his keys as his nerve was quickly diminishing.

'Well... er,' he stuttered trying to find the words, 'You have... er... obviously... er... upset her,' he pushed his glasses up his nose and a bead of sweat ran down the side of his face, he was unable to meet Aunt Violet's stare as she exited the car.

'Everything you say will be wrong, a wrongness in everything that you say,' Aunt Violet chanted bitterly.

Mr Johnson look utterly baffled by what Aunt Violet had just said and he stood still, holding open the car door, flabbergasted. He began to puff out his large, rounded lips making them vibrate as he did. Mr Johnson responded then like he was possessed, he just couldn't stop himself, 'You're totally off your rocker, you silly old bat!' his hand flew up to mouth in an attempt to stop the already escaped words.

Aunt Violet continued up towards the house with a wry grin.

***

'557!' Elliot declared triumphally as Freddie collapsed face down on the floor, 'That's 100 more that yesterday, mate!' he congratulated Freddie.

Freddie just held up his thumb while he lay panting on Elliot's cabin floor. Elliot let out a little laugh as he threw Freddie a little towel to wipe his brow as he got up.

Elliot then asked, 'How many times a day do you need to train again, Fred?'

'Whenever I'm not studying my Sargent says,' Freddie paused, thoughtful for a moment, 'So, A LOT!' he exclaimed, wiping the towel all over his head and then picking up a barbell with his left hand and started to press the weight above his head. Elliot shook his head in wonder, glad Elves didn't have to meet such physical requirements.

Little T exploded through the door like a lightning bolt. The boys froze and watched him as he panted and puffed trying desperately to catch his breath.

'Its…' he puffed, 'It's…' he panted, 'It's Abigale!' finally got out, 'We need help!' He rested his little hands on his knees and bent over trying to regain his voice.

Elliot jumped up, a look of fear across his face, 'Where?' he said firmly.

'The girls' cabin.' Little T got out in between breaths.

Elliot and Freddie hurried out the door, 'Get Mama Gilbert!' Elliot shouted behind him to Little T. Little T took a couple of deep breaths and rocketed back out the room.

***

Mama Gilbert lifted her best china tea pot, 'You know my dear, Munchkin County don't make these anymore,' she turned the pot to display a forest with a bright-yellow brick road going through it with tiny flying monkeys in the sky.

'It's 'Your Majesty' now, Mama Gilbert,' Noralynn corrected.

Slightly embarrassed Mama Gilbert's cheeks glowed a bashful pink, 'Apologies, Your Majesty,' Mama Gilbert bowed regretfully, 'It only seems like yesterday you were my star pupil!' she bowed again, 'I forget myself.... Tea? Your Majesty?'

'We all make mistakes,' Noralynn said arrogantly, although there was an unfamiliar tightness in her chest. 'Just boiled water, thank you,' she clipped, looking around Mama Gilbert's cabin in appalled awe at all of her clutter, 'You have been busy over the years, haven't you?' she added in a back-handed rhetorical compliment.

Mama Gilbert, seemingly oblivious to Queen Noralynn's inflections, poured her a cup of boiling water. She took her seat on her giant comfy chair, settling herself into the back of its right-hand corner, her feet just dangling over the edge, pointing her toes up and down as she quietly sipped her tea.

Noralynn fidgeted from side to side on the little stool, her patience beginning to wear thin. 'How have you been, Mama Gilbert? It's been so long,' her words dripped with insincerity and false opulence.

'Oh, I'm fine, Your Majesty,' replied Mama Gilbert in a sing-song, happy-go-lucky voice which seemingly irritated the Queen more.

'It's seems we are in unprecedented times,' Noralynn continued in a bid to try and entice Mama Gilbert into conversation.

'Really?' Mama Gilbert looked up towards the ceiling as if see was trying to think of these unprecedented times, 'How so?'

'Well…' Noralynn wasn't prepared for this to be such hard work. She remembered Mama Gilbert to be an eccentric and forgetful teacher, but this was ridiculous, 'Having our first Never-Believer amongst us and facilitating her safe return.' Noralynn winced, the pain of another lie travelled up her arm causing her hand to shake and the cup and saucer to clatter. Her other hand shot up to steady the cup, shooting Mama Gilbert a look to see if she had noticed.

Mama Gilbert took a deliberately long sip of her tea holding her china cup and saucer still in her hand. She lifted the cup up admiring the ruby slippers painted on its side, in turn making her look at her own sapphire, sparkly shoes in delight.

'Mama Gilbert?' Noralynn said curtly, her shoulders relaxing as Mama Gilbert gave the appearance of obliviousness.

'Well, she not the firs…' Mama Gilbert was cut short by the tiny, panicked voice.

'Qu-i-ck!' Little T shouted breathlessly, 'Emer-gen-cy!' Little T inhaled deeply, 'She's hurt!' he finally blurted out.

With that Mama Gilbert leapt out of her comfy seat, tossing her precious china cup, which landed perfectly back in its place next to the yellow brick road teapot. With no regard for her company, she grabbed a tiny purple bag with the Believer rings incrusted in gold glitter on the side.

'Lead the way Mr Glitterfluff Thunderlily!' she asserted with impatience.

Cringing, Little T took some deep breaths and turned around and headed out the door in front of Mama Gilbert.

Noralynn rolled her eyes, she slowly and awkwardly rose from the little stool, glad they had rushed off to not witness her ungracefulness. Slowly placing down her china cup, she knew to save face she must also follow, and at least appear to help.

Noralynn now regained of her gracefulness glided out of

Mama Gilbert's cabin and followed Little T's taillight down the train's carriages. The train's vibrations picked up strength as Noralynn walked through rocking her from side to side. Every time she had to reach out to steady herself she let out a sound of annoyance. The train's energy got stronger and stronger tossing Noralynn around like a rag doll.

Noralynn let out a scream, 'STOP!'

The train shuddered to an almost stop, recapturing its gentle hum.

'I know what you're doing,' Noralynn groaned through gritted teeth, her whole body seething. Placing her hands flat against the mahogany carriage wall, she took in the vibration of the train. Removing one hand and with one delicate finger she traced over the cast-iron wings that adjoined the hinges of the train and window clasps.

'You know,' Noralynn suggested, her voice dripping with sinister intent, 'A little remodelling wouldn't go amiss.'

With that she dug her nails into the soft varnish of the mahogany walls and dragged them horizontally down the wall. The train shook as if releasing a pained cry.

The beautiful symmetry of Noralynn's face now looked old and odd as her evilness was laid bare. A smile that held years of jealously and bitterness was plastered across her tainted face. The smirk held her triumphant win over the train as she now traced over her scratch marks. The power felt so good, she felt it rush through her veins and leaned her head back and laughed a deep, cold, and venomous laugh.

As her head came back into alignment she caught her reflection in the high sheen of the reds and browns of the wood. The train showed her a truthful reflection free from the glamour-magic that the royal role possesses. She saw every line of bitterness creased upon her face, every hate-act, every lie-burn, every mean and vindictive infection was there for her to see.

Her hands went to her face instantly in a panic, the reflection was too real. She felt her smooth, firm, youthfulness underneath her fingertips, her perfect face was still intact. She was relieved by what she felt but knew in her heart the reflection was her destiny should she ever fall from the throne.

Noralynn defiantly waved her hand making the image disappear. She walked toward the open cabin doorway where she could hear the dramatic cries of teenage girls, the buzzing of Pixie fire flight and the muttering of Mama Gilbert's desperate healing spells, with the stench of cinnamon drifting out the door. As she stood in the doorway she realised the grey clad girl laying lifeless on the floor must be Abigale.

The screeching of Clara and Annie was vexing to Noralynn as they hugged each other wailing on the iron-grey bed. The 3 T's and Little T were dotted around the room in various dramatic pensive statuettes, that Noralynn would swear were in mockery.

The giant oaf boy that stood to attention at the foot of the green bed appeared to be waiting to be called to duty and Elliot, *my Elliot,* Noralynn thought surprised at his presence. It had been ages since she had seen her brother in person. She walked over towards him, he shook his head at her quickly, signalling her to stay back. He actually looks worried, Noralynn thought. Noralynn was now worried.

She looked back at him over her shoulder. He seemed transfixed on the girl lying on the floor. Noralynn would need to speak with him again if this didn't pan out in their favour. Hopefully, the girl wouldn't make it, and all would return to how it should be.

Mama Gilbert was beginning to get upset as nothing seemed to be awaking Abigale. Mama Gilbert looked up to the sky as if pleading with somebody, then back to Abigale, chanting, over and over. Nothing.

'Noralynn,' Mama Gilbert finally spoke, 'Is there nothing you can do?' she was practically begging.

Noralynn spun around with a look of audacity on her face that Mama Gilbert had dared to call her by her first name in front of students.

'Curhummmm,' Elliot cleared his throat loudly getting Noralynn's attention, and nodded his head instantly towards Abigale. Noralynn corrected herself and plastered a caring smile across her face.

'I really don't see what I can do,' Noralynn moved closer to Abigale, 'Royal magic might not work on a Never-Believer,' she finished hesitantly.

Little T was sitting high on Clara's shelf amongst her pink sparkly headbands and swirls and twirls of pink ribbon. He was surveilling the Queen and Elliot's secret nods, looks, and sounds. Elliot nodded more forcibly towards Abigale to the Queen, in a silent insistence that she help her.

The Queen knelt by Abigale's side, 'There's only one spell that should work…' she looked at Mama Gilbert, 'Pathway of Light?' Mama Gilbert nodded knowing exactly what Noralynn was thinking of and took Noralynn's hands. Noralynn and Mama Gilbert chanted in a unity of haunting harmony. They chanted for what seemed like an age…

Nothing.

Mama Gilbert's face drained of colour, both her and the

Queen looked exhausted. Mama took a deep breath ready to give the unearthly news to the group.

Noralynn whispered to Mama Gilbert, 'I've never known this not to work,' Noralynn looked down at her hands, confused, tired, and concerned, 'It always works.'

Mama Gilbert looked up to Clara and Annie, 'I'm so sorry girls... I... I really don't know how to say thi...'

'Christmas and dangly bits, stop what you are doing!' insisted Professor Mortley as he bounded into the room. He headed straight to Mama Gilbert. Bending down he whispered secretly in her ear. Nodding to everything Professor Mortley was saying, Mama Gilbert was injected with a new lease of life. The colour restoring to her cheeks she leaned down repeating the whisper, this time into Abigale's ear, laying one hand over her heart.

'Stand back,' Professor Mortley ordered everyone. 'Now!' Professor Mortley ordered Mama Gilbert.

Mama Gilbert shot a purple beam of fairy light directly into Abigale's heart. Causing her little body to convulse and lift off the floor. The light turned blue and encircled Abigale, suspending her above the floor. The light flickered as it faded Abigale floated gently back to the ground. The room was silent as they all watched and waited.

Professor Mortley walked towards Abigale's body, slowly and carefully looking for any signs of life. Closer and closer, taking one hand out of his pocket and unconsciously bringing a sparkly, green Christmas tree marshmallow to his mouth. Just as it was about to reach his lips Abigale jolted upright with a cough and a sneeze of blue glitter, causing professor Mortley to jump back in shock and plant the green sparkly marshmallow firmly in his face.

Chapter 25

Mitsey vaulted past Mrs Johnson causing her to trip as she stormed towards the kitchen. She considered kicking the vile little dog as it yapped past her, but it was gone before she had time to action the thought. Mrs Johnson gripped the Dove grey speckled-countertop so hard the tips of her fingers turned white. *Aunt Violet needs to go*, she confirmed to herself. *Mr Johnson shall tell her tonight*, this thought made her feel much calmer.

Aunt Violet bent down and stroked an excited Mitsey at the bottom of the stairs. The little Jack Russel yapped in delight to see her, bounding around in a figure-of-eight through her feet. Aunt Violet clicked her fingers sharply, a blue spark crackled and snapped and Mitsey sat instantly to attention.

'That evil little dog should be locked in the garden!' declared Mr Johnson from the doorway, both hands this time flying up to cover his mouth as the words flew out without his permission. Mrs Johnson turned round aghast at Mr Johnson's outburst. Aunt Violet gave Mitsey a knowing smile and it was almost like he smiled back at her as she gave him a little wink.

Standing straight Aunt Violet spun around to Mr Johnson, 'How very dare you! You pitiful little man!'

Giving the performance of a lifetime Aunt Violet stormed upstairs to her room. Mitsey ran up to Mr Johnson and barked at him as if telling him off himself, then bounded up the stairs after Aunt Violet.

Mrs Johnson stared at Mr Johnson, silenced with incredulity at the idiocy of his words, he walked towards her his hands still covering his mouth and eyes bulging in shock. Angrily whispering, as not to let Aunt Violet hear, Mrs Johnson began to attack Mr Johnson.

'You stupid man, what on earth has gotten into you?'

Mr Johnson kept his hands over his mouth and just shook his head, scared to take his hands away for fear of what might come out.

'Speak man!' the whisper slightly evading Mrs Johnson voice as her anger began to build again.

Mr Johnson couldn't hold it any longer, the words pushed past his hands, 'Me stupid? You vindictive woma…'

Mr Johnson's cold eyes bulged out of his rounded face, he couldn't grasp his own insanity as his bulbus lips moved without his consent. The words now being muffled again by his fat fingers as beads of sweat continued to drip down underneath his glasses.

Fear gripped him as Mrs Johnson came closer and closer her sharp pointy face looking distorted in temper. Her rounded nose twitching from side to side as if she were breathing in Mr Johnson's contempt.

Mr Johnson was backed up against the black door frame of the kitchen, Mrs Johnson leaned right into his face. Mr Johnson could feel her unusually cold breath on his face and the chill of the tips of her murky, grey hair touched his face. Keeping constant eye contact with Mr Johnson, Mrs Johnson screamed into his face, 'Peter!… George!…'

Mr Johnson closed his eyes and winced as her icy spittle blasted in his face.

Aunt Violet sat in Peter's room, at his dark-grey desk. The top of the desk was covered in engraved pencil markings of 3D rectangles. Aunt Violet caught sight of her refection in the in the little window, the only source of light in Peter's grey room. She reached up and pulled out the hair pin that was holding her perfectly coiled bun in place. Her white hair tumbled down around her shoulders, streaks of flame had started to appear, a mixture of blonde, bronze, and red gleamed against the white. Fine lines around her eyes had started to disappear and her face look smoother, less freckled. The enchanting consequence of using her magic after all this time.

Aunt Violet heard the commotion of Mr and Mrs Johnson downstairs, she couldn't help an ironic smile as she reassured herself that it's only what he deserved, remembering the look of madness on his face as she cast the spell. She patted her lap for Mitsey to jump up. He also felt softer somehow.

Aunt Violet twirled the strands of coloured hair around her fingers remembering what it was like before. She couldn't help Abigale, could she? There was just no way she could go back, Aunt Violet was hesitant. *Not after all this time?* She listened to the arguing downstairs; she heard the boys bound down the stairs like a pair of elephants making the walls slightly shake with the heaviness of their steps.

In the distance she heard Mrs Johnson, 'Peter, tell your father I shall not be communicating with him.'

Mr Johnson retorted, 'George, can you please tell your mother, that I don't give a da...'

'PERCY!' Mrs Johnson shouted.

Aunt Violet looked down at Mitsey on her lap, 'Maybe old Percy is now enjoying his new verbal freedom,' Mitsey let out a little bark in agreement and snuggled into Aunt Violet's lap enjoying her warmth.

'What do you think Mits?' she asked the dog already knowing the answer, 'Time to head home and face the music?' Aunt Violet stared at herself in the window's reflection for a long time. With every thought of returning to her old life another strand of colour appeared, another line of meanness gone, the grey fading by the second.

From a hidden pocket in her black shawl, she pulled out an old black-and-white photo, the edges worn, faded from being handled too much, from being loved too much. A crystal tear glistened down Aunt Violet's face as she spoke to the girl in picture.

'She looks just like you, D,' Aunt Violet wiped the tear away with the back of her hand, 'I'll do it... I owe you that.'

Aunt Violet had then made a vow she never thought she would have to make, a vow to return to The Faedora and help Abigale.

***

'Mama, I remember everything,' Professor Mortley gushed once they reached the privacy of his office, 'It's Viola, Mama Gilbert, she is related to Abigale, she is alive!'

Mama Gilbert looked puzzled and exhausted after the afternoon they just had, 'Who's Viola, again?' Mama Gilbert knew she should know who she was, but she just couldn't remember.

Mama Gilbert yawned stretching her delicate arms up to the ceiling, she couldn't remember the last time she had felt this exhausted.

'I've given permission for Abigale to sit in on tomorrow's les...soooons,' she told Professor Mortley mid-yawn, making her way to the Professor's large, red, leather office-chair.

Professor Mortley was pacing in front of his large desk, his appearance fixed in a teenage holographic form. His dusty-brown hair looked wild, as did his hazel eyes with the flecks of deep brown taking prominence with possible conspiracy theories racing through his mind.

His chocolate-brown suit looked slightly baggier, and he had an energetic spring in his step. He began to go off on a tangent trying to unravel the riddle of who could have taken their memories and when.

'Mama, who could have done this?', 'Why would someone have done this!?' he questioned over and over. 'What would the person have to gain?' Professor Mortley looked up to the ceiling as if he were trying to figure out the answer to how much the sky weighed.

He turned round to see why he wasn't getting any reaction from Mama Gilbert. Peering over the stacked-up papers and files on his desk he saw Mama Gilbert fast asleep in his large, red, leather office-chair. Her head was tilted slightly backwards as she released tiny, soft snoring puffs. Her normally beauti-fully presented lilac-hued hair looked dishevelled, and the long cascading sleeves of her lilac and pink jewel-encrusted dress draped over the arms of the chair trailing on the floor.

Professor Mortley walked slowly over, grabbing a large, dark-brown, fleece-blanket, and ever so gently laid it over Mama Gilbert. Making sure to tuck her in nice and tight, giving her forehead a kiss of good sleep.

He, however, had work to do. He started looking through

and cross-referencing all the files and logs of all the students and guests that had ever been let aboard the Faedora.

***

Abigale sat on the edge of her bed, both hands holding on tight to the coloured ties at the end of her plaits, she looked on at what was unfolding.

'Ok Clara, cast the spell, I'm ready!' said Annie, closing her eyes and holding out an emerald-green notebook.

'If you're sure, Annie?' Clara wanted to check one last time, it was her first time casting a real spell, on a real person. Abigale looked on in awe at her two friends.

'Sure!' Annie confirmed with a nod, 'It's the only way we can find out what the Queen is actually up to. I can look at the spell without being enchanted, we only have twenty-four hours until the Pink Moon.'

Nodding, Clara passed Annie the mug into her spare hand. Inside the mug were Abigale's hair, and the teardrops.

Clara began to chant, 'Tell me your secrets I'm making an enquiry, write every detail down in this diary.'

The mixture began to stir by itself and swirled around in the mug. The emerald-green notebook flashed, and Annie took a deep breath and downed the mixture in one gulp.

They all waited.

'I think we're good,' said Annie smiling, 'You did it Clara!' They hugged each other tightly.

'Phew!' Clara breathed out in relief her whole body dramatically collapsing inward, 'I thought I was going to turn you into a stick, or something.' The girls all looked at each other and started laughing.

'What a day!' Annie said laying back on her bed and then turning onto her side to face Abigale.

Abigale was laying in her grey bed, the rough cotton blanket pulled up and tucked under her arms. Abigale was looking up to ceiling staring, hardly breathing as she entered her stillness.

Annie watched, 'You ok, Abs?' she asked still worried about her friend.

'Yeah,' she said vacantly, 'I'm excited Mama Gilbert has let me come and watch class tomorrow,' she said plainly.

'You don't sound it!' Clara exclaimed in a giggle joining in.

'It's just,' Abigale paused thoughtfully, 'It's our last day together,' she finished sadly.

The girls then all laid back on their beds staring off into the space, thinking about the enormity of what Abigale had just said. Clara jumped up and peered down at Annie.

'What?' Annie said surprised.

'Just checking you're not a stick.'

The girls then giggled again. They talked and laughed long into the night, making every second together count until the sleepiness overtook them.

Chapter 26

'How do I look?' Abigale asked as she spun around in her grey pleated dress, knee-length grey socks and black patent shoes.

Annie was sat on her bed putting on a pair of shamrock-green pumps with sprinkle laces. Clara turned over still tucked up in her in her soft baby-pink duvet with the white lace trim pulled up to her nose.

'Ermmmmm,' Annie was trying to think of something encouraging to say.

'Honestly?' Clara said gruffly from beneath her duvet.

Abigale looked down at the grey with a glum face. Then in a light-bulb moment she ran over to her shelf and grabbed the sparkly-green and dazzling-pink hair-ties and attached them to the bottom of her plaits. Then spun around again. 'How about now?'

Clara and Annie answered in smiling agreement, 'Perfect!'

As Abigale and Annie grabbed their things, Abigale walked over to Clara's bunk, 'Are you sure you're going to be OK?' she asked Clara, concerned.

'I'll be fine,' Clara let out a few fake coughs and splutters, 'I just need to rest, I'm sorry I'm missing your day at school,' Clara let out a few more fake coughs and pulled up her duvet to hide her face.

'Let's go,' Annie said encouragingly, pushing Abigale towards the door and giving Clara an over-exaggerated wink behind her back.

Abigale reached down for the doorknob and pulled the door open, to be surprised by the boys standing outside the door. Elliot and Freddie stood looking shocked that the door had opened. Little T hovered running his hand through his hair, he had been using the shine of the door as a mirror.

'Oh, hey guys,' Annie said a little shocked they were there too. Freddie straightened his back and looked forward.

Elliot then spoke, 'We thought we'd walk you to class.'

His jet-black spiky hair was moulded to precision making his bright-green eyes more striking than usual. He was dressed in a brilliant white shirt and had wide-legged baggy, dark-blue denim jeans on, held up by the black leather belt with Believer emblem.

His diamond-shaped face with Greek-shaped nose looked masculine with a strong jawline beginning to form. To Abigale, he was breathtakingly handsome.

'How nice, let's go,' Annie said hurriedly, grabbing the arm of a stunned Freddie and pulling him away from the door.

Little T buzzed behind them, 'Hey!' he called, half looking back at the girl's door, 'What's wrong with Clara?' he said, sounding slightly disappointed.

'I'll explain later, come on, we'll be late,' Annie said leading off down the carriages.

Abigale closed their cabin door behind her and turned towards a waiting Elliot. Slowly her gaze came up to meet Elliot's. They both stopped, just looking.

'Hey,' Elliot said softly.

'Hey,' Abigale replied, feeling her cheeks flush with heat.

Elliot stood slightly to one side giving a kind of half bow and gentlemanly extending an arm in the direction they needed to go, gesturing for Abigale to lead the way.

***

Once the cabin door clicked closed, Clara leapt out of bed and began frantically getting dressed. Pulling on a pair of fuchsia velour jogging bottoms and matching hoodie. Clara began spinning and pirouetting around the cabin. Tidying, picking up and replacing all their knick-knacks and thingy-ma-jigs, getting the area ready for her to create her own personal magic.

Once everything was put away and the beds were made and the area was clear, she leapt up to her bed and pulled down bag after sparkly bag, arranging them around the room.

'Ready, steady, let's go!' she shouted to the empty room.

***

'How are you feeling?' Elliot asked Abigale as they ambled towards the classroom, not want to rush the journey.

'Errrmmm,' Abigale thought carefully for a second before answering, the heat filling her cheeks once again, 'Much better, thank you,' she looked down bashfully, 'Thank you for being there.'

'You sure gave us all a shock,' Elliot replied with light relief. 'Any idea what happened?' he asked trying to sound casual.

'No, not really,' Abigale answered innocently, 'My chest suddenly felt icy cold, and it went dark,' Elliot listened intently, 'Then…' Abigale trailed off and stopped herself.

'What?' Elliot pushed.

Abigale looked up into Elliot's bright-green eyes, she had become accustomed to the heat in her cheeks, giving her a cherry glow, 'It's silly,' Abigale said dismissively looking down at her black patent shoes, not wanting to appear foolish in front of him.

Elliot instinctively placed a reassuring hand on her elbow. No sooner than his hand touched the greyness of her dress, blue sparks crackled and fizzed, giving Elliot an electric shock that made his hand shoot back.

Abigale jumped back in horror. Elliot laughed as he shook away the sting from his hand, 'I've heard love being like a bolt of lightning, but I thought that happened metaphorically not in real-life!' Realising what he had just said it was Elliot's turn to blush as Abigale smiled as she peered at him out the corner of her eye.

'So…' Elliot pressed again, trying to get information on what Abigale saw, desperate to change the conversation as the burn on his cheeks persisted.

Giving her a gentle nudge with his shoulder for encouragement, this time the sleeve of his white T-shirt protected him from the blue electric shock, 'What happened?' he said, his confident smile winning her over.

'Well…' Abigale hesitated, 'I swear I saw my mean Aunt Violet?' she said while shaking her head in disbelief, 'But she looked soooo different, younger and really colourful,' Abigale half laughed at herself, 'It couldn't be her though, if you saw her you'd know why,' shrugging her shoulders she said, 'Told you it was silly.'

Elliot opened his mouth to speak but was stopped by Little T appearing in the doorway, 'Come on you two love birds,' Little T started blowing kisses at Abigale and Elliot, causing Abigale's face to turn bright crimson. Elliot ran in front then, trying to swat Little T with his books.

Abigale slowly crept forward and stood in the doorway of the classroom. Never had she seen such a beautiful classroom or even thought that classrooms could be beautiful. She saw six single mahogany desks in two rows of three, the wood flowed with life through the school-room cabin.

Swirls of reds and browns formed shapes and symbols on the walls. Abigale only assumed they must have some kind of magical meaning. Three large oval windows beamed light into the room reflecting light like lasers off the desks.

Annie was sitting with her back straight at one of the front desks, Elliot slid into the desk behind her, and Little T was lying on the desk behind him, in front of an open book magically making the pages flick backwards and forwards.

The seat next to Annie was empty she assumed this must be Clara's desk, and Freddie, just like Annie, sat to attention in the desk behind. Leaving the seat next to Little T empty. Abigale walked over to the back of the class to take that seat.

'No, no, Abigale dear,' Mama Gilbert spoke, who was perched on top of the giant desk at the front of the room. A desk that was the length of the huge blackboard on the wall behind, 'Take Clara's seat at the front, this may be your only time to be here.'

Abigale pushed back in the seat and walked hesitantly to the front of the room. Annie looked over her shoulder, her large brown eyes sparkling behind her thick-rimmed glasses and smiled encouragingly.

'You're going to love this, Abs,' she said excitedly.

Mama Gilbert walked over to the blackboard and spoke as she wrote in flowing italics, *Glamour 101 – Fairy Filters*.

Mama Gilbert turned towards the class and put one hand up the cascading sleeve of her lilac dress and pulled out her wand. There was a communal intake of breath as no one had seen Mama Gilbert's wand before. The wand looked like a lilac crystal cylinder, just over a foot long that sparkled without the need for light reflection. The light seemed to dance within the cylindrical, like a dazzling glittered kaleidoscope.

Mama Gilbert waved her wand across her face from left to right and chanted, 'Disguise me now let's copy and paste, Glamour a bird upon my face.'

The wand swept past Mama Gilbert's head changing her face into a beautiful white swan's head. Her neck now elegant, long and bestowed with gleaming white feathers, her turquoise eyes large and almond-shaped, raising up at the ends and pointing downwards towards her honey and apricot-coloured beak. Little T, Elliot, Freddie, Abigale, and Annie sat silently absolutely mesmerised.

Mama Gilbert let out a large noise, *'SQUUUUUUAAA-AAARRRRRKKKKK!!!'*

'Ahhh!' Freddie let out in a high-pitched cry being taking by surprise by the squark from Mama Gilbert.

The rest of the class began to laugh, Mama Gilbert swished her wand back, swishing right to left this time, returning herself back to Mama Gilbert.

Freddie's cheeks glowed as he let out a nervous laugh trying to join in with the others and brush it off. Mama Gilbert began chanting again.

'Disguise me now, let's copy and paste, glamour Professor Mortley upon my face,'

Mama Gilbert swished the wand from left to right metamorphosing into Professor Mortley. Mama Gilbert shook her head making her now dusty-brown hair flap on her head. Her cheeks rounded with bold, fleshy-lips, and she pulled out a green, sparkly Christmas tree marshmallow and took a big bite leaving a green, sparkly moustache behind. Mama Gilbert then licked her lips repeatedly.

The class erupted into laughter. Abigale was hopelessly in love with everything she saw, she was fit to burst. She had never believed that these kinds of warm, colourful feelings existed. She had never believed she would ever be part of a world like this. Her skin tingled with joy as if happiness was radiating out of every pore. She felt different. Something had changed.

The laughter was prematurely cut short by loud, slow, clapping. Everyone turned towards the door.

'You really are excellent at that, Mama, such a wonderful teacher.'

'Thank you, Your Majesty,' Mama Gilbert waved her wand back returning herself to her natural form, then curtseyed as the Queen made her way to the front of the class.

'You certainly have a wonderful bunch of students here.'

As the Queen spoke she sashayed down the middle of the desks, pausing and placing a hand on Elliot's shoulder, placing an emphasis on him. An action that reminded Little T he needed to speak to Elliot about how he obviously knows the Queen.

The Queen turned then, returning to the front of the class where she faced everyone. Standing in between Annie and Abigale, she looked down at Abigale.

'We seem to have an intruder in our midst,' she smiled a tight, short, unwelcoming smile, 'We don't seem to have formally met?' she chanted.

Abigale stood up nervously, not really knowing what to do, 'Abigale Johnson, Your Majesty,' Abigale said softly while performing a little perfect curtsy.

'Let me have your palm,' the Queen asked as if she had a bitter taste in her mouth.

Abigale looked to Annie for what to do and Mama Gilbert moved forward protectively as Abigale reluctantly held out her hand. The Queen reached out and grabbed Abigale's hand impatiently, blue sparks crackled and forked from Abigale's palm. The Queen retracted her hand and held it close to her chest, shocked and furious.

'How dare you, you insolent girl,' the Queen couldn't control her reaction as she spat the words at Abigale.

'I'm… I'm… I'm so sorry, Your Majesty,' Abigale begged as she shot her hands to her side, on the verge of tears, 'I… I… don't… I don't know… how.'

'Your Majesty,' Mama Gilbert interrupted, standing in between Abigale and the Queen, 'My apologies, Abigale must have picked up some residual magic from my wand, being at the front and all,' Mama Gilbert guided the Queen away from Abigale, then is a hushed tone whispered, 'She is a "Stoney", they can't do magic,' a desperate ploy to take the Queen's attention away from Abigale.

'How can we help you today?' she continued, 'Class…' Mama Gilbert tried to command the attention of the room, 'Have I ever told you that our benevolent and forgiving Queen was my star pupil when she was on the Faedora.'

Feeling the weight of the whole classes eyes burning into her skin and seeing Abigale weeping quietly into her hands bent over on her desk, the Queen knew she had to do something to save face.

'Of course,' she said trying to regain some composure, straightening her shoulders, 'They were the best days, Mama

Gilbert is a wonderful teacher,' she nodded towards Mama Gilbert, the tight smile still in place.

Mama Gilbert carried on putting on her best royal voice, 'Your Majesty, by what do we owe the pleasure of your company today?'

'I've come to collect the lovely Annie,' the Queen said regaining herself now and beginning to chant. 'As you know, she is helping me with the Pink Moon spell that we are going to use to send Abigale back to her rightful home,' she smiled insincerely.

Everyone then looked a little sad and the Queen beckoned Annie to leave class, 'Annie, shall we go?'

This was not a question. Mama Gilbert went to talk but the Queen held up her hand to silence her. Annie began to clamber all her books together, dropping them as she did.

Freddie instinctively got up and helped Annie collect her books from the floor. 'Here,' he said quietly to Annie, she looked up and smiled anxiously, 'Be careful,' he whispered.

'Look after Abs for me ok, don't forget about the party,' Annie whispered back.

'Let's go, Annie,' the Queen ordered as she began to glide towards the doorway outstretching her hand to touch Elliot's shoulder again as she passed.

Elliot, however, kept his head down and shrugged away her hand from touching him. Looking hurt, the Queen turned her head and carried on exiting the door with Annie running after her.

'Little T,' Mama Gilbert directed, 'Come dear, come glamour yourself…'

Chapter 27

Aunt Violet had awoken as if having never slept. Having listened to Mr and Mrs Johnson argue all evening she was beginning to regret casting on Mr Johnson. Mr Johnson's evil had risen to new heights with the torrent of hurtful words he was powerless to stop. He was now revelling in his spiteful and shocking words and their effect on Mrs Johnson.

The sleepless night however, had little effect, as Aunt Violet managed to get out of Peter's low bed with an unusual vigour. It had been years since her bones had not ached from the night's rest.

Mitsey still slept soundly at the base of the door, ready for action should intruders enter their midst. Aunt Violet smiled, another thing she hadn't done for an eternity, as she remembered that was how 'P' described him after she brought him back from Neverville. He could never sleep until Mitsey had taken his protective place at the foot of the door.

Sitting at Peter's table she ran her fingers through her hair. Gone was the dry, wiry feel of her thin, white, old lady hair, in its place luscious locks of fire. She reached out for her long paddle-brush and began to brush her mane. Only a few streeks of the brilliant white hair remained. Now a full head of shiny flame locks. Reds, golds, and blondes with a hint of burnt orange that reignited her ferocious blue eyes to be utterly piercing. The once lined skin was smoothing out with every moment that passed, old freckles blending together to give a lightly tanned complexion.

Aunt Violet heard Mr Johnson bellow from downstairs meanly at Mrs Johnson, 'Whoever taught you to cook woman? This is not even good enough for that wicked dog!'

As the words left his mouth another streek of white melted away and was replaced by another dazzling strand of colour. Aunt Violet started to feel bad for Mrs Johnson, which actually took her by surprise. It had been so long since she had allowed herself to feel anything at all.

Waving a finger gently from side to side she chanted, 'Take back what was done the magic that was cast, recant my words and make it happen fast.'

Hmmm my chants certainly are a little rusty, Aunt Violet reflected as she sat listening and waiting for it to take effect.

'Peter, can you tell your father that he will be making his own breakfast for the foreseeable future, until his attitude changes,' Mrs Johnson said full of contempt and snootiness.

'Dad, Mum said, you ain't eating,' Peter reiterated.

Aunt Violet listened harder for Mr Johnson's reply, it was silent for what seem like an awfully long time.

Then, 'Yes dear, you're right, of course,' mumbled Mr Johnson. Aunt Violet could feel the deflation in his voice.

Aunt Violet saw the last streek of white vanish and began to think of the enormity of what the day ahead had in store. The Pink Moon would be at its strongest within the midnight hour and there was only one spell that evicts someone from the train without the train's permission, and that spell was in *The Book of Lost Fae*.

Aunt Violet took out the old picture again and traced over the face slowly with her finger as she allowed her mind to remember, *Delphine*.

Bang! Bang! Bang!

Aunt Violet was brought back to the present as the door rattled with the pounding of George's chubby hand. Mitsey jumped to attention and began to bark crossly having been awoken from his slumber. Without waiting for a response George opened the door, his mouth full of bread that he was spitting everywhere.

'Mum said do you want breakfast?' he mumbled through his too full, too small mouth.

Grabbing her black shawl Aunt Violet wrapped it round her head trying to hide her newly vibrant head of hair. She held up a finger quieting Mitsey. Putting on her sternest and most clipped Aunt Violet voice she replied, 'No, thank you George, I shall be leaving shortly.'

George stopped chewing and looked at the woman in front of him in stunned silence as he processed this information.

'George!' Aunt Violet shouted breaking his trance, 'Tell the other one he can have his room back, I'm no longer in need of it.' She stared at him hard and then began to walk to him in a bid to release him from his hypnotic state.

With that George had his light-bulb moment, he slammed the door and ran down the stairs screaming, 'Mum! Mum! Mum! I've got the best news... Can I have some bread?'

Aunt Violet heard the celebration downstairs when George announced she was leaving. She began to put her things into her large, grey, canvas travel bag with grey, leather handles. Pulling her black shawl down from her head she unveiled her now full, red, and burnt-orange mane. Aunt Violet knew she couldn't let the Johnsons see her transformation.

Opening Peter's silver wardrobe, she began to rummage through the clothes and shelves. Finally, she found what she was looking for. Aunt Violet expertly twisted and pinned her new hair into a perfectly formed bun and then placed the grey beanie hat over her head hiding any trace of colour. Wrapping her black shawl around her shoulders and pulling on a grey trench-coat, Aunt Violet looked around the room reflectively. This would be the last time she would ever be in this house, she vowed. Mitsey knew instinctively it was time to go and was at the door ready to head into battle.

Aunt Violet opened Peter's door, turned right, and headed down the grey stairs towards the black front door. Mrs Johnson rushed out of the kitchen followed by Mr Johnson, Peter, and George.

'Sorry to see you go, Aunt Violet,' Mrs Johnson said beaming, finding it just too hard to hide her elation. 'Percy shall take you to the bus station,' she nudged Mr Johnson to get his shoes and coat on.

'Goooood Bye Aun-tie Vi-o-let,' Peter and George said in smarmy unison.

'No need,' Aunt Violet said not turning back to look at them. Opening the front door and allowing Mitsey to exit first, 'I'll be getting the train,' she shouted back as she slammed the black front door behind her, knocking the Never-Believer knocker clean off the front door and leaving the Johnsons utterly flabbergasted.

***

Professor Mortley was a holograph possessed, frantically checking paper after paper. He was flickering between man and boy, holding up pieces of paper and then walking round to the front of his desk and laying each sheet of evidence horizontally onto the shiny vertical wooden floor. Professor Mortley walked around and around the papers looking for a sign. The swirls within the wood twisted and turned with him as if they too were looking for answers.

'There's something there, I just can't see it,' Professor Mortley said, he licked the top of his bold, fleshy-lips, where a thick layer of green, sparkly, marshmallow Christmas tree residue sat.

The trains vibrations hummed louder in response. Professor Mortley then walked back over to his desk and tried to reach over for a scroll right at its other side, knocking a heap of papers onto the floor. Professor Mortley looked up at the clock that sat in between his thimble 'Kiss' and his 'Lost Boy' tapestry on the wall and could feel the minutes and seconds slipping away.

He sunk to his knees, feeling beaten and exhausted. Reaching for the knocked-over papers and shoving them back together in a messed-up pile, 'I'm never going to find it,' he let out with a sigh of defeatism. He was losing hope.

The train then shook so hard that Professor Mortley had to hold on the edge of the desk, 'Ok, OK,' he patted the train, 'I'll keep looking!'

Professor Mortley tried to pull himself up. The train then shook again, harder.

'Whoaaaaa!' Professor Mortley fell to floor on top of the newly scattered papers. 'Jeeze, take it easy, will ya?' he said beginning to get cross.

The swirls within the wood turned into little arrows pointing to where Professor Mortley should look. Professor Mortley pushed himself up onto his elbows and looked where the arrows were pointing. He scratched his head, trying to see what the train was seeing.

Then, 'Shimmering Christmas baubles!' he exclaimed, clambering over to the sheet of paper with a long list of names and grabbing it holding it up to the light.

'It can't be,' his voice was full of disbelief, 'She wouldn't,' Professor Mortley walked over and grabbed other piece of paper and compared what he had found, 'They couldn't have...' his voice trailed off as he was trying to put all the pieces together in his mind.

'Who couldn't have?' Mama Gilbert twirled into the room, Professor Mortley didn't even hear her as he studied what was in front of him.

Mama Gilbert walked over to his desk and looked at what he was looking at, 'Professor, what have you found?'

'Mama, be prepared to be knocked off your tinsel toes!'

'Professor, you're frightening me.'

'To be honest Mama, I'm a little frightened myself,' Professor Mortley admitted biting the corner of his bottom lip.

Mama Gilbert rested her hand on Professor Mortley's and looked at him over her little rounded spectacles, giving his hand a squeeze, encouraging him to go on.

'There was only two other Fae that were on the train when Viola and Delphine disappeared, and we lost our memories,' he held up the pieces of paper in his hand so Mama could read the evidence.

Mama Gilbert drew in a quick intake of air shocked as she read the names, her eyes welled up as this was the first time it really hit her how much danger Abigale could be in.

'We need to help Abigale, no matter what the cost,' Mama Gilbert said firmly to Professor Mortley.

Professor Mortley's door then opened and in zoomed the 3 T's with a swish, a swoosh, and a whizz. Chanting as they entered, doing their usual dance across the ceiling.

'A note from the Queen, the Queen has note,' they sang.

Tatum dropped a white scroll tied up with gold lace down to Professor Mortley. Fumbling as he tried to catch it, the 3 T's laughed malevolently.

Mama Gilbert finally caught the scroll, discarded the gold lace, and read aloud, 'Pockets, it has come to my attention that to harness the full power of the Pink Moon we need to move the ceremony forward to the midnight hour tonight. Please make sure the Never-Believer is ready, regards, Queen Noralynn.'

Mama Gilbert looked at the Professor, concern plastered across her face.

'Thank you T's, leave us please,' Mama Gilbert said dismissing the Pixies, who flew out the door like three nuclear missiles, slamming the door behind them.

Mama Gilbert threw the scroll in the bin, 'We're in trouble, P,' she said apprehensively.

Professor Mortley nodded in agreement, 'You need to get your memory back, have you nothing of Viola's? Nothing royal?' he asked in hope.

Mama Gilbert shrugged her shoulders doubtfully, 'Unless...' she pondered for a second and started running out the door, 'I'll be back P, hopefully I can find it in time.'

'Go, go!' Professor Mortley shouted after her, 'I'll prepare the children.'

Chapter 28

'Thanks guys you really didn't have to walk me back, I knew the way,' Abigale said, pausing outside her cabin door. Elliot, Freddie, and Little T, all hovered waiting for Abigale to open the door.

Abigale looked at them as if they were mad waiting there. Freddie then spoke breaking the awkward silence that was forming, 'Annie gave me strict instructions that I must walk you inside the door,' he then did a mock salute making them all laugh.

Who knew Freddie was so funny, Abigale thought while holding her cheeks that actually ached from smiling. *I'm really going to miss these guys,* her smile faded a little as she turned to open her cabin door.

Before she did Little T flew in front of her, 'Allow me, madam,' he said bowing and knocking on the door with his usual rhythm. Three quick knocks and two slow. Abigale looked as him as if he had lost the plot, *these guys get weirder and...* before she could finish the thought, the door flew open, and Abigale was dragged inside.

'Surprise!' yelled Clara, 'Happy Birthday!' she shouted, absolutely beyond excited.

All the boys cheered and shouted together, 'Happy Birthday!'

Clara then shouted, 'Hugo, play party music!'

Abigale jumped as music started to play out of a tiny box on Clara's shelf. She looked around in total amazement at what

Clara had created inside their cabin.

Pink satin banners hung from the ceiling with, 'Happy Birthday Abigale,' embroidered in purple silk thread. Each banner arched perfectly into the next, with purple and pink teardrop chains dripping from links causing a pink and purple glitterball effect around the room as the light touched them.

An arch of pink and purple latex balloons framed the arched window with other balloon clusters positioned all over the room. Clara had covered Annie's bed and made it into a buffet table, adorning every party food a person could wish for. Sausage rolls, party rings, cheese, and pineapple sticks, with a pile of alternating pink and purple plates with white serviettes in between.

Clara leaned over Abigale, passing a purple sash over her head, placing it across her grey-pleated dress and patting into place. Looking down Abigale saw embroidered in big pink letters, 'Abs Birthday Girl.'

Abigale was silent, she walked over with her back to the group and reached up to feel the teardrop chains, twisting it so it danced to light. Clara was taken aback shrugging her shoulders at the boys in bewilderment. Abigale was still watching the light.

'I'm sorry, Abs, I thought you'd like it,' Clara said sadly, feeling ever so guilty for getting wrong.

'Like it?' Abigale said finally. 'I LOVE IT!' Abigale shouted. 'It's the most wonderful, beautiful, stupendously glorious, kindest…' she said pausing, 'It's the most phenomenal, sensational thing I have ever seen in my whole entire LIFE!' Abigale threw her hands up in the air enhancing the meaning of her words.

Then, she stopped to look at the shocked faces of her friends.

She looked down at herself to see if something was amiss and then back to the astonished faces before her.

'What?' she started turning backwards and forwards looking at herself now seriously self-conscious, 'What guys? What? Tell me!'

Clara was the first one to break the silence, 'It's that... Abs you're glowing!'

'Glowing?'

'Yep bright blue, all around you!' Little T added.

'But how?' Abigale questioned, worried that she couldn't see it.

'It seems to be fading,' Clara said, filled with curiosity.

'I've got an idea,' Freddie said, 'Give her, her present!' he nudged Elliot.

Elliot dug into his pocket and pull out a cluster of royal-blue thread plaited together in the shape of a bracelet.

'It's the best I could do, considering,' bashfully he reached forward to give it to Abigale.

'WOW! I'm going to need to invest in some sunglasses,' commented Little T, as they all covered their eyes as Abigale beamed.

'Yep, just as I thought,' Freddie said, 'She glows when she is happy.'

As the shyness set back in the light faded again, she let Elliot tie the thread around her wrist, but her thoughts were now consumed with why she glowed. *How could she glow? She was a Stoney*, she thought. *Maybe it was the residual magic Mama Gilbert spoke about? What if it wasn't though... Surely she couldn't be...*

'It's been quite a day,' Freddie broke her chain of thought, finding a new confidence it seems within this group.

'Really? You must tell me everything,' Clara said leading Abigale to her bed to sit down and mouthing to Little T silently, 'Where's Annie?'

Little T did his best charade of a wicked witch pretending to fly around on an imaginary broomstick and a dramatic evil laugh. Clara laughed at him taking Little T totally by surprise. Nodding in acknowledgment, Clara continued to lead Abigale to the bed to hear about how the school day went. Once seated, with the boys mulling around the room and holding on to her green and pink sparkly hair-ties, Abigale retold the events of her first Fae classroom experience.

'Hugo, quieter!' Clara shouted halfway through Abigale's story, 'So let me get this straight, you got taught how to glamour, met the Queen, who you then almost shocked to death with blue sparkle fingers, then, she made you cry, then, she took Annie, and then you find out you glow!' Clara shook her head incredulously, 'You must be utterly buffuzzelled!'

Overhearing the story, it jogged Little T's memory, he needed to speak to Elliot. Elliot was sitting next to Freddie on the floor next to the buffet table, helping themselves to the food every five seconds. Little T chose this as his opportunity to get some answers and flew over and perched himself in between the sausage rolls and cheese and pineapple sticks. Freddie and Elliot looked up and smiled warmly at Little T offering some pastry from a sausage roll.

Elliot looked over towards Clara and Abigale making eye contact with Abigale and then smiling to the floor.

'Yuk, you two are so gross,' Little T stated pretending to throw up into a pretend bowl.

'You're just jealous, T,' Freddie said trying to defend Elliot,

'Just 'cause Clara won't give you the time of day!' Freddie and Elliot did a cheers using their sausage rolls and shoved them whole into their mouths.

'Actually, Freddie, Clara just fell about laughing at my comedic genius,' Little T boasted, 'But what I want to know is... what is Elliot's relationship with our dear evil queen!'

Elliot nearly choked on his sausage roll as Little T began to question him.

'So, Ells... she's a bit old to be an ex?' Little T laughed at his own wit as he said it.

Freddie patted Elliot's back to stop him from choking. Elliot soon fell quiet, but Freddie too had noticed the shoulder squeezing and noticeable attention the Queen had directed towards Elliot.

'Leave it alone T, it's not your business,' Elliot said with an unusual hardness.

'Well, considering the Queen wants to get rid of Abigale who you're making googly eyes at, I think it is our business!' Little T spoke back with equal vigour and opened his arms showing the inclusion of the group in his question.

Freddie lowered his head, he had nothing to add as he believed Little T, on this occasion, was right. 'Maybe I'll go and ask Abigale and Clara to join the conversation with us!' Little T went to get up from the buffet table.

'Stop!' Elliot said his voice in a raised whisper as hard as it was before, 'She's my sister, OK!'

Little T's mouth dropped open in astonishment, Freddie then looked up with the same look of incomprehension.

After a moment Little T's thought process began to kick in, 'Your sister!' Little T also now speaking in a loud whisper, 'Then why is she against us and not helping us!' Little T then looked to Freddie, 'She is enchanting Annie to do Faedora knows what to Abigale, tomorrow,' Little T was going off on a tangent, throwing question after question at Elliot. Elliot lowered his head as he listened to Little T go on and on.

Freddie then lifted his head, his face full of disappointment, 'She is tricking Annie,' he paused, 'She is doing something bad.'

Elliot looked up and met Freddie's eyes feeling how disappointed he was in him. Elliot couldn't help the emotion rise within him.

'You wouldn't understand, you just don't get it,' Elliot said shaking his head, his voice wavering. Elliot tried to calm himself not wanting the emotion to spill out on to his cheeks. Freddie's eyes and disappointment bore into him.

Little T's questions were relentless 'Why, Elliot, why, why, why, Elliot?!'

'Because blood is thicker than water, T!' Elliot shouted at Little T, then he got up and stormed out the room.

'Woah!' said Annie as Elliot raced passed her, 'Tadah!' Annie jumped into the room, 'Hope I haven't missed the cake!' she said with a big smile on her face, 'Happy Birthday.'

'Hugo, off!' Clara yelled, the room went quiet.

Annie looked around at the surprised, glum, and shocked faces, 'Not the mood I was expecting. What's happened?' she asked the room.

'I glow blue!' Abigale replied, still confused with how she actually felt about it.

'When she is happy!' Freddie added trying to impress.

'Really! OMG, when did this start? How long did you glow for? Tell me more! How? Let me get my boo…'

'Elliot is the Queen's brother!' Little T shouted interrupting Annie.

'Noooooooooooooooo,' said Clara in a deep, disbelieving tone. She got up to go sit down where Elliot once had, grabbing a sausage roll with intrigue on her mind.

'Looks like we had a mole in our midst!' Annie blurted out sitting down next to Freddie. 'Good job we have this!' she said holding up the green diary she used with her time with the Queen, 'Abs get over here birthday girl!'

Abigale got up slowly and walked over to the group, she couldn't help still looking back at the door hoping Elliot would walk back through it. But he didn't.

The door creaked open slowly and the group looked up all with different expressions on their faces, each person's opinion full for all to see. Abigale was hopeful it was Elliot returning, but instead of jet-black perfectly cropped hair poking round the doorway, it was dusty-brown and wildly unruly.

Professor Mortley walked in slowly greeting the children, 'Hi guys and gals, celebrating are we?' he surveyed the room, eyes bulging he said, 'Ooooooooue Party rings! May I?'

Before any of the children could answer the checky face of a little boy had shoved three into his mouth, crumbs spilling everywhere.

'They threw me a birthday party,' Abigale said sadder than expected, the tumbling crumbs from Professor Mortley made a strange ache in her heart as George sprang to mind. It brought about her stillness for she just couldn't fathom why she felt this way about a brother who was always so mean to her.

'Happy Birthday my dear,' Professor Mortley commented while reaching for a handful of sausage rolls. 'I just love birthdays, nearly as much as I love Christmas!' he laughed to himself and gave an unexpected shake of his bum and shuffle of his arms, 'No music?'

'It's not actually my birthday,' Abigale couldn't help but smile, 'I've just never had one.' Abigale was so proud of her friends, nothing could really ruin this day, 'This is just the best day ever!' Abigale began to glow blue again.

Professor Mortley lowered his head, completely missing Abigale's happiness glow, remembering why he was there. 'Actually kids,' Professor Mortley continued keeping his head down, incurring a sombre tone which left the whole group feeling kind of miffed that he was missing what Abigale could do. Professor Mortley continued, 'I don't come baring good news.'

Abigale's glow went out and he lifted his head to see the mix of curious and worried faces.

'Oh no, what's happened now, are the royal family upset we know their little secret?' Little T rolled his eyes, obviously thinking he knew everything.

'No, Little T,' Professor Mortley's face started to flicker as it did when he was stressed.

Clara, Annie, and Abigale shuffled closer to each other and held hands and Freddie stopped eating and stood to attention. Seeing the kids' faces, he couldn't quite bring himself to yet say what he needed to.

'You know what? Let's enjoy the party first!' Spotting the music player on Clara's shelf he shouted, 'Hugo! Party music please!' and with that he started shaking and twisting, making the kids giggle at his awkward moves. Professor Mortley got all the kids up dancing and smiling.

After a while of dancing, Abigale noticed Professor Mortley

standing quietly by the door watching the room. He looked older, sadder. Abigale walked over and quietly stood next to him.

'You look like her, I never noticed it before,' he said eventually.

'Who?' Abigale questioned, confused.

Professor Mortley turned towards Abigale avoiding the question and quietly said, 'You need to be ready by midnight my dear,' he choked out the words, he felt the weight of knowing who she really was heavy upon his shoulders, with no way yet to help her.

'Midnight?' Abigale repeated with a sigh, taking in a deep breath, and trying to give the Professor a positive smile.

'Midnight,' Professor Mortley confirmed. Clara and Annie began beckoning Abigale to come dance.

Abigale glanced up at Clara's clock, five hours. That wasn't long enough.

Chapter 29

Noralynn was sitting in Elliot's room waiting for him. As she looked around the room she reminisced about when she was a student at the Faedora. She began to straighten and smooth over his bed, her face crumpled up in disgust.

How can he live in such squaller? she thought.

Picking up empty packets of Flyers crisps and Jack and Giant magic beans with her fingertips, she placed them ever so elegantly in the bin. She jumped as Elliot stormed into his room and threw himself face down onto his bed. With his head buried, he allowed the tears to seep out into the navy-blue cotton of his pillow, unaware he was not alone.

He breathed in and out deeply trying to regain some calm as his shoulders shrugged uncontrollably. He then jumped as he felt a hand stroke down his back but did not want to lift his head and show the flowing tears as he knew exactly whose hand it was.

Lifting his head to finally meet his sister's worried gaze, he said angrily through his tears, 'You've ruined everything!' He then shoved his head back deep into the wet tear-stained pillow.

'Elliot, I'm sorry, you know there's nothing I can do,' Noralynn tried to explain, her words were sincere, and heart felt, 'We couldn't keep it a secret much longer,' she paused trying to give him a chance to think, 'Could we?'

Elliot sat up and crossed his legs on his matching navy-blue duvet resting his back against the wall, 'We could have tried!

And YOU could have tried harder with Abigale.'

He couldn't stop tears leaking from his now reddened eyes, but somehow this made their sapphire green colour even more piecing.

Noralynn tried again, 'You know Uncle Horith. I have to do what he and the Council say,' she looked down at her hands picking at her perfectly manicured fingers, 'I have to…'

'Noralynn, you're the Queen!' Elliot stated interrupting her, 'You can do whatever you want,' he challenged.

'It doesn't work like that… the politics are….' she stumbled to find the right words to say, 'You know I hate it.'

'Leave then!' he dared.

'I can't do that either, Elliot,' Noralynn said, beginning to lose her patience with the teenager before her. 'I have to tell you something,' she knew now this was going to go down badly before she even spoke the words.

'What?' he spat.

'The council have asked we move up the Never-Believer's assisted exit,' she said cautiously, 'The eviction will be in the hour of midnight,' the look on his face said it all, he hated her. She felt a sharp pain in her heart as his eyes bore into her.

'She has a name,' Elliot said with distain, but Noralynn carried on as if he said nothing, losing her sisterly sympathy the more he carried on with his dramatics.

'Elliot, you have known about this from the beginning, this is no surprise that she has to leave the train.'

Elliot said nothing.

'Nothing to say?' she took a deep breath and rose to leave from the chest of draws she was resting on, 'I still expect your full support, Elliot. You've learnt the spell?' Elliot nodded

229

reluctantly. Noralynn rolled her eyes, 'That Annie girl is never going to get it right by herself.'

'Don't speak about her like that, you know what you're asking me to do?' Elliot asked with desperation in his eyes, as if pleading for her not to include him.

'Yes, Elliot, I do,' Noralynn responded, taking on her queenly persona and royal tone, 'I'm asking you to stand with YOUR sister, YOUR Queen, and to send back someone who doesn't belong in this world, who will never belong in this world, and protect where you come from, you barely know the girl.' As Noralynn reached the door she took one last pot-shot to ensure Elliot was in her corner, 'What would Mother and Father do?'

Elliot dropped his head to his chest. Noralynn looked to the sky in silent forgiveness. The tension in the room between the two was immense, an unspoken history and an unspoken bond of siblings divided.

Noralynn couldn't waste any more time and spun round to head out the door, virtually knocking into Freddie and Little T. Freddie bowed without a thought, whereas Little T's effort was much less regal or respectful. The Queen didn't have time to reprimand him, she had to be ready to lead the chant. Without acknowledgement the Queen coasted off down the carriages.

The boys stuck their heads around Elliot's door. Elliot wiped his face with the backs of his hands trying to hide any evidence of upset.

'Ahem, ahem' he coughed, 'Damn pink glitter, think I'm allergic,' he said as the boys sat down with an awkward sadness.

Freddie and Little T looked at each other guiltily after seeing how upset Elliot was. Freddie started, 'We're sorry mate, aren't we T?' Little T flew forwards to speak but Elliot held up his had to stop him.

Elliot looked at the doorway his sister had just left through. He knew he had made a choice, he now needed to come clean with his friends and hoped they would help and understand.

Elliot took the deepest breath and told Freddie and Little T everything he knew.

Freddie looked down at his watch, 'So we only have four hours left?'

'Flabber-me-Thunder-Fluff, that's not long!' Little T was stunned into silence.

***

Abigale, Clara, and Annie sat in a circle inside the blue and gold circular rug. Their legs were crossed, but they sat close enough so their knees were touching each other. The green diary and a pencil lay in the middle of them.

'Ready?' Clara said to Annie handing her the diary and pen.

'Let's do this!' Annie said confidently, Clara loved this assertive side of Annie, if anyone could help Abigale it would be her.

The three of them held hands and they chanted the rest of the Dear Diary spell 'Tell me your secrets I'm making an enquiry, write every detail down in this diary, pen it all down even what we don't see, make this a magical window for all to see.'

With that Annie's eyes glazed over, her head rigid, focused. Opening the book and gripping the pencil she began to write at lightning speed. She began to get faster and faster, that as she scribed across the pages, little swirls of lead smoke arose from the pencil's nib. Abigale and Clara gave each other an

231

astonished look as Annie seem to be utterly possessed as she wrote.

Then, without warning the pencil nib snapped and Annie lay the green book back down in the circle. The cloudiness cleared from Annie's eyes, and she began to blink furiously. Clara and Abigale were still frozen in amazement at Annie.

'Well, did I do it?' Annie asked her hopefully, rubbing her eyes beneath her glasses.

'Let's find out,' Clara said reaching forward and opening the book, the girls huddled around and began to read together.

As they read the looks on their faces changed from that of amazement to that of concern and fear. Annie leaned across and ripped out one of the pages and ran over to her bookshelf and pulled out the oldest and most dog-eared book on the shelf.

There was not a hint of sparkle, or anything remarkable about this book. It was just old and battered. A dirty, brown colour with loose pages within the spine. Annie grabbed another piece of paper and began to flick through the pages and wrote down corresponding words from the diary to the old book. Annie worked almost as quickly as she did under the spell. Abigale and Clara got up from the floor and walked over just as she was finishing. Holding it up a tear escaped from her eye.

'It's worse than I thought,' she said wiping away the tear with the hem of her emerald petticoat.

'What is?' Clara queried, beginning to chew on her perfectly manicured nails.

'The spell, the one I've been learning to help Abigale transition back to the Never-Believer train…' Annie gulped loudly, 'It's a demonic fairy exorcism spell.'

'That doesn't' sound good,' Abigale sat on the bed, wondering how this could get any worse.

'She'll be OK though, won't she Annie?' Clara questioned, but her heart felt like she knew the answer.

Annie shrugged. In truth, she didn't know.

'What if I just don't do it?' Annie said sitting up defiantly, 'I'm just not going to help! To hell with the Queen and her fancy fourth-floor magic and recommendations!' Annie couldn't help feeling a tiny tinge of self-pity.

Abigale held Annie's hand and squeezed it, 'I can't ask you do that, Annie.' Abigale then said with conviction, 'In truth,' she paused, 'I don't belong here, I'm a Stoney,' she smiled, 'I'm a Never-Believer, I'm never going to be one of you.'

'Abigale…' Clara came over and sat by her feet, 'You are one of us I can just feel it, you just have to…'

'Clara, it's fine, I'm sure the Queen knows what she is doing,' Abigale grabbed and squeezed Clara's hands too, 'After growing up a Johnson I'll take my chances with a demonic exorcism.'

'We will never see each other again,' Clara couldn't hold it in any longer and the tears tumbled down her rosy cheeks.

Abigale grabbed hold of her pink and green hair-ties and said, 'You will be with me forever!'

Jumping up from the bed Abigale ran over to her pile of grey pleated pinafore dresses, 'Clara, scissors please!' Clara jumped up to the shelf and twirled down handing Abigale the scissors looking puzzled.

Snip, snip, snip, and with that Abigale turned round with a giant smile and held out each hand, Annie and Clara rose up and walked over to get a closer look, in each hand Abigale held a large stony-grey button cut from her dress.

'Sorry it's the best I could do,' she said as she handed them each a button.

Clara and Annie looked at the buttons and closed their hands tightly around them holding them to their hearts. They then held out their other arm to embrace Abigale.

'Group hug!' they all shouted through laughter and tears.

Knocking on their cabin door grabbed their attention and Professor Mortley's head came round the door, complete with green, sparkly moustache.

'It's time, Abigale, you need to come with me,' he said solemnly, 'I'm sorry girls,' he said trying to stop his own heart from breaking as he saw their reaction.

'We only have two hours!' cried Annie with a look of horror.

'I'm sorry, I have to prepare Abigale for what's to come,' he paused, 'Abigale, please,' he waited for Abigale to reach the door.

Abigale turned and flicked her sparkly green and pink hairties and with the bravest of smiles, beamed, 'I will never, ever, ever forget either of you!'

She then walked out the door and as it closed behind her, Abigale fell heartbroken into Professor Mortley's awaiting arms.

Chapter 30

Mama Gilbert was frantic to the point of being crazed. Draw after draw was pulled out in her cabin and delved into as if her life depended on it. The cascading sleeves of her lilac dress had been tied in a knot and beads and sequins were flying everywhere as they hung and knocked against Mama Gilbert and whatever other object they encountered.

They swung in pendulum fashion as her arms explored deeply into each draw of her most precious possessions. Mama Gilbert hurried over to her table and flicked through the pages of her Grimoire of Light. Lighting the three candles, which were positioned triangularly around the book, with three clicks of her fingers she began to chant in Fae.

'Fundst de carborum declareded, Fundst de carborum declared.'

Mama Gilbert opened one eye and looked to see if the spell had worked. Nothing. Again, she chanted, louder and with more passion, 'Fundst de carborum declareded,'

Mama Gilbert again opened one eye and quickly flicked from side to side. All the objects and ornaments in her room begin to vibrate, louder she chanted, 'FUNDST DE CARBORUM DECLAREDED!'

Every object in her cabin lifted off the floor, shelf, or table, or wherever it had been strewn, and began to encircle. Spinning like a mini tornado. The spiral of objects began to twirl faster, quicker, and harder.

Mama Gilbert ducked down under her table, the wind generated from the hurricane of her most treasured belongings blew out the candles on the table and her Grimoire of Light gusted shut. The spell took control of the room.

The cyclone spun, twisted, and turned drawing up everything into its thunderous spiral of might. Books flew off the shelves in a queue of swirling urgency. Mama Gilbert's teapot with the yellow brick road, poppy fields and flying monkeys were absorbed into the power of tornado. The teacups with the Ruby Slippers, Tinman, Scarecrow and Lion danced their way into the chaos.

Mama Gilbert was on her knees under the table, her head ducked within her hands holding on to her now very dishevelled, blustery bun. Whirling and spinning, banging, and crashing, Mama Gilbert held on to herself under the table for dear life.

Then, calm.

Stillness had arrived. The quiet deafening, and Mama held her head tight for a few moments more.

'Mama?' came a quizzical voice breaking the silence, 'What are you doing under the table?'

Mama Gilbert clambered out from under the table to find the voice calling for her.

Taking one look at the face before her she opened her arms wide for the force of the embrace that was heading her way.

'Clara, my dearest,' Mama's soft, velvet voice was filled with concern as Clara hugged her with all her might, gently sobbing into her hold.

After a few minutes Clara lifted her tear-stained face, 'Mama, Professor Mortley came to take Abigale, the transition is now, they moved it to midnight,' desperation was clinging to every syllable.

'Midnight?!' Mama Gilbert was shocked, and again she was filled with urgency, 'That means we only have one hour to find it!'

Mama Gilbert looked around her cabin which was now spotlessly clean and tidy but still no sign of what she was looking for.

'Mama, what is it? What's wrong? What are you looking for?' Clara urged.

'I need to remember, my memory has been erased, Clara,' Mama Gilbert went over and held Clara's arms and explained, 'I need the Believer bracelet, the one with the blue stones inside each of the circles,' Mama Gilbert began to head for the draws again.

Clara thought for a second and then lifted her arm, 'Do you mean this one?'

Mama Gilbert ran over and grabbed the silver bracelet on Clara's wrist. The silver caressed Mama's skin and she was catapulted backwards by the light into her extra-large, purple, comfy chair and was struck motionless. Clara shook Mama as she lay comatose repeating the name over and over.

'Viola, Viola, Viola,' and memories came flooding back.

***

Annie sat on her bed with the diary in her hand, reading the transition spell and its translation over and over. This was a demonic spell, she could feel it her bones as the words slithered inside her skin each time her eyes rolled over the pages. Her fingers felt numb as if ice were beginning to run through her body.

'The fourth floor was not worth this, the Queen is not worth this.'

There was a gentle knocking at the door, giving Annie a welcome break from her thoughts.

'Come in!' she called blankly, looking up to see who it was, 'Come in!' she yelled again. And then, a large hand and a warm unsure smile stuck their head around the door, 'Freddie,' Annie acknowledged, feeling her fingers thaw, 'Come in.'

Freddie walked in slowly leaving the cabin door ajar and sat down on the bed next to Annie.

'I just... ermm... I thought I'd...' Freddie searched for the right words.

Annie leant over and rested her head on Freddie's arm. Freddie froze for a second not knowing how to react, but as he felt the weight and warmth of Annie leaning against him, he relaxed and allowed her just to lean.

They both just sat, quiet and thinking until a now familiar and unwelcome voice arrived in the doorway.

'Annie, it's time to prepare,' the Queen ordered in her usual tone, exuding royal bitterness.

'I'm ready, Your Majesty,' Annie replied solemnly.

The 3 T's hovered in the doorway behind the Queen looking in at Freddie and Annie giggling and laughing, 'Funny. Big Tooth fairy that one, that one's a funny Tooth fairy,' they said spitefully for Freddie to hear.

'T's,' The Queen ordered, 'It's time to keep the fairy in the house!' and with that the 3 T's darted off at record speed.

Annie and Freddie looked at each other puzzled, 'Annie, come, now!' the Queen beckoned Annie like a Bactrian Basilisker.

Annie got up and walked towards the door leaving Freddie looking at his oversized feet. Swiftly, Annie spun on her heels and rushed over to Freddie, planting a tiny, gentle kiss on the cheek just above his strong, chiselled jawline.

'Thanks Fred,' she whispered, then heading back towards the door, she turned back quickly just before she disappeared, smiling brightly at him.

Freddie's hand had risen up and caressed the very spot her kiss had touched. He stared at her shocked and dazed, like he couldn't believe if that had just really happened.

Annie wondered if that silly smile on his face meant that like her, she would never forget this moment.

And with that, she was gone.

***

Abigale sat in Professor Mortley office chair staring into space. Her heart ached at the thought of leaving everything that was, her everything, behind.

She pictured her old room, remembering sitting at her grey dressing table trying to smile that painful smile. The smile that reached the corner of her eyes, the smile that here, came so very easily.

Abigale pictured her brothers, Peter, and George. Peter with his pointy nose, face, and chin. His spiky mousy-brown, grey-tinged hair with his cold grey eyes. She heard his voice in her head, *Guttergale, Guttergale, that's where you belong, in the gutter, Guttergale,* followed by a mean, hollow laugh.

She imagined George standing just behind him, shoving piece after piece of bread into his hamster-style cheeks. His little rounded nose bobbing from side to side as he munched, continually pushing his black-rimmed glasses up so his steely grey-blue, beady eyes could get a better look. Crumbs flying everywhere onto Mrs Johnson's plush grey carpet.

And Mrs Johnson, how she thought she missed her, but she didn't miss her. Abigale missed the person she wanted her to be. What the Believers had, what the Fae had. But Abigale was a Never-Believer, a 'Stoney' and try as she might, she just didn't believe she fitted in anywhere. Abigale's whole chest began to hurt as the ache radiated from her heart.

The train began to shake, to hum as if trying to comfort Abigale. To convince her that she did belong. She leaned forwards and placed both her hands fully on Professor Mortley's giant mahogany desk, blue sparks crackled and fizzed from her fingers, like tiny bolts of forked lightning. The trains vibrations increased. Abigale removed her hands as the sparks zapped over her fingers. She thought she could hear the train's voice telling her to stay, telling her to be brave, telling her to just believe.

Professor Mortley bounded through the door his face old and tired-looking, gone was the mischievous boy, the hologram had stopped and an old tubby man in a brown, too small, suit, with tangerine-waistcoat, stood before her, looking utterly helpless.

'Abigale, I'm sorry we have to go now to the transitioning cabin.'

Professor Mortley looked at Abigale and he wished harder than he had ever wished before for the magic to come.

The train vibrated harder, more violently. Professor Mortley tapped his desk to try to soothe it, but the vibrations continued.

'Professor?' Abigale asked softly.

'Yes, dear?'

'Thank you.'

Abigale's words were like a flying marble to the heart as they both headed for the door.

Chapter 31

The wind blew with a force that Aunt Violet hadn't felt in a foreverness, it felt like it too was against her, trying to rip the warmth from her body. Picking up Mitsey, she held him close to her chest, both appreciating each other's heat.

The air smelled musty as the duo looked around the dirty, old platform. Paper, cans, and Never-Believer's rubbish blew across the deserted, dark platform. The rubbish of grey lives, the remnants of life in Neverville. The platform lights flickered, strobe-like and eerie.

It had been over forty years since Aunt Violet had stood on this platform, making the same promise as she did all those years ago, that this would be the last time she would stand on a train platform again. Aunt Violet looked up and down the rails, waiting for the train to arrive.

I hope I remember, she thought. *I hope it remembers me,* she wished.

Aunt Violet saw the silver, bullet train approaching on the horizon and pulled off Peter's woolly hat and removed the pin out of her perfectly woven bun. Her mane of burnt orange and red hair was released from its hold, a stark contrast against the grey, flickering background behind her.

Placing Mitsey back down on the concrete floor he barked loudly at the approaching train, he too feeling full of ominous premonition.

Aunt Violet's hair flickered and tossed around wildly,

whipping at her cheeks, and making them rosy as strands lashed across her face. The Neverville wind fought against her, but the more it beat against her, the better she felt, the younger she felt.

Aunt Violet stood defiant against the elements feeling a long-forgotten power restoring to her body. Like a flame dancing across the surface of coal, Aunt Violet stood rebellious, staring down the approaching train. Fierceness raging in the ferocity of her eyes, she was ready for a battle.

The sleek, silver train pulled in silently to the platform, its newness making the platform and station look even more drab and grey. Aunt Violet checked the time, 11:11pm, she still had time. She hesitated before stepping from the safety of the grey concrete onto the metallic floor of the train. These were not the trains she remembered. The quietness of the electric, the smoothness of the rail, the smell of people other than smoke and steam, everything unfamiliar, everything alien.

Mitsey ran into the train and turned to her, he barked in urgency for her to board the train. Aunt Violet breathed in deeply hoping to smell the smell she had smelt all those years ago. But it wasn't there, there was nothing there. The train was absolutely deserted.

Looking around Aunt Violet hugged herself as she walked in between the seats of the empty carriages, trying to decide if the train being empty was a help or a hindrance. The electric doors opened silently and predictively as she approached each one counting as she went.

'Nineteen, twenty, twenty-one and twenty-two.'

Aunt Violet had reached the end of the train, she looked down at Mitsey and then out the window of the end carriage's train door. All she saw was the track that they'd left behind.

Over the modern train speaker system, she heard the guard announcing the next station they were approaching.

'Grey Valley approaching, Grey Valley, this is the 11.02 to Greystone,'

Aunt Violet looked up again for the time 11:45pm. The time was ticking away too quickly. She held her hands up and placed them on the window of the new, modern, silver train. That's when she felt it. A hint of a vibration. The smoothness gone, blue sparks, crackled and fizzed from her fingers and the vibrations increased.

'There you are,' she whispered to the door.

She pressed her hands harder against the glass. Sparks and lightning bolts began to fly out of her hands like fireworks. She focused and dug as deep as she could, but the train wasn't budging. Aunt Violet felt the power and magic flow through every fibre of her being, getting stronger and stronger.

A current of electricity outlined her body and fizzled and crackled as the circuit got brighter and louder. Aunt Violet stood back from the door now smiling, brighter and younger, remembering exactly who she was, where she came from and more importantly who she was now fighting for.

'You're going to make me do it the hard way, ah?' Aunt Violet spoke to the door.

Mitsey was prancing around her feet excitedly, knowing what was coming. Looking down at her beloved companion for conformation, Mitsey nodded back to her in agreement. They both backed away from the door, then with all the strength and speed they could muster, they both ran full pelt towards the last carriage's steel door.

Chapter 32

'Oh my, Clara! Abigale is Viola's great-niece!' Mama Gilbert finally awoke from her trance springing from her comfy chair and untying her cascading sleeves and pulling out her wand.

'What?' said Clara, 'Who's Viola?'

Clara was totally lost, shattered and magically and emotionally drained, she plonked herself down on to the little stool by Mama Gilbert's comfy chair.

'There's no time to rest, my dearest, it's time to save your friend,' Mama Gilbert held up the bracelet in the air like a trophy, 'After all she is royalty!' Mama Gilbert announced.

'Royalty?' Clara was still looking a little puzzled, 'What? Abs?'

Mama Gilbert rushed over to Clara's side and bent down clasping her hands over hers and holding them tightly.

'Abigale is a Bellflower, Clara,' Mama Gilbert paused as she let the information sink in for Clara, 'Remember I told you the story about the Royal Family before Noralynn, but I couldn't quite remember their names,' Clara nodded in stunned silence, 'Their names were Viola and Delphine.' Mama Gilbert threw her hands up in the air in an act of realisation, 'Viola is Abigale's aunt, or is it great-aunt?' she questioned herself then stopped dead as it hit her like a tonne of bricks and her face fell, 'That means Abigale...,' Mama Gilbert trailed off.

'That means Abigale what?' shouted Clara on the edge of her seat.

'That means Abigale is Delphine's granddaughter…' Mama Gilbert trailed off again, 'Where is Delphine? No one has mentioned her….' The question was filled with sadness as if she already knew.

Seeing a sadness capture Mama Gilbert, Clara found a new lease of life. She this time grabbed hold of Mama Gilbert, bringing her back to the here and now.

'Let's go save Abigale!' Clara asserted.

'How long do we have?' Mama Gilbert asked.

'15 minutes, it's 11:45!'

Clara and Mama Gilbert turned to head for the door. As they opened the door and tried to walk through the doorway they were thrown backwards by some kind of invisible wall. They tried to exit the cabin again, but the unseen wall held strong, that's when they heard it.

A haunting melodic high-pitched chanting, 'Time to keep the fairies in the house, in the house we keep the fairies.'

The 3 T's hovered the other side of the invisible magical wall holding Mama Gilbert and Clara in the room.

Clara cried out in a rage, 'Let us out, you spiteful little Pixies.'

The 3 T's just laughed and giggled, chanting repeatedly, 'Time to keep the fairies in the house, in the house we keep the fairies,' their voices harmonious and lyrical.

Mama Gilbert pulled Clara away from the doorway and out of the ear shot of the 3 T's.

'We need to make them fight,' Mama Gilbert whispered, 'We need to make them break the chant and their unity, then

I can overpower their spell.'

'How are we supposed to do that? We are running out of time!' Clara said in a panicked and desperate whisper. Mama Gilbert held up her hands in a gesture of not knowing the answer.

Clara walked back over to the door, watching the 3 T's dance and spin and giggle in their triumph.

'How can you do this?' Clara voice cracked.

Mama Gilbert came up behind her putting an arm around her shoulder in comfort, pulling her in to her embrace. Mama Gilbert looked down at the bracelet in her hand and then up at the clock as it flicked to 11:50pm, time was almost lost.

'Prepare to fire!'

The 3 T's stopped chanting, Clara lifted her head from Mama Gilbert's shoulder, and they both looked through the doorway to see what the commotion was.

'FIRE!' the little voice yelled.

Tiny, little, silver pointers that were like miniature, steel arrows started to hurtle through the air at the 3 T's fast and hard. The three Pixies tried to dodge and out-manoeuvre the shots fired. Until Tiana was hit on the top of her tiny little green thigh and started shrieking in pain. Tiana held on to her leg as she tried to fly but she couldn't, she started to fall towards the floor.

The silver pointers just kept on coming as Tatum and Tamsin flew down to catch Tiana, one of them at her either side. They grasped her arms and like rockets they tore off away from the secret assassin.

Mama Gilbert waved her wand over the doorway removing the 3 T's incantation and slowly, very slowly they exited Mama

Gilbert's cabin. Looking around they could see nothing and no one. Then, one of the winged-hinges in the mahogany carriage creaked and a secret compartment lifted.

'Private Tyson Glitterfluff Thunderlily reporting for duty, Mama G!' Little T saluted Mama Gilbert and Clara.

'T, how did you do you this?' Clara said beaming at him.

Holding up his golden Feather Blow Dart and green bag full of silver pointers, 'Pixie Olympic dart blowing champion second year in a row!' he bowed and smiled at his own achievement.

'Ohhhhh I could just kiss you!' Clara bent down and kissed Little T right on the lips. Little T then dramatically pretended to faint and pass out on the floor.

The train started to shake angrily, 'Quick what's the time?' Mama Gilbert shouted.

'11:58pm' cried Clara, 'We are not going to make it....'

'We need to try!' Mama Gilbert began running through the carriages followed by Clara and Little T.

Chapter 33

Abigale stood where it all began, in front of the large Victorian mahogany door. The red and brown swirls whizzed around displaying montages of angry Fairies and Pixies out of its swirling wood grain. The train vibrated angrily making everyone uneasy and nervous. Everyone, except the Queen.

'Abigale, please stand to the left of the doorway,' the Queen ordered, devoid of emotion or feeling, 'Elliot you this side of me, and Annie you here, we need to make a circle around her and the doorway.' The Queen drew a chalk circle on the floor around Abigale, 'Do not step out of the circle!' she warned.

Professor Mortley looked at his watch, *11:59, times up,* he thought as he gazed down the carriages hoping for Mama Gilbert to appear.

'Freddie, you're going to need to stand back, over there by Professor Mortley,' the Queen ordered.

Abigale looked absolutely terrified as the Queen took Annie and Elliot's hands and told them to start the spell.

'All together now,' the Queen commanded looking at Annie and Elliot, '*Abalienare ne hic, Per illud aere.....*'

'STOP!' shouted Annie.

'Bravest Annie keep going!' the Queen chanted.

'It's not working anymore Your Majesty, when a godmother knows she is being charmed the chant no longer works,' Annie said proudly, starting to stand strong. 'I'm not sending Abigale back, I want her stay, she should be with us!'

Annie stepped out of the circle and went and stood by Professor Mortley who instinctively stood in front of her.

Anger rose within the Queen, she held Elliot's hand tighter and glared back at Annie, 'We don't need you, you're a foolish girl,' she turned back to face Abigale, and roared 'Elliot! Again! Begin!'

They began to chant the spell, the train began to shake violently, Elliot couldn't get the words out properly and the Queen began to shout at him again.

'Elliot, concentrate!'

Elliot could feel his heart pounding in his ears, he felt like his whole body was going to crumble as he battled with himself. He looked into the eyes of his angry, pleading sister and then locked eyes with Abigale as he fumbled over the words of the spell.

Abigale smiled and then mouthed 'It's OK,' to him. Elliot closed his eyes and tears escaped as he realised, he just couldn't do it, and stepped out of the circle releasing his sister's hand.

'Elliot, what are you doing!' she screamed at him, angrier than she had ever been, more hurt than she could ever be.

'I can't do it Noralynn, I want Abigale to stay,' Elliot turned his back to Noralynn and went and stood next to Annie, behind Professor Mortley.

'I don't need any of you!' Noralynn yelled, 'I have enough power to do it myself!'

Yelling could then be heard in the distance, Professor Mortley turned to see Mama Gilbert, Clara, and Little T running towards them.

'Please Noralynn,' Professor Mortley held his hands up in a

prayer position to plead with the Queen, 'Please, Your Majesty, stop this, let's just see what they have to say.'

'Please Nora,' Elliot pleaded.

Noralynn looked away unable to comprehend the insubordination. Her fingers began to crackle and fizz with white light.

Mama Gilbert, Clara and Little T made it to the transitioning carriage, Mama Gilbert hung on to Professor Mortley's shoulder gasping for breath and holding up the bracelet.

She breathlessly said, 'She… is… a… Bellflower,' holding out the bracelet to Noralynn, 'Please Noralynn, just let her put on the bracelet and you will see!'

Mama Gilbert held out the bracelet to Noralynn. Tiana swooped in and took the bracelet and rocketed away down the carriage way.

'Don't worry I'll get it!' Little T shot off after her while Noralynn laughed wickedly.

Noralynn turned towards Abigale, she extended her arms and began to chant the spell hard and fast, the white electricity increasing from her fingers. Abigale started to rise off the floor, her head flew back so quickly it might snap. She too became encircled by forks of white electricity.

Starting to release moans of discomfort Abigale rose higher off the cabin floor, her head being pulled back harder. The train shook more and more violently, trying to fight Noralynn as hard as it could. Annie and Clara began to scream at Professor Mortley and Mama Gilbert, tears streaming down their faces.

'Help her!' shouted Clara.

'She is hurting her!' yelled Annie.

Professor Mortley and Mama Gilbert didn't know how to help. They tried to approach the magic circle, shouting for

Noralynn to stop, but were propelled back. Noralynn's electricity got more powerful and striking, crackling, and snapping. Noralynn fell to her knees as she chanted over and over in a hypnotic frenzy, while screams of pain escaped from Abigale.

'Something isn't right!' shouted Elliot, 'Somethings wrong!' Elliot looked around the cabin, everyone absolutely petrified at the scene unfolding before them.

Elliot decided he needed to act and ran towards Noralynn hard and fast. He knocked her clean out of the magic circle, sending the Fae Crown flying. Abigale collapsed to the floor while Noralynn was twitching and sweating, every inch of her exhausted from trying to cast the spell.

Annie and Clara rushed to check Abigale who was lying on the floor contracted and moaning in pain. Elliot and Professor Mortley tried reviving a wiped out Noralynn.

'It should have worked, I should have been powerful enough,' Noralynn mumbled beginning to awaken.

'Silly-billy girl,' came a bubbly jolly voice from the back of the carriage, practically laughing, 'I told you ,Commander, she wasn't up for the job.'

'Fairy Godmother Cindercrest, Commander Alaris, I'd hoped I was wrong about you two' Professor Mortley said a little crestfallen.

Mama Gilbert stepped back grabbing Clara and Annie and pulling them behind her, holding her wand to her chest knowing this certainly wasn't over.

Chapter 34

'*Wallop!*' Aunt Violet and Mitsey smashed into the train knocking them both clean out.

The force of the collision thrusted them backwards onto the floor, Mitsey let out a tiny little yelp as they landed.

'I certainly don't remember it hurting this much,' Aunt Violet said to Mitsey rubbing her head giving him a quick, blurry, once-over to make sure he was ok.

Rainbow colours then filled Aunt Violet's peripheral vision, as they do when you are slightly dazed. Yellows, oranges, reds, blues, and lilacs, the whole spectrum surrounding everything she could see. As the rainbow of dazzling lights began to dissipate, she began to see more clearly.

There it was, the old Victorian mahogany door, swirls of reds and browns looking just as beautiful as they had always done dancing within each other. The cast-iron wings as hinges and the prism of light surrounding the door.

Like Abigale before her, she was drawn forwards towards the door. Aunt Violet traced her finger over the hinges and then laid both of her palms flat on the door.

'Hello, my old friend,' the door of the train shook, and vibrated, and blue sparks began to fly from Aunt Violet's fingers.

She began to nod her head and her face became harder and sterner, she seemed to push her hands more firmly into the wood as the train spoke to her.

'How many are behind the door?' Aunt Violet asked, the

panic beginning to rise in her voice.

The train shuddered and Aunt Violet nodded. 'And Abigale?' she questioned, Mitsey barked impatiently at Aunt Violet.

'Shhhh Mitsey, Abigale is unconscious,' Aunt Violet paused, listening hard. 'We need to stop the Fairy Godmother casting the spell,' she began to pace the carriage trying to think of a plan, 'They only have a short amount of time that they will be able to harness the Pink Moon power, I need to get in there.'

Aunt Violet bent down to Mitsey, 'When I get sucked in,' she stopped, and then pulled the spotted little Jack Russell in close, 'You wait here like a good boy, OK Mit's? I'll come get you when it's done,' Mitsey whimpered worriedly, nuzzling into Aunt Violet.

Aunt Violet rubbed her hands together quickly and sparks began to fly from the friction. She then rubbed and rubbed; blue lightning bolts began to fork from her hands as she walked back over to the train door.

Placing her palms back on the train, sparks and lightning rods started flying everywhere. She leaned into the train and whispered, 'We hold off the spell and then you throw me in,' the train shook powerfully in contemplation, 'I will be fine!' Aunt Violet confirmed, yelling over the noise, in a jokey, half-confident, half-not way.

'We hold it off then you throw me in...' she repeated this time serious and authoritarian. 'They're starting, get ready my old friend.'

The swirls on the train started to spin and swirl so quickly it was like its whole molecular structure was charged and ready.

Aunt Violet pressed her palms into the wood and blue lightning encompassed the whole door, the lightning fizzed, crackled, crashed, and banged so loudly that Mitsey's bark could not be heard. The sound was deafening as the blue electricity pulsated through door.

'Hold…,' she shouted to the train, 'Hold on…' the train shuddered and shook so fiercely planks started to break away.

'Almost there, keep going…' Aunt Violet shouted, Mitsey was barking in a frenzy, he saw Aunt Violet weakening. Then, Aunt Violet screamed, 'NOW!'

Silence.

Mitsey sat and let out an almighty, heart-wrenching howl and waited.

***

Professor Mortley noticed that Noralynn had regained some of her strength and Elliot was still trying to help her stand.

'What are *you* doing here?' Noralynn questioned, trying her best to sound regal.

'What am *I* doing here?' Fairy Godmother Cindercrest scoffed, exchanging amused looks with Commander Alaris, 'It is *I*, who should be asking you, Your Highness, what *you* are doing here?'

The Fairy Godmother was virtually skipping around the room, her pink ringlets bouncing everywhere. Looking down and inspecting the circle chalked on the floor, she tutted animatedly, and laughed. Professor Mortley exchanged looks with Mama Gilbert, they were in seriously trouble.

'I have everything under control, I…' Noralynn tried to stand up free from Elliot and pushed him aside to confront Godmother. Noralynn lost her footing and ended up tumbling back down causing Freddie to leap out and catch her.

'You boy!' shouted Alaris.

Alaris stood tall, dressed from head to toe in his military fatigues. The Tooth Fairy fatigues were a mixture of dark, navy blue, royal blue, and silver, to help them camouflage at night. Alaris's oak eyes bore into Freddie as he watched him struggle to hold the Queen's weight with one arm.

Normally considered handsome with his chiselled cheekbones and strong jawline, oh so like Freddie's, Alaris look frightening and austere.

Freddie, using all his strength to hold the Queen with one arm, stood to attention saluting as best he could.

Alaris towered over Freddie, he leaned into Freddie's ear, 'Drop her!' he ordered.

Freddie's face drained of colour as he hesitated, torn between not following the order and dropping a woman, a weakened woman, but a woman that was his Queen. Not following an order went against everything he was being taught, everything he had ever believed. The decision he made now was going to effect the rest of his Tooth Fairy career.

Freddie then felt a warmth on his shoulder, he turned and saw Annie's hand resting there, she was standing strong beside him.

'I'm sorry, sir, I will not drop the Queen!' Freddie said in his best army voice.

Annie squeezed his shoulder in support. Then another hand came on the other shoulder, it was Elliot, he started to help take his sister's weight and released the strain from Freddie. Pride waved over Professor Mortley.

'You're finished in the Tooth Fairy Academy, boy!' Alaris threatened Freddie.

Freddie held still and saluted again, this time mocking Alaris as the strength of his friends washed over him making him his bravest self, 'Sir, yes, sir!'

Alaris's face turned bright red, he was just about to explode when the Godmother interrupted.

'Alaris my love muffin, leave the boy alone we can deal with him later,' she twirled and pirouetted in front of him, her pink ringlets catching Alaris's nose making it twitch and her hand gently stroked his face. 'Come, it's time to start,' she beckoned Alaris over, a little more seriousness in her joviality.

Looking at Freddie he threatened, 'This isn't over, boy!'

Professor Mortley grabbed Freddie and pulled him back to the group, trying to make sure he didn't anger the Commander even more.

Godmother Cindercrest had drawn a series of circles in chalk around Abigale where she lay, still unconscious in front of the transitioning Victorian door. Clapping and laughing and giggling at her artwork she sniggered, 'Time for this Stoney to go back where she came from!'

The train ferocity increased again in protest, an archway of rainbow light began to beam through the cracks of the transition door. The door began to crackle and fizz. Alaris walked over to the Godmother and questioned quietly, 'Is that supposed to be happening?'

'Just give me the baby teeth, they will help harness the power of the Pink Moon, the train won't be able to stop us,' the Godmother said confidently, blowing him a kiss, 'Then the Kingdom will be ours, my King Alaris!' she let out a girly giggle as she curtseyed.

'My Queen,' Alaris grabbed her kiss out of the air in his palm, he then kissed it and placed his hand on his heart, bowing, sealing his pledge of love.

'Erk, gross!' said Clara, putting two fingers up to her mouth and heaving her chest.

The Godmother began to take the little teeth out of a dark blue, velvet bag and placed them on top of the white-chalk lines, spacing them out evenly around Abigale, who was still out cold.

The train began to shake with such violence that Professor Mortley and Mama Gilbert exchanged looks of fear, they had never seen or felt anything like it before.

Pulling the children and Noralynn towards the back of the cabin Mama Gilbert stood guard, wand at the ready to protect the children at all costs. Noralynn began to regain her strength and came forward next to Mama Gilbert.

'It's time to pick a side Noralynn, are you their queen or ours?' Mama Gilbert said with a fierceness Noralynn had never seen before, the lioness had come to the fore.

Wow! thought Professor Mortley, even he'd never seen Mama like this.

Godmother Cindercrest took her spot in front of the door, her body now full of seriousness and began to chant the demonic fairy spell. A beam of pink light shone upwards towards the sky from the chalk circles surrounding Abigale.

As the Fairy Godmother chanted, the baby teeth shot out red beams of light that began merging with the pink rays. Abigale started to rise off the floor again with her body being outstretched, her head again being tilted backwards hard and sharp. The sparkly pink and green hair-ties dangling from her plaits behind her head as she turned slowly in mid-air within the magic circles.

The train shook and the floorboards under the Godmother began to shake and crack, lifting from their nailed position. The Godmother chanted harder and faster.

'Oooowwwwww!' Abigale screamed in pain as her body convulsed.

'STOP!' Professor Mortley ran forward in hope to somehow do something.

Alaris struck him before he could reach the Godmother. Mama Gilbert shot out her arm and a beam of purple light bolted from her wand, producing a lilac mattress to soften Professor Mortley's landing on the cabin floor. He bounced off and rolled to the opposite corner of the carriage, just to the right of the transitioning doorway.

Fairy Godmother Cindercrest seemed to be becoming flustered her chanting becoming even harder, trying to make the spell take hold.

Professor Mortley was lying face down on the floor trying desperately to think of what to do next, that's when he saw the shadow of feet underneath the mahogany transitioning door. He pressed his face to the vibrating carriage floor trying his best to look for a clue of who it could be, then came the forks of blue lightning, and he knew exactly who it was.

'*Viola*,' he whispered to himself astounded, hope refilling his heart.

Professor Mortley caught Mama Gilbert's eye and mouthed the word, 'Vi-o-la' to her.

Not really understand what he was trying to say, Mama Gilbert looked at him confused and then he signalled pointing down to the bottom of the doorway. Mama Gilbert then saw the blue electricity for the first time, she knew then. Professor Mortley saw her face light up with restored confidence.

Fairy Godmother Cindercrest's face had been distorted with her determination and the evilness contained within the spell. Her full and rosy cheeks now looked mottled and flushed. Her eyes looked swollen and red, the glint and sparkle had totally gone. Her smile that had once reached from ear to ear was now a hard and tightened grimace. Her shiny, pink ringlets, dull and frizzy, she began to take on the appearance of a crazed, pink clown.

More and more she kept going. Walking forwards towards Abigale's body trying to push and crush her out of the train with the power of the spell. All the while screams, and gasps were coming from the onlookers as Abigale let out groans of pain as the spell was trying to expel her body from the train.

Alaris checked his watch, 00:55am, his face had also changed from his chiselled good looks, being full of confidence and arrogance, to having now suddenly aged with worry and concern. It is becoming all too much as he watched his love be all-consumed by the evil spell, a spell that won't reach its magical peak.

There were only five minutes left for the Pink Moon's power to be harnessed, he couldn't watch the Fairy Godmother any longer, he tried to get her attention, 'Tula, it's not working you only have five minutes!' he yelled to her.

'It will my love, I've almost got it!' she said with a frenzied determination.

Fairy Godmother Cindercrest was too consumed by the spell and proving she could overpower the train that she didn't notice the increasing blue electricity for what it was. It had started to creep up the Victorian mahogany door, branching out around the room.

Fairy Godmother Cindercrest drew in a deep breath, she seemed to pull herself inwards, gathering more power together. The Godmother braced and beamed the full-strength of her magic at Abigale. Abigale let out a blood-curdling scream as the light turned blood red and rebounded straight back at the Fairy Godmother knocking her out and rendering her unconscious within the red light.

'Tula! Noooooooo!' Alaris tried to run to her but the power in the red light was too strong and violently catapulted him across the room.

Blue lightning bolts then began to fly across the cabin radiating across every wall.

Professor Mortley got up and began to run towards the kids and Mama Gilbert.

He shouted to warn them, 'Get down, take cover!'

They ducked into the corner and Mama Gilbert drew the mattress back with her wand, creating a wall of springy defence.

The room then flashed with piecing blue strobe-light, making everyone cover their eyes, followed by the loudest explosion as the transition door flew off its cast-iron, winged-hinges.

Mama Gilbert and Noralynn hugged the children tighter together, while Professor Mortley looked on bravely though his fingers. The mattress bounced and pounded as pieces of doorway struck it and rebounded off. Clara and Annie screamed, Elliot and Freddie held on tight as they were gripped with fear. All of them terrified of what had caused the explosion and was happening to Abigale.

Suddenly, the mattress was ripped from them. Mama Gilbert

stood up ready to fight, her wand held high.

Abigale was still suspended in the tubular red light as was the Fairy Godmother who was unconscious on the floor. Alaris was lying face down on the carriage floor, his hands tied behind his back with a blue electric current encircling his wrists holding them together.

Again, the blue strobe flashed like lightning, making everything look in slow motion. From behind a large piece of mahogany wood slowly rose a flame-haired warrior raising her hand with a blue, electricity ball poised to project at them.

Upon seeing the flame-haired warrior, much to the shock of those Mama Gilbert was protecting, Mama Gilbert lowered her wand and Professor Mortley jumped up waving his arms and clumsily ran towards her.

As Professor Mortley got closer, the ball of electricity dissipated and the warrior outstretched their arms, to which Professor Mortley ran into them lifting the warrior clean off the floor in a hugging embrace.

'Viola!' Mama Gilbert exclaimed in wonder beginning to follow Professor Mortley.

'Viola?' Noralynn queried in a combination of disbelief and amazement.

'Who's Viola?' whispered Elliot confused.

Annie shrugged her shoulders, while Clara whispered secretively acting like she had known the whole time, 'Oh, that's Abs's Great Aunt Viola.'

Mama Gilbert picked up her pace as Aunt Violet came into full view and couldn't contain her happy tears as she embraced her.

'Oh,' Mama cried in pure joy, 'My dear, dear Viola,' they hugged tightly and then locked eyes, eyes that drank in every inch of each other's face. It was an unspeakable connection, Aunt Violet couldn't' speak, but Mama knew. Mama Gilbert squeezed her hands, 'Save Abigale first, we have later.'

Professor Mortley was glued to Aunt Violet's side, the holographic boy in full force, sticking close, terrified he might lose her again.

'We are going to need everyone,' Aunt Violet said finally, she looked up at Abigale suspended in the light, her heart aching for her, 'We need to make a circle around them.'

Mama Gilbert turned towards the children, 'Children we...'

'We are in!' Clara and Annie stepped forward holding hands not needing for Mama to finish the sentence.

Freddie then stepped forward and saluted Mama Gilbert, 'Freddie Wildthorn reporting for duty, ma'am!'

Elliot stepped forward next to Freddie, 'Without a doubt,' he confirmed.

Unexpectedly a voice came from behind, pulling down one of her pairs of glasses, 'I hope you're going to clean this lot up after you!'

'Petula?' Aunt Violet uttered in astonishment.

'Look what the Bleeding Jackalopes dragged in!' she smiled hugging her old friend, 'Room for one more?'

'Please, Pet,' Aunt Violet squeezed her hand, 'Thank you.'

'Welcome home,' she winked at Aunt Violet.

Everyone began to take their places around Abigale, around the red light. Professor Mortley turned back and held out his hand.

'Noralynn?' there was a hopeful expectation in his voice.

Noralynn's head was bowed, her white, satin fishtail dress covered in soot and dust, her platinum-blonde hair looking wild and unkept. Noralynn lifted her head then, her face tear-stained, dirty, and haunted.

'Please Noralynn, for me,' Elliot pleaded holding out his hand too.

Chapter 35

Noralynn limped forward reluctantly and took Professor Mortley and Elliot's hands completing the circle around Abigale and Fairy Godmother. Aunt Violet bent down and picked up the Fae Crown, which then sparked with blue light, she walked over to Noralynn and held it out to her. Noralynn's eyes turned cold and stared at Aunt Violet full of hate and snatched the crown from her hand.

'Thank you, Your Majesty,' Aunt Violet said with earnest and gratitude.

Noralynn stared forward ignoring Aunt Violet's words. Accepting Noralynn's actions Aunt Violet resolutely went back to her position in the circle.

'I know some of you don't have your magic colour yet,' Aunt Violet said to the group, 'But, you need to focus on one of our lights. Mama Gilbert's is purple, Miss Petula's is gold, the Queen's is white and mine is blue.'

All making eye contact the group nodded to each other in affirmation that they were ready.

Aunt Violet then spoke again, 'Mama G, Pet, Your Majesty, full power, magic and light Believer promise. Everyone else, join in the chant when you know it.'

Mama Gilbert, Miss Petula, Noralynn and Aunt Violet all bowed their heads and started to chant in a delicate whisper:

Magic and light we believe we are you,
Join us together and let the love flow through,
Earth, wind, fire, and water,
Father, son, mother, and daughter,
We promise to follow the light and let the magic lead the way,
We promise to Believe our hearts completely Fae.

The words soft and graceful as they found a joint rhythm. Finding unison their chant became harmonious, each voice complimenting the pitch of the other.

Aunt Violet's heart began to glow blue, then, Mama Gilbert's purple, Petula's gold, and finally the Queen's white beam shone through. The train hummed along with progression of the chanting.

Annie joined in the adult chorus and looked down at her chest and saw a flicker of green. She closed her eyes tightly and concentrated as hard as she could.

Clara and Freddie then join in the Believer promise and colours of pink and yellow joined the kaleidoscope of the group.

Professor Mortley knew that he wasn't magical like the others. But still, he chanted with such passion, hoping his words would help Abigale. To his surprise a blue light began to beam from his heart just like the others, he looked up to Aunt Violet, who smiled and squeezed his hand. Professor Mortley puffed out his chest becoming the baritone of the harmony with all his might.

Elliot squeezed his sister's hand and then joined in with a matching white light. All of them then chanting and believing. The prism of light hit the darkness of the red surrounding Abigale and the Fairy Godmother, pushing, and banishing it away. An unlikely wind picks up within the circle, beginning to swirl the colours together around red, squeezing and squeezing.

'Hold tight!' Aunt Violet shouted, they all tightened their grip within the circle.

Then, like and eruption of gas the light burst, blowing back the circle and causing everyone to take a few steps back. When they all opened their eyes, Abigale was lying on the floor next to the Fairy Godmother. Aunt Violet ran over and slid Abigale's head onto her lap. Both Abigale and the Fairy Godmother lay motionless.

'What happens now?' Annie asked Aunt Violet.

Aunt Violet stroked a strand of Abigale's hair away from her eyes and face and said, 'She needs to Believe.'

Clara then burst forwards 'She does Believe, she does.'

Annie and Clara sat either side of Abigale. Clara lifted and straightened Abigale's plaits with the sparkly pink and green hair-ties, a blue spark then flew from Abigale and shocked Clara.

'Mmgh,' Abigale murmured.

'See!' Clara exclaimed excitedly, rubbing her hand from the shock.

'Abigale… Abigale can you hear me,' Aunt Violet said gently, giving Abigale a gentle shake.

'Mmmghh… Where am I?' Abigale said hoarsely.

'The Faedora, with Annie and Clara,' Annie said urgently and excitedly beaming from ear to ear. Aunt Violet smiled at them, remembering how it felt to be them.

Abigale opened her eyes wider seeing her friends and then smiling she questioned, 'They didn't send me back?'

'Oh, they tried!' Freddie said peering over Annie's shoulder, waving goofily.

'Good job your aunt showed up to save us all!' Elliot added unknowingly.

'My who?' Abigale looked confused.

'Hello, Abigale.'

'Aunt Violet? Noooooo,' she uttered in disbelief. Abigale just stared at her, she couldn't believe it.

'Hmmm, you haven't seen me like this before, have you?' Aunt Violet smiled and flicked her flame hair. Thinking for a moment, she then, put on her best Aunt Violet voice, 'You insolent, stupid girl.'

'Oh wow! It is you!' Abigale and Aunt Violet giggled making the past melt away.

Abigale hadn't realised how much she had longed for a familiar face. Reaching out she touched Aunt Violet's now fire-coloured hair in wonder and gently stroked her youthful, transformed face.

'We have lots to talk about,' Aunt Violet said gently smiling, she opened her arms for Abigale. Abigale hesitated for the slightest second, not knowing if this was who she remembered, but she needed her she knew that. Finally, Abigale embraced her, her family.

Aunt Violet helped Abigale get to her feet, she was feeling stronger and stronger by the second. Abigale looked down at herself and her dress, socks, and shoes.

'I'm still a Stoney then,' she said slightly glum-faced with a half-smile.

Yelling started coming from the back of the carriage, a forgotten little voice was approaching quickly.

'I've got it!' the voice yelled repeatedly. Aunt Violet froze and her fingers crackled as she pulled Abigale protectively behind her.

'I've got it!' Little T cried again triumphantly. He was dangling the Believer royal bracelet around his neck. Stopping dead in his triumphant tracks he surveyed the scene. 'What on Fairy Faedom has gone on here? Who the Glitterfluff are you?!' he said pointing to Aunt Violet.

Everyone laughed then as Little T had missed everything. Mama Gilbert walked over to Little T and took the bracelet from around his neck and handed it to Aunt Violet, 'This my friend, is yours.'

Mama Gilbert went to hand the bracelet to Aunt Violet when a bolt of white lightning shocked through the middle of them making them both jump backwards.

Aunt Violet instinctively formed another electric power ball in her hand, 'Noralynn, we don't have to do this,' Aunt Violet said protecting Abigale.

Noralynn shot another bolt of lightning, although unexpectedly shooting past Aunt Violet. A pink bolt of light then came firing back.

Everyone had forgotten all about the Fairy Godmother, who had awoken on the floor, who was now stood in unison with freed and recovered Alaris.

Noralynn shot lightning bolt after lightning bolt at the pair walking towards them refusing to be gotten the better of, again. The Fairy Godmother shoved Alaris, to his dismay, into Noralynn's path, knocking her to the ground. The Fairy Godmother smiled a triumphant smile and raised her hand to finish Noralynn.

Aunt Violet shot two currents of the blue electricity out of her arms catching the Fairy Godmother unaware and holding her within the current, 'Now, Nora!' shouted Aunt Violet,

'Bind her wrists,' Noralynn, shot out the white electric handcuffs and finally restrained her.

'Are you ok, Your Majesty?' Aunt Violet asked holding out a hand to help her up.

'I had her, I didn't need *your* help,' Noralynn spat bitterly, refusing Aunt Violet's hand of help, then stormed out of the cabin.

Aunt Violet looked sad, yet resigned, and didn't try to rebuttal Noralynn. Abigale went to her and hugged her again looking over at Alaris and Fairy Godmother Cindercrest.

'What will happen to them?' Abigale asked.

Professor Mortley scratched his head, 'Well normally they would go before the Fae council,' he pondered for a moment.

'I'm sure Uncle Horith and Troma will know what to do them!' Elliot said, looking mighty worried for them, but relieved as well.

Mama Gilbert smiled at Elliot, 'No doubt your uncle will be here soon, Elliot. Now, before we were rudely interrupted,' she turned to Aunt Violet and passed the royal Believer bracelet, 'This belongs to you Viola.'

'Actually,' Aunt Violet said with a meaningful smile, 'This should be yours, Abigale,' she leaned in and whispered, 'It was your grandmothers,' Aunt Violet fastened the clasp, adjoining the Believer rings together. As the clasp fastened the bracelet began to fizz and spark.

'Stand back everyone!' Aunt Violet warned.

They all took a step back and Abigale looked a little terrified as the sparks got bigger. Blue light beamed out of the blue sapphires within each circle of the Believer crest. The blue beams of light began to swirl around Abigale and trace over every inch of her skin. Abigale felt scared, but it also felt good. She allowed the power to rush over her as every part of her glowed brightly.

'Just go with it!' Aunt Violet encouraged, 'Believe!'

No sooner were the words out of her mouth than Abigale pirouetted high into the air. A whirlwind of colour surrounded her, bursting blue, spectral rays of rainbow lit her up from head to toe.

Gone were the black-patent plain slip-on shoes, the grey knee-length socks, and the pleated charcoal-grey dress. The light began to reveal who she truly was. A flash of blinding illumination exploded from the bracelet on Abigale's wrist, and she floated elegantly back down to the floor.

Abigale looked down at herself, taking in a sharp intake of breath as she smoothed her hands down the most beautiful tea-shaped dress. Strapless, yet high on the chest with a straight edge that rested flat just below where the collarbone meets. The dress pulled in at the waist and then flared out to meet her calves, modest and regal.

The material shimmered a dazzling baby blue but as the light touched it, it became monochrome and luminescent, picking up every colour she could ever dream of.

Abigale gently lifted the skirt of the dress to see her feet. Her legs seemed to be covered in glitter as they sparkled all the way down to her toes. But there, at her feet were the most spectacular shoes she had ever seen. A pair of crystal, kitten heels that sparkled like they were covered in diamonds. Never in her wildest dreams could Abigale have dreamt of such beauty.

Annie, Clara, Little T, Freddie, and Elliot stood with mouths open as they witnessed Abigale's transformation.

'That didn't happen to me when I wore it!' Clara said jokingly as they admired the striking girl before them.

Miss Petula, Mama Gilbert, and Professor Mortley stood beside Aunt Violet, bearing witness to Abigale's transformation. All were smiling smiles where the edges reached the corners of their eyes.

A wave of panic then went over Abigale's face, she reached up to feel her hair. Following the plaits down each side of her head and bringing them forward from behind her, she checked to make sure the pink and green sparkly hair-ties were still there.

Abigale gave them a quick squeeze in relief that they hadn't changed, 'Still there,' Annie said flicking the green hair-tie.

Abigale smiled and Clara came to her other side, 'Can't get rid of us now,' she said taking her turn to flick the pink hair-tie.

'Never!' Abigale exclaimed, drawing them in.

'Group hug!' shouted Little T as they all rushed over to embrace.

Aunt Violet looked around at the devastation of the transitioning cabin and walked over placing a hand on what was left of the mahogany wall.

'Sorry my old friend,' she stroked the wood tracing the swirls with her finger as if they were playing an intimate game.

'No worry with all that,' Professor Mortley came over taking out the biggest sparkly, green Christmas marshmallow from his trouser pocket, 'I know three little Pixies who have some making up to do!' Taking a giant mouthful, he called, '3 T's!'

Swishing, swooshing, and whizzing down the carriages came the 3 T's. With his mouth full, Professor Mortley nodded to Mama Gilbert.

In her most professional teacher voice Mama Gilbert

commanded, 'Take care of this will you T's,' pausing and smiling as their little faces shrunk, 'Oh and Little T, make sure they do a good job, you're in charge!'

Little T exploded in excitement and pulled on a green hard hat and began ordering his sisters around with sheer ecstasy.

Leaving the cabin, all hand in hand, Professor Mortley buddied up to Aunt Violet, 'You are staying, aren't you?' The holographic face of the vulnerable little boy she rescued all those years ago now apparent and his eyes pleading with her.

Aunt Violet looked at him for a long time, 'I hope so P, I do hope so.'

One week later

'Mama Gilbert, have you heard anything yet?' Little T was darting around the room not being able to contain himself much longer as Mama Gilbert walked into the classroom.

'No, Little T, nothing yet,' Mama replied in a low hesitant tone, her head low devoid of her usual jolliness.

'Elliot, have you heard anything?' Annie asked turning round to face him.

'No, nothing,' he replied sadly, 'My sister won't even take my calls.'

Little T flew up and sat himself on his shoulder, patting him, in a sign of solidarity and friendship.

'Freddie, how about you?' Clara asked hopefully.

'Nothing, Clara. The new Commander is keeping very tight-lipped. All I know is that I have double work now as I'm being fast-tracked to First Lieutenant.'

'That's amazing Fred, well done,' Annie smiled, giving him a tiny wink.

'Maybe they have been sent to the land of lost,' Little T said dramatically, 'Or maybe Viola has been stripped of her powers and sent back to Neverville?' Little T pretended to pass out in shock on Elliot's desk.

'She's a blue blood they can't do that!' said Annie, 'Can they, Mama?'

Mama Gilbert broke up the chitter chatter, 'That's quite

enough of that, stop all this filly-flabbering, and no Annie, they cannot do that,' Mama Gilbert then paused and thought, 'Not that I've ever known anyway, we will know when we know,' she added then, more confidently, 'Now then, who is going to list for me all the love potions that make "True loves kiss" happen?'

Freddie and Annie's hand shot up into the air.

***

'Lead Chancellor Horith can you please bring the Council to order!' spoke a tiny, little, elfin man at the front of the room. He banged the gavel hard on the desk three times, making his blue and gold ceremonial hat fall in front of his eyes.

White tuffs of hair poked out of the sides and around the gold trim of the hat. The rest of the hat was of royal blue with the five circles of the Believe emblem embossed on the top in gold, and a gold knotted-tassel hanging from its tip.

His white tuffs of hair seemed to come from every available angle as the old Elf tried his hardest to look serious and important, while continually lifting the gold-trim from his view and straightening his hat.

The courtroom was packed to the rafters, full of members of the Fae. The old Elf judge at the front of the room sat in a high, white oak dock, together with a strange-looking lady, a maybe Elf, that had a huge drooping nose that was practically elephant in shape. She had bright-green spiky hair, and fluorescent-pink, dangly parrot earrings, which hung off the pointiest of maybe Elf ears.

Abigale could have never imagined such an Elf. The judge's dock was surrounded with a semi-circle of white oak desks that he presided over. The half to left were the Fae Council, Queen

Noralynn and Chancellor Horith. Then to the right, Professor Mortley, Aunt Violet and Abigale.

Members of the Fae then filled every possible gap that was left, with the Pixies zooming from the beams overhead. Never had Abigale seen such an array of magical beings, of Fae, of Believers.

Aunt Violet nudged Abigale. 'Stop staring,' she whispered.

'Chancellor Horith?' the judge said impatiently.

'Sorry, Your Honour,' Chancellor Horith responded respectfully, 'As you can appreciate this is an extremely sensitive and unprecedented predicament we find ourselves in.'

'Viola my dear,' the judge's face changed, becoming kinder, gentler as he addressed Aunt Violet, 'What is your view on situation at hand?'

'Objection, Your Honour,' bellowed Chancellor Horith, his angry angular face looking flushed, 'You're clearly biased towards the defendants.'

'As so it seems are you, Chancellor,' the judge stared down at Chancellor Horith. 'I think you'll be hard pressed to find anyone in the Fae who isn't biased in this instance,' summarised the judge. 'You are therefore, stuck with me.'

'Your Honour, please,' pleaded Chancellor Horith.

The judge held up his hand silencing the Chancellor, 'Viola, my Quee… my dear,' he corrected quickly, 'Would you like to speak?'

'I would, Your Honour, thank you.'

Aunt Violet got up from behind a large, oak desk where she sat in between Professor Mortley and Abigale. She gave Abigale's hand a reassuring squeeze and took her place in front of the judge. The judges' seat was so high up that she had to tilt her head backwards to see him.

'If you don't mind Your Honour, I'd like to address the Queen and Council?' Aunt Violet's crystal blue eyes sparkled vibrantly against her mane of fire, luminous, and mesmerizing to any and all that dared to meet them.

'Of course, my dear, proceed,' the judge himself was spellbound by her beauty.

Abigale sat totally still, astounded by the woman that stood in front of her. Still baffled that the velvety, soft words and pure kindness that came out of this woman could be her Aunt Violet.

Even more shocking, was that the little dog curled up on her lap, snoozing soundly, was the same bitter and snappy Jack Russell that had once tried to take her hand off one summer visit. Abigale and Mitsey had within this last week become inseparable, Mitsey enjoying every ounce of love and affection Abigale had to offer, and Abigale had plenty of that to give.

Professor Mortley grabbed Abigale's hand, at first Abigale thought it was for her reassurance, but as she looked at him taking bite after bite of green, sparkly Christmas tree marshmallow, she was sure it was more for his benefit. Abigale sat and watched on as Aunt Violet began to address the Council.

'Chancellor Horith, Troma, new members of the Council and Your Majesty,' Aunt Violet curtseyed to Queen Noralynn, 'Thank you for allowing me to speak. I know you are all still in shock at my return, and some of you, that I am indeed alive. It is with great sadness that I have to inform you of the death of my beloved sister, her royal highness Delphine, Abigale, Lumina Bellflower.'

Aunt Violet's voice wobbled with emotion as she spoke about

her sister for the first time in years. There was a sharp intake of breath around the courtroom. Along with lots of mumbling, whispering and the odd cry of shocked heartbreak, upon hearing the conformation of her sister's death.

Abigale's eyes widened as she heard her name within her grandmother's.

Taking a deep breath, Aunt Violet smiled and turned signalling to where Abigale was sitting, 'However, it is with great happiness that I introduce to you all to her granddaughter, Abigale,' the room erupted again in whisper and murmuring.

'Objection, Your Honour, we are not here for storytelling,' Chancellor Horith insisted meanly and without sympathy.

'Chancellor Horith, should you interrupt her highness...' the judge coughed quickly trying to cover up his mistake. 'Should you interrupt Viola again I will hold you in contempt!'

Picking up on the judge's mistake Chancellor Horith's overly large ears flapped in disapproval as he leaned over and muttered something inaudible to the Queen.

Noralynn had not looked up throughout the proceedings, she sat silent next to Chancellor Horith. Placing a hand on Chancellor Horith's arm as if to quiet him, he sat back quietly in his seat and waited for Aunt Violet to speak again.

The judge nodded towards Aunt Violet, and she continued, 'I would like to convince the Fae Council and the Queen that I am not back for the crown,' she paused to let her words sink in, 'And that it is the furthest thing from my mind,' Aunt Violet pledged with utmost sincerity. 'I would just like to be able to live with my grand-niece and our friends in peace on the Faedora, helping the next generation of Fae,' Aunt Violet paused again, 'I thank you for your time.'

Aunt Violet then curtseyed to the Queen and Council and returned to her seat.

'Professor Mortley, what say you?' the judge looked at Professor Mortley. Chancellor Horith began to stand to object, 'Sit down Horith!' the judge commanded before he could fully rise.

Professor Mortley stood up nervously and addressed the judge, 'Your royal judgeness,' he bowed, 'It would be my, and the whole of the Faedora staff's pleasure to have past Queen Bellflower as a permanent member of our family, thank you your magical great judgeness,' Professor Mortley bowed again and took his seat. Aunt Violet couldn't help but smile to herself.

The judge looked over at the council members and the Queen, 'Queen Noralynn, Chancellor Horith, what say you?'

The Queen leaned over and whispered into Chancellor Horith's ear, nodding, and agreeing, Chancellor Horith then turned to address the court.

'We feel the unexpected return of Viola Bellflower, is unsettling to the whole Believer community. Viola Bellflower and her so proclaimed great-niece, have been living as Never-Believers for over forty years. This so-called niece,' Chancellor Horith stopped and peered disapproving at Abigale and Aunt Violet, his face full of contempt, 'Was born a Never-Believer and has only been in this world for a mere two weeks,' pausing for effect as the mixture of Elves, Fairies and Pixies around the courtroom seemed to whisper in agreement.

The Chancellor continued, 'How are we to know that once Abigale has learnt the ways of the Fae they will not want to take the Crown and lock up all of the Believers and turn us all GREY!' he added emphasizing the 'grey' sending shockwaves around the court. Even the judge gulped loudly at Horith's words.

'Your Honour,' Aunt Violet stood up, 'We just want to be together, judge, we mean no other upset, we will not make any claim for the crown!' Aunt Violet was making a desperate plea.

Horith then turned on Aunt Violet, 'But isn't that why you left in the first place Viola?' the Chancellor asked accusingly.

Aunt Violet hesitated, 'What…? No…' she stuttered.

Flicking through the paperwork on his desk, Horith pulled out an old piece of paper and held it up to the court, 'Your Honour, the court would like to enter into evidence proclamation 1473, where Queen Bellflower intended to unite Believers and Never-Believers,' the room gasped.

'Is this true, Viola?' the judge asked, his face saddened.

'Your Honour, my intention was to join…'

Chancellor Horith interrupted, 'See, Your Honour, she doesn't deny that she wanted to turn us all grey!'

'No, that's not… that's not what that was, it… it was to integrate, to help Never-Believers… Dominic and I…' Aunt Violet tried to find the right words.

The Queen leaned in again to Horith and the Chancellor interrupted again, 'Your Honour,' the Queen dabbed her eyes, 'The Queen is finding this all very distressing… now Viola is bringing up the Queen's deceased brother in her ill intentions,' the Chancellor shook his head showing his disgrace theatrically at Viola's actions.

Aunt Violet raised her voice, 'How dare you…' she spat venomously, her fingers twitching with blue electricity. Professor Mortley grabbed Aunt Violet's arm trying to stop her doing something she regretted.

'You see, Your Honour, she obviously has a temper, not fitting for the Fae.' Horith smiled with victory having shown Aunt Violet in a bad light, 'She is clearly dangerous and should not be allowed to remain within our realms.'

Panicked, Aunt Violet whispered to Professor Mortley, 'What about article 57? I can't let Noralynn do this, can I invoke article 57?' before Professor Mortley could get any words out of his mouth, Aunt Violet shouted, 'I invoke article 57!'

A hushed silence fell across the courtroom as everyone froze into a stunned silence. Noralynn then, finally, raised her head and stared at Aunt Violet with a wicked smile. Professor Mortley held his head in his hands.

'We have no objection to article 57 being invoked, Your Honour,' Horith said almost laughing, 'We would like to draw the opposition to the newly amended subclause 57.a456 and clause 57.b789.'

Chancellor Horith smugly passed over two huge manuscripts to Professor Mortley, both making a little thudding sound as they landed on the oak desk.

Aunt Violet sat down looking perplexed, 'What have I done, P?'

The judge then spoke, 'In light of both parties agreeing to article 57 being invoked, I hereby give the defendants until the eve of Fae graduation for the terms to be met, if they are not met by said date, then all parties of defendants shall be stripped of their power and returned to live out their lives as Never-Believers.' The judge hit his gavel on the desk, rose and left the dock.

Abigale leaned over and asked, 'What just happened?'

Aunt Violet and Professor Mortley looked over to the Queen,

the Chancellor and the Council who were all shaking hands and congratulating each other.

Noralynn sauntered over smugly, her glide looking smooth and menacing. The Fae Crown now seemed to look far too big for her head as it sparkled coming towards them.

Noralynn handed Professor Mortley a piece of paper, 'When you've finished reading,' she looked towards the giant manuscripts, half laughing, 'This is my choice.'

Professor Mortley took the piece of paper and looked at it, reading the inscription he sat back down looking utterly defeated as Noralynn laughed evilly. Then, addressing Aunt Violet, 'I look forward to beating you, Viola. Again.'

The Queen turned and sauntered away to continue celebrating with her uncle. Aunt Violet leaned across the table and read the piece of paper. 'What does this mean, P? What's going on?' Professor Mortley sat there speechless.

***

Miss Petula burst into the classroom, 'Have we heard anything yet?' her voice filled with hopeful optimism.

Mama Gilbert, Elliot, Freddie, Little T, Annie, and Clara, all jumped and turned to look at her hopefully as she walked through the door. Then, slumped back in their chairs to face forwards in disappointment at it not being who they wanted it to be.

'I'll take that as a no then!' Miss Petula took a seat at the back of the class and joined the silence.

After what seemed like an age the group heard footsteps coming towards the door and the muffled chatter of heated voices. Miss Petula got up and joined Mama Gilbert at the front of the class pre-empting the need for support.

Professor Mortley was first around the door, his holographic face fixed on an old and tired man. Aunt Violet was next, her flame-hair looking wild and unkept, her face vexed and troubled. Abigale then emerged her eyes slightly swollen, and her cheeks obviously tear stained.

Professor Mortley walked straight over to Mama Gilbert and rested his head on her shoulder. Instinctively, Mama Gilbert raised a hand to his head to comfort him while the other went to her pocket to hand him a sparkly, green Christmas tree marshmallow.

Aunt Violet stood at the front of the classroom to address them all, 'I'm deeply sorry,' she paused finding it hard to say the words, 'It seems I underestimated the Queen's hatred of me, still after all these years.' Aunt Violet's eyes filled with tears, 'They tricked me into entering a contract I didn't realise or think to think they had updated.'

'Oh, my god we are all going to die!' Little T said dramatically.

'You may wish that,' Professor Mortley said in a sad and defeatist tone.

'What on earth has happed?' Mama Gilbert said concerned.

'I invoked article 57.'

Mama Gilbert and Miss Petula sucked in a deep, sharp intake of air.

'But what does that mean?' asked Clara, not having the slightest clue what article 57 was.

Aunt Violet looked down and then took a deep breath, 'I am to now face the Queen on the eve of your graduation and complete the six levels of the Royal Inheritances,' Aunt Violet looked over at Miss Petula and Mama Gilbert as the information sunk in.

'You can do that, right?' Annie said unsurely, 'What about Abigale? You'll be able to stay right?'

'This is where, I am so deeply sorry to you all,' Aunt Violet continued, 'Yesterday they changed the clauses to the article and added a few amendments,' Aunt Violet pulled out a piece of folded up paper from the pocket of her pale-blue trouser suit.

'Clause 57.a456 states that the graduating year must decide if they are on the side of the Crown or the challenger within twenty-four hours of the article being invoked and thus, all eventualities will herby be incurred by the side you decide,' Aunt Violet paused to let the information sink in.

'So, let me get this straight,' Little T interrupted, 'We have to decide if we are on your side or the Queen's and whatever the consequences are for the loser they also apply to us?'

'Correct, Little T,' Aunt Violet confirmed.

Little T was stunned into silence.

Elliot lifted his head and his eyes locked with Abigale's as tears streamed down her face, she reverted to standing deathly still.

'Also,' Aunt Violet continued slightly clearing her throat that felt like it was closing in, 'The graduating class needs to complete the Royal Transition Quest as a group and the recipients are to be of the Queen's choosing.'

With that Elliot stood up and stormed out of the classroom.

Freddie then said what they all were thinking, 'So, the Royal Transition Quest is to turn a Never-Believer into Believer, right?' Aunt Violet nodded again in affirmation.

'Who then, who did the Queen pick?' Freddie asked.

Abigale finally broke her stillness and stepped forwards. She walked over to Aunt Violet and taking her hand, Abigale took a deep breath then blurted it out, 'My family, we have to turn the Johnsons.'

To be continued...

Acknowledgements

I'd like to start by thanking James Essinger, managing director of my publisher The Conrad Press Ltd. Without James and his team *Believe* would not have been possible. Thank you James for your attentiveness, straight-talking and belief in making my dream a reality.

My warmest thanks to Charlotte Mouncey of Bookstyle designs. Thank you so, so much for creating a beautiful front cover for *Believe*, for typesetting and for going through and making all the amendments that were needed. Furthermore, thank you for being kind and approachable, which is so important being a new author, thank you for seeing my vision and making it a reality.

Thank you, Karla Harris, for helping me edit *Believe* and all your positivity, helpfulness and making the editing process feel like I was doing it with a friend I'd known forever. Also, for your kindness in not acknowledging my many mistakes and grammatical errors. Thank you.

Thank you Zoe Verner and Karla Harris for all your help with the PR and book launch. Your support and advice have been invaluable to making *Believe* a success. I can't wait to work on more books with you in the future.

Thank you to my beta readers, who didn't know they were beta readers, my daughter Charley and friends Sam, Carolyn, Kate, and Mr Willis. Thank you for giving me the confidence to publish *Believe* and for being the best friends, I love you all.

Last, but by no means least, thank you to family. Firstly, my beloved husband, Norman. Thank you for allowing me to pursue my dream, for standing by me and always believing I could do it. Thank you and I love you more than you will ever know.

Secondly, thank you to my mum, Geraldine, for giving me quiet when it was needed, encouragement when I was down and for giving me the genes of the great family storytellers that came before me.